THE
SECRET
MISTRESS

BOOKS BY ELLIE MONAGO

The Marriage Test

THE DIVORCE SERIES
The Custody Battle
The Divorce Lawyer

THE SECRET MISTRESS

ELLIE MONAGO

bookouture

Published by Bookouture in 2025

An imprint of Storyfire Ltd.
Carmelite House
50 Victoria Embankment
London EC4Y 0DZ

www.bookouture.com

The authorised representative in the EEA is Hachette Ireland
8 Castlecourt Centre
Dublin 15 D15 XTP3
Ireland
(email: info@hbgi.ie)

Copyright © Ellie Monago, 2025

Ellie Monago has asserted her right to be identified
as the author of this work.

All rights reserved. No part of this publication may be reproduced, stored in any retrieval system, or transmitted, in any form or by any means, electronic, mechanical, photocopying, recording or otherwise, without the prior written permission of the publishers.

ISBN: 978-1-83618-701-1
eBook ISBN: 978-1-83618-700-4

This book is a work of fiction. Names, characters, businesses, organizations, places and events other than those clearly in the public domain, are either the product of the author's imagination or are used fictitiously. Any resemblance to actual persons, living or dead, events or locales is entirely coincidental.

ONE

MAREN

"Hi!" I say to the pair of strangers at my door. They have the wrong apartment, but I can't help smiling warmly since one of them is a little boy, bashful and beautiful, half hiding behind his mother's skyscraper legs.

She's strikingly pretty: tall and willowy, dressed head to toe in black. Her style is edgy and downtown, the spiky bracelets on her wrists matching the protrusion of spikes all over her stiletto boots. Her caramel hair is long and deliberately frizzy, shaved on one side, wild on the other. I wonder who's expecting them on my floor, as I strongly suspect this building is out of her neighborhood. Out of her element.

"You have amazing eyes," I say. They're sea-glass green, made more dramatic by the contrast with her tanned skin.

"Thank you," she says. "I'm Jade." Had she been named after her eyes? "And this is Tai." She urges him forward slightly and then pauses, as if waiting for recognition. Should I know them?

Of course not, though he's so precious that I wish I did.

"Hi," he says, softly enough that I'm basically lip-reading. And when I smile at him even wider, he seems to cower more.

Oh no, have I become the kind of person who frightens small children with my overenthusiasm? Lately, I've been a bit off my social game. But at least I've started getting out again, engaging with people after cloistering for so long.

"Who are you looking for?" I ask Jade. I can try to direct her to the correct apartment.

"You," she says. "You're Maren, aren't you?"

"I am." I stare at her, confused. She came here for me? Normally Javier, the doorman, would have called to see if he should send her up.

Jade is looking at me with that steady green gaze of hers, like I'm supposed to be piecing things together. I really have no idea who she is or what she might want, but she seems so sure. I haven't been sure of anything for months. I wrack my brain, scrambling for some mental purchase, groping for a semblance of memory. If I'd seen them before, surely I'd remember?

Maybe not. Grief sharpens feelings and dulls intellect.

She stares at me. I stare back. It's becoming a stalemate.

Suddenly, I locate a snatch of an image, like a page ripped from a magazine, the edges jagged. But it's not still. It's not a photo; it's a video. Jade's in motion, dashing out of the frame.

That distinctive hair flying behind her as she flees the church. The utter devastation of a day confirming that my world had been reduced to rubble.

Jade sneaked in and then stole away from my husband Corey's funeral. If she hadn't wanted me to see her then, why is she here now?

I get this strange feeling in my stomach, like something momentous is about to happen, and meanwhile I'm dressed in my workout clothes because I've been trying for the last hour to get myself to take the elevator to the gym. I never used to have motivational problems, but even though I'm better than I was, I'm just... different. You can't lose the love of your life and remain unchanged.

"Why are you here?" I say fearfully.
"Because Tai is Corey's son."

TWO

MAREN

I couldn't have heard her correctly. Corey doesn't have any children. I would know because neither do I, which is a wound that I've done my best to suture over the years.

"I thought about texting you first," Jade says, "but it was going to be a shock either way. One look at Tai, though, and you'll see that it's true. He's not the spitting image of his dad, but the resemblance is..."

She continues talking; I've lost the ability to listen. I refuse to look at Tai, so instead my eyes are trained on Jade. Her lips move as if in slow motion.

Head-to-toe black. Is that because she's in mourning? For my husband, her lover? As in, Corey had a mistress and got her pregnant?

No, it can't be.

Corey loved me beginning to end. Our marriage was the envy of all our friends. Friends I couldn't bear to see after his death because they reminded me agonizingly of him, because everything did.

It's been more than five months since Corey died. For the first four, it was a challenge to get out of bed; I rarely left my apartment. I didn't want to talk to anyone or be anywhere. Life felt bleak and meaningless, a black-and-white movie. Lately, though, I've been trying to force some color back into it. Once I gain some sense of purpose, I can feel like myself again, instead of like an understudy who's been cast in the part of Maren.

I stare at Tai. I try not to stare at Tai.

I've always wanted to be a mother, but that feels like a pipe dream now. I'll be forty-one soon. My closest friend, Alyssa, says it's not too late, that I should hurry up and start dating again, which is unfathomable.

It hasn't been easy, being around Alyssa, whose husband, Sean, worked with Corey. Sean's an asshole, even Alyssa says so (Alyssa says so the most), and yet he's still alive and well, while my incredible husband is six feet deep. The injustice of that—

Focus, Maren. Focus on the woman and the child in front of you.

Corey's child?

There's no way. If Jade is telling the truth, then my entire life with Corey—my entire life, period—was a lie.

"I don't understand where you came from," I say, "but I'm sorry, I need to go." I make a move to shut the door, and Jade puts out a hand to block me.

"No, I'm sorry," she says, and while that may be, she's clearly standing her ground. "We should meet up sometime soon, without Tai. I'll show you the proof. I can tell you everything."

I'm looking past her, studying the whorls in the wallpaper, trying to keep myself from spinning out.

"Tai is Corey's son." Her tone is gentle, sympathetic. But firm. She's not going away, not for long.

"No," I say, in a moment of strength and clarity. Corey isn't here to defend himself, so I have to. I know my husband. "You need to go. Now."

She nods calmly. Of course she's calm. She knew this was coming; she's had time to plan.

Meanwhile, I'm the victim of a sneak attack. It's never once crossed my mind that Corey would have an affair, let alone a child.

That's because he didn't.

Why is she lying? What does she want from me?

"I'll give you a few days to take this in, okay?" she says. "Then I'll text you."

As in, she already has my number? The same way she had my address and was able to get past Javier?

It's terrifying, knowing someone you've never met can get to you anytime they choose.

I break out in a cold sweat, hit by the realization that Corey's not here to protect me anymore.

I'm all alone.

THREE
MAREN

"Sorry I'm late," Jade says, bustling in, removing her scarf. It's an unusually cool day for early April, and she's all in black again. I'm in a silk blouse and heels, with jewelry like armor.

There's a coffee in front of me, untouched in its paper cup. I bought her one, too. I was raised to be nice, always. But that conditioning might not be serving me well right now. I have to be tough. Let her know that this ends today. No more harassing texts. No more pictures.

Oh, God, those pictures.

"I love bagels," she says, "but that's a big line."

"I should have bought you one. I just didn't think..." I trail off. What I mean is, she's so skinny; she doesn't look like someone who touches carbs. Or maybe she just has a fast metabolism. Or she hasn't been able to eat since Corey died...?

No, I'm the one who's been wasting away these past months. Not her.

"Thanks for meeting me," she says. As if she would have taken no for an answer. "I'm sure this can't be easy for you, but hopefully we can make it quick."

"I'd like that," I say, folding my hands together primly to stop them from shaking.

I knew Corey. I know myself. This is bad math. Jade could never be part of the equation.

"I always respected your marriage," she tells me. "I never asked Corey to leave you."

I'm stunned. What a piece of work this woman is. It's like she expects me to thank her.

"This doesn't have to change anything for you," she says. "You had a great marriage. Corey always said that. He loved you very much."

"Loved?"

"I just mean he's not here anymore to love either of us."

"Are you saying he loved you?" I can't believe the words that are coming out of my mouth.

She nods, without pride or shame. Just... matter of fact. "He talked about you a lot, though. All good things."

What man would talk to his mistress that way? What mistress would put up with it? There it is, my answer. She has to be lying.

"Corey knew how to compartmentalize," she says. "He loved you, but he also loved Tai. Very much. Corey's been in Tai's life since the day he was born. He wasn't just a sperm donor, if that's what you're thinking. He was a father. He and Tai were incredibly close."

"How old is Tai?" I shouldn't be asking. It'll only encourage her and prolong the interaction. Even now, though, I want to keep this from getting ugly. I can't help wanting to end on a good note, with no one getting hurt. But there's just something about Tai.

I should have deleted those pictures she sent, the ones of Tai and Corey together. Instead, I've looked at them a hundred times. My eye wasn't lingering on Corey; it was Tai who drew me in.

"He's four," she says.

"He's beautiful." It comes out mechanical, though I very much mean it. I'm speaking with difficulty, as if lockjaw might set in from the pain. Not the pain of Tai being Corey's son, since that can't be true; I won't let it be true. It's the pain of knowing Jade gets to be Tai's mother. It's likely that I'll never get to experience that myself.

"Thank you." She looks down at the table, and I have the sense that she's steeling herself. "Corey didn't provide for Tai in the event of his death."

There it is. She might talk a good game about love, but in the end…

"So you're here because you need money?" I keep my voice and face neutral. I'm no idiot; I thought this would be coming.

"I'm here for Tai. To claim his inheritance."

"There's a reason it's called the last will and testament—as in, it represents the will of the departed. You and Tai were never mentioned in Corey's." That comes out mechanical, too, for a different reason. I'm reciting my prepared statement.

"Corey didn't think to update his will, and I never thought to ask. Corey was young and healthy." She's looking at me as if for confirmation; I'll give her nothing.

"Is Corey listed on Tai's birth certificate as the father?"

"No."

"Because you weren't sure if Corey was the father?" I feel a little bad, battering her like this, but she's the one who started it.

She's trying to contain her offense at the suggestion. "I know Corey's the father. I just didn't want it on the birth certificate because I wanted to make sure I'd always have sole custody."

"You thought Corey might sue for custody?"

"No." She's visibly frustrated, as if I'm supposed to be trying to understand her. As if I'm just going to roll over and let her have her way.

"I'm guessing you don't have any DNA testing to prove Corey's the father, either."

"We didn't do testing. I knew Corey was the father. He knew it, too. There was never a question."

Well, I've got questions. But her answers have been most reassuring. We should be able to finish this today.

"You saw the pictures." She's turned pleading. "You saw Tai the other day. There's no question Tai is Corey's son."

I shake my head. That's an emphatic no. I can't allow myself to crumble and cave and open my heart and checkbook just because Tai's a little boy, an innocent, and New York is expensive, and I do have plenty of money. But I believe in justice, and in honoring the wishes—and the memory—of the dead.

I believe in Corey, and I know that he updated his will last year. Neither Jade nor Tai earned a mention.

Because none of this is true.

"There was no good way to tell you about Corey and me," Jade says. "I wanted to be kind. I gave you a head start."

"What does that mean?"

"I skipped the funeral." She's lying; I saw her there. I feel a tiny note of pleasure since now it'll be easier for me to dismiss her. Small lies suggest bigger ones. "I'm not a patient person, but I waited to approach you. As months went by, I realized there was no settlement, that he hadn't made any financial arrangements."

I'm watching her closely. She fibbed about the funeral, but I can see her sincerity and her pain. Her desperation. Now it's all becoming clear. "I can tell you believe what you're saying." My tone drips with compassion.

"Excuse me?"

She's obviously sick. She managed to take pictures of Corey with Tai—maybe there was a Toys for Tots event through Corey's work, since one of the photos she sent me also features

Santa—and then constructed some sort of alternate fantasy life. She thinks she's telling the truth because she's mentally ill. I need to treat her with kid gloves.

She must be picking up my drift because her expression turns indignant. "I'm not crazy! Corey and I were in love."

"It doesn't really add up, though, does it? No woman would be with a man for years, listening to him talk about how great his wife is, okay with being a permanent sidepiece. Especially not after having his child."

"I wasn't a sidepiece; I was an independent woman." She seems a little frenzied as she repeats, "I'm not crazy."

"I didn't say you were." Her agitated response seems to be proving my theory, though. I do hope she gets the help she needs, but that'll be from a psychiatrist, not from me.

Suddenly her entire demeanor changes. She's the one oozing sympathy. "I get it, Maren. You're probably still in denial from losing Corey, and then I show up. So you want to deny this, too. But on some level, in your gut, you have to know I'm telling the truth."

"I'm sorry, but that's not what my gut is telling me."

"You want me to go away, right?" she says. "I'm happy to do that. All I want is what's fair. This can be totally amicable."

My eyes widen. Was that a threat? "So you'll only leave me alone if I pay you off?"

"I'm asking you to do the right thing. I know you're a good person. Corey told me you are. Tai is Corey's son, and he should be provided for."

"You're his mother. Don't you provide for him?"

"Do you have any idea how much it costs to raise a child?"

I feel abashed. I grew up like any regular middle-class kid, but when I got together with Corey, I hit the jackpot in every way. Only my luck ran out the day Corey died.

Well, if I'm honest, it ran out years before that—the day Corey told me that he'd changed his mind about having a baby with me. Was that because he was having one with Jade?

Oh my God. The timing... He said that about five years ago. And Tai is four.

Is it possible that the math does add up?

"If you had a child of your own, you'd fight for his well-being, wouldn't you?" Jade says. "You'd be doing exactly what I am."

I feel a surge of fury, but I'm not sure who the target is.

"I'm sorry," Jade says. "I know having kids of your own must be a sore subject. I shouldn't have—"

"No, you really shouldn't have." Only how would she know what a sore subject it is unless Corey had told her?

I don't like what my gut is saying right now.

I push my chair back with a loud scrape. I look her right in the face and say in a clear crystalline voice, "None of this can be true."

"I have hundreds of pictures I can show you." She picks up her phone and starts hurriedly swiping.

"It doesn't add up." It's my party line, my best defense.

"My name is Jade Bastone." She's speaking quickly. "Google me. Hell, commission a full background check. I'm a decent person who just happened to fall in love with another woman's husband." I'm looking past her, the sidewalk outside beckoning. "I'm sorry, Maren. When Corey was alive, you weren't real to me. He was more real to me than anyone I'd ever met, which is nuts since he wasn't my type at all. I bet that's what you've been telling yourself when you look at me: that it couldn't be true because I'm not his type. That Corey and I don't make sense."

I don't say anything, but of course that's crossed my mind.

"I had a relationship with Corey for six years, off and on, but mostly on," she says. "Even when we were off, he stayed involved with Tai. He loved us, Maren. A lot."

I want to go, but for some reason, I can't seem to walk away. My feet won't cooperate. Or is that my gut?

"Corey and I didn't have a formal financial arrangement," she says. "I never asked for one, and he didn't offer. I guess I didn't want our relationship to seem transactional, but now I realize how stupid that was. We should have had a child support agreement in place. I didn't protect my son in the event of... well, you know the event." Tears leap to her eyes. "He helped me out every month, but it wasn't a lot of money. I kept living in the same apartment in Brooklyn. It's rent-stabilized."

I don't want to hear this. Her life is her life, and it should never have intersected with mine.

"You do know your husband. You know the man Corey was. So you know that he would want his son to be well taken care of."

"I can't do this," I say. "I can't believe you."

"You can't. And yet, you do."

"I think this conversation is over." I wish I hadn't led with "I think." I wish I'd sounded firmer.

Now she's going to keep coming for me.

FOUR
MAREN

I stumble up the street toward the midnight blue town car and yank open the passenger side door. I'm out of breath even though I've walked less than two blocks through the thicket of pedestrians, mostly tourists, beneath the myriad billboards for Broadway shows, all while trying not to breathe in through my nose. (I don't know which smell is worse—urine, sewer, exhaust, or hot dog carts.) I'd picked a part of the city that I don't frequent, a place where I have no personal associations. It's impossible for Jade to ruin Times Square.

Emmanuel looks over from the driver's seat, his dark eyes bright with concern. He's been worried about me for the past two days, ever since I told him about Jade's appearance on my doorstep.

He and I have done so much grieving together, much of it unspoken. We both miss Corey terribly. Emmanuel's been our family driver for almost ten years, so he and Corey spent countless hours together traversing the city, countless hours engaged in conversation. Corey used to joke that Emmanuel knew where all the bodies were buried.

It doesn't seem like a joke anymore, now that Corey's dead. Now that I've met Jade.

Emmanuel's five years older than me, though his courtly manner can make him seem even older and definitely wiser. While his face is handsome and barely lined, his hair has a smattering of gray amid the black coils. The gray predates me. It's probably because he and his wife, Zauna, went through so much in Nigeria and in the subsequent process of immigrating to the U.S. They're incredible parents to two incredible daughters.

Corey and I used to host Emmanuel and his family at least once a month for dinner. I've loved watching his girls grow up. But since Corey's death, it's just too painful for me to witness what I don't have.

I haven't explained it outright to Emmanuel, but I know he understands why the dinner invitations have stopped. These days, he's the only one who makes me feel understood. Who makes me feel safe. He's my family now.

"Anything I should know?" I ask, trying to smile. It's one of our customary greetings, a reference to the fact that while Emmanuel waits, over the course of a day, he reads the entirety of the *New York Times*. That's remained his ritual for the past decade.

"Not a thing," he says firmly. "What should I know about...?" He's sensitive enough not to say her name.

"I'll tell you sometime." I lean my forehead against the cool glass of the window. "Could we just go home, please?"

"Of course." He starts the engine.

I close my eyes, even though that makes me more sensitive to every lurch of traffic since I can't see what's coming. I didn't see Jade coming, that's for sure.

Off and on, for *six years*?

It's unfathomable. Yet she looked so credible, so convinced

of the story she was selling. And I just can't stop seeing those pictures. Despite myself, she's getting to me. Because Tai is.

My eyes snap open. We're just turning onto Third Avenue, and I can see the iconic Chrysler Building in the distance, standing sentinel. I love this city. I moved here for Corey. But now I'm hollow, and New York feels haunted.

"You're one hundred percent sure you've never heard—or overheard—the names Jade and Tai, that you never even suspected that Corey was involved with someone else?" I say. Emmanuel and Corey had been incredibly close, much more than an employer and employee.

"One hundred percent." His tone is unequivocal and his eyes are on the road. Is he avoiding looking at me? Could it be that his allegiance to Corey survives death?

No, there's no way. Corey wasn't a liar, and neither is Emmanuel. Which means that Jade must be, even if she doesn't know it.

What if a mentally ill woman is after me? Well, after my money. She told me outright that if I pay her, she'll go away.

Is that considered extortion? Maybe I should go to the police.

I'll only do that if she keeps bothering me. I don't want to make trouble for someone who's unwell, especially when that someone is the mother to such a beautiful little boy.

She's beautiful, too. I wouldn't blame any man for being attracted to her.

"Do you think Corey would ever have cheated on me, just for a night even?" I ask. Maybe he and Jade were together one time, and given her age, she's quite fertile. I'm probably a decade older. She could have gotten pregnant and never even told Corey. The whole bit about him acting as Tai's father could have been made up, a way for her to strengthen her argument for a cash grab.

I could forgive one moment of weakness. It wouldn't have to change my whole way of seeing him or our relationship.

"Corey would never cheat on you," Emmanuel says firmly. Too firmly?

"Do you swear?"

He laughs, a deep, resonant baritone, and extends his hand toward me. "Pinky swear." I laugh as we entwine our fingers.

Once both his hands are back on the wheel, my mood dips again. I don't want to believe what Jade was telling me because it's so much worse than mere infidelity. To believe Jade would mean accepting that Corey hadn't only been leading a double life; he'd been leading the life that I always intended to have with him. We tried for years to have a child of our own. Then about five years ago, he'd had enough. He refused to do IVF and wouldn't consider surrogacy or adoption.

"I love you," he said. "I love our life. We're each other's family. I don't want everything to be about conceiving."

I'd been filled with panic but tried not to show it. "I'm not saying that a child is the only thing I want. But it is what I want the most."

"Tell me the rest of your bucket list. I'll make every other thing happen."

I stared at him. Was he hearing himself? Did he actually think anything could substitute for the experience of loving, nurturing, and raising another human being? "Paris in the spring," I said flatly.

"Done." He didn't even realize I was being sarcastic. "I really think it's better this way."

I was speechless.

Which he seemed to take for assent. "Having children is like the world's biggest roulette wheel. You have no idea who you're going to get. Why introduce that kind of uncertainty? And stress? And chaos?"

"Because it's parenthood. Because..." I couldn't even explain it. It was pure feeling.

A feeling he clearly didn't share.

"I thought we both wanted kids," I said. "I thought we were in this together."

"We are in this together." He came toward me. His face, voice, and body language were in congruence; they all told how completely he loved me. "We're in this life together. But it's not going to include a child. I need you to accept that."

It was the cruelest thing anyone had ever said to me. That moment had been a kind of death.

"We tried," he said, "but it wasn't meant to be. You're disappointed, I know. It's painful to want what you can't have, which is why I'm proposing that we put all our energy into wanting what we do have. Let's want each other. Let's want sex and freedom and trips to Paris. Let's live high."

I went along because what was the alternative? I couldn't imagine twisting his arm into fatherhood. That wouldn't have been good for him or me or the child. I never even thought of leaving, not with the way I loved him. The way I still love him.

So I worked at enjoying my life—our life together—by having more adventurous sex, planning romantic dates, taking lavish trips, throwing parties in our Manhattan apartment and our Hamptons house, eating at the world's greatest restaurants, shopping at Bergdorf's, and convincing myself that I wasn't empty, I was full.

That was five years ago, and Tai is four.

Could Corey have stopped trying to have our baby because Jade was pregnant? In one life, he was a father; in the other, he was still free. They say you can't have it all, but maybe you can, if you're leading a double life.

I'd put all my faith and trust in Corey, I gave up all the other lives I could have led just to stand beside him, but what if it wasn't worth it? What if he lied and cheated and stole childbearing years from me?

Five years ago, I was thirty-five. If I'd left Corey then, I could be a mother by now. Whether Jade is telling the truth or not, I'm still alone. I have nothing, and no one.

Emmanuel looks over and sees that I'm crying. He hands me a tissue. "Come to dinner tonight," he says. "Everyone misses you."

"I can't, but I miss them, too." Dayo's fourteen, Blessing's eleven, and they're both forces of nature, just like their mother, Zauna. Emmanuel is the steady hand. "Tell me everything they've been up to."

He smiles. "It's my pleasure."

We're not far from home but I already know I'm going to stay in the car awhile just to listen longer. I'd invite him up, but he prefers the car. He gets a little nervous when we head into the apartment. I think I'm the only woman who he spends time alone with outside of his wife and daughters.

"It's amazing that Blessing's only eleven and already knows what she wants to do with her life," I say to Emmanuel. I have yet to decide what I'm going to do with the rest of mine. "You're going to have a doctor in the family!"

"She's ambitious, that one." He glances at me. "Come see her, Maren. I'll text Zauna and she can cook something special."

"No, I wouldn't ask that of her. She's already so busy." Zauna is incredibly warm and friendly, but we've never exactly been friends. Maybe it's because I find her a little intimidating. She's a devoted public school teacher and a devoted mom and a nonstop whirling dervish. Her work is demanding and exhausting, but it's also a source of great pride and fulfillment. Even before Corey died, I was a little envious.

I guess I'm lucky, having no one to worry about but myself, being able to indulge my misery for so long without having to concern myself with working to pay my bills, but it's a double-edged sword. My home is a refuge, yes, but it's also way too quiet. I wish someone depended on me.

If anything happened to Emmanuel, Zauna would have to keep going. She'd be needed by her kids and her students. She's vital. There wouldn't be enough hours in the day for her to sit and cry, whereas I've had so many hours. Far too many hours.

I'm already dreading the moment when I go upstairs and shut the door and am left alone. I don't want to get out of the car, don't want Emmanuel to go.

With Corey gone, a private driver is an absurd extravagance. But I can't bear the idea of losing Emmanuel, too.

Finally, I can feel that it's time. We've been idling near the building for long enough. I need to quit stalling.

"Take care of yourself, Maren," he says.

"You, too." We share a smile and then he gets out to open my door for me. I'd rather do it myself, given our friendship, but he prefers formal rituals.

Once inside, Javier wishes me a good afternoon from his post at the front desk. I'm about to head for the elevator, but then I find myself hesitating. Turning back. And on a whim, I ask the question that I probably shouldn't. After all, Emmanuel's already told me what I wanted to hear, and I should leave well enough alone.

Instead, I say, "You know the woman who came to see me a few days ago? The one with the partially shaved head? She was with a little boy."

"Sure, I remember."

"Had you ever seen them before?"

He nods. "Not the little boy, but the woman. It was just the one time, but it was definitely her. She was here with Corey. When she came by a couple of days ago, she said she wanted to surprise you. She asked me not to call up since you really like kids and you'd like meeting her son."

"When was she here with Corey?" My throat is dry; I'm choking on the words. "What were they doing together?"

"It was a year ago, maybe? He was telling her it was okay, she should come upstairs, and she was saying no, she'd just wait for him in the lobby. 'Out of respect,' she said, that was the phrase. She said it a few times before he took no for an answer. She stayed behind, so that's how I got such a good look at her. He went up and grabbed something and then came back and they left."

She didn't go upstairs. Out of respect... for me?

Corey and Jade had been close enough to argue. Intimate enough.

I see it dawning on Javier what he's just said, drawing the obvious conclusion that he'd probably drawn then and forgotten. But he hadn't forgotten Jade. A woman like her is memorable.

"It's probably not what you're thinking," Javier says, which only makes it worse. It confirms that he's thinking it, too.

"Thanks, Javier," I whisper, as the walls collapse around me.

FIVE
MAREN

"I was a little worried," Alyssa tells me once we're settled on our favorite Central Park bench. "I thought you'd gone MIA again."

"Sorry," I say. "Things have just gotten a little complicated."

"Oh?" She perks up. Alyssa claims drama is good for the complexion, though really, that glow of hers is from a combination of facials, lasers, microneedling, and whatever else her cosmetic dermatologist chooses to throw into the mix. (Alyssa will try anything once.) Even in the most direct sunlight, she appears poreless and incandescent.

She's attractive in a very effortful manner: an ombre blonde with bright red lips and a killer bod (if they're implants, they're world-class), always dressed in high fashion, never jeans or athleisure. She's the kind of woman who unselfconsciously references her "signature scent."

But she's also got a truly good heart. She was the first finance wife to accept me fully, without an audition, and because of that, the others followed suit.

I'll always be grateful for the way she handled my reemergence after Corey's death. I alternately ignored and avoided her for the first few months, but she never gave up or made me feel guilty. She kept inviting me to events long after everyone else had stopped. Not that I blame them—widows are murder on a dinner party.

"So what's going on?" Alyssa asks eagerly.

I breathe deep, taking in the fresh air and the beautiful setting. I love the Shakespeare Garden in spring. The minor bulbs are tiny and numerous, creating a carpet of flowers. Daffodils, tulips, roses, peonies, azaleas, and violets are all here, waving at us in the breeze.

"Don't keep me in suspense! Remember, I left my kids for this!" Alyssa grins in jest.

She can be free at a moment's notice because, while her children are three and six, they each have their own live-in nanny. She once joked, "Some people get lawyered up; others get knocked up. Me, I'm nannied up."

We're very different people. If I'd been fortunate enough to have kids, I wouldn't want to miss a minute.

Since Jade and Tai showed up, my wound at not having a child has been ripped back open. Last night, the pain was so acute that it was like I was hemorrhaging. In my fitful dreams, Tai's face featured prominently.

I'm not going to get to raise Corey's child. She will.

How could he have done this to me?

"Seems like you need a minute," Alyssa says. "I'll fill in the gap with Asshole's latest crime…"

She launches into a story about her husband, Sean, whom she affectionately (and at times not so affectionately) calls "Asshole." Part of why I couldn't go straight back to hanging around Alyssa after Corey's death was because of the Asshole anecdotes. While Alyssa's marriage is one of the most solid around and her acerbic humor is an essential trait, while I can often enjoy living vicariously through a woman who says the quiet parts out loud, I was just too raw in those first few months. I knew that I had to keep my distance when I had the truly vile thought, "Why couldn't God have taken Asshole instead of Corey?"

"I'm ready now," I say. She adopts an overexaggerated listening posture, leaning toward me, ear cocked. But she quickly drops the pose when she realizes just how serious it is, as I tell her about my interactions with Jade, as well as what I've found out about the difficulty of proving paternity (or hopefully disproving it) from beyond the grave. Corey was cremated and lives in an urn on our bedroom mantel.

Alyssa rolls her eyes. "Of course she doesn't have any actual proof, because she's lying. But she's planted reasonable doubt, and she knows you'd have a hard time fully disproving the claim. What a genius scam she's running."

"You really think it's a scam?"

"Absolutely!"

I wish I shared her conviction. Jade had seemed so sincere. Not to mention, sincerely bereaved over Corey. Javier identified her, and she's got pictures of Tai with Corey. My gut says that she's telling the truth. But then, my gut thought Corey was an honest man, too. All those years together and I never once suspected him.

"Some sort of affair probably went on." There, I'm the one saying the quiet part out loud. "What I don't know is how long it really lasted—I just can't believe it was six years, I would have sensed something—or whether Tai really is Corey's son."

"There is no way. Corey worshipped you."

"Thank you." Tears prick my eyes. Because there is a rather obvious way that Tai is Corey's son, and if that's the case, then what am I supposed to do? I can't just bury my head in the sand. Jade won't let me. She's made that clear. And can I really let an innocent little boy suffer for the sins of his parents?

"No, thank *you*. For being an example for the rest of us. Do you know how many times I've told Asshole, 'Treat me like Corey treats Maren. WWCD—as in, What Would Corey Do?'" She smiles and reaches out to stroke my arm like I'm a cat. "I know what I saw, and believe me, I'm no sucker."

I feel my spirits lift slightly.

"Jade's probably one of those predators who reads the obituaries to look for marks. Did you know there are people who use other people's tragedies as opportunities?" I can see Alyssa warming to her theory. "They come out of the woodwork after terrorist attacks or natural disasters, when the loved ones are grieving and vulnerable. Jade must have realized her son looked a little like Corey and saw her chance. She's probably done it to a bunch of other widows, too."

"She's already sent me a few photos of Corey and Tai. She said she has hundreds of others."

"Deep fakes are everywhere now! Anyone can get the software. She probably wrote it off as a business expense. Didn't she make it absolutely clear that she's after your money?"

I'm not sure why I'm having any desire to defend Jade, except for Tai. I don't want him to have a con woman for a mother. When I first laid eyes on him, he was cowering behind her. I hate the idea that he's been frog-marched down other widows' hallways.

"It just seemed like she was telling the truth," I say.

"She's probably a failed actress. No, an actress who's succeeding wildly, if she's convincing people to give her a cut of their estates."

"If she's an actor, then maybe Tai is, too. I mean, maybe he isn't her real son." I don't have to know him to want a good life for him.

"Don't let some con woman mistake your compassion for weakness, Maren."

"I don't think I've been that compassionate, actually." I'd felt a little guilty about it later, how I treated Jade in the bagel shop, questioning her sanity, but if Alyssa's right, then Jade's the one who should be found guilty in a court of law. She's defrauding people.

Even if Alyssa's wrong, even if Jade is telling the whole truth, then Jade should feel guilty for having a protracted affair—and unprotected sex—with a married man.

What are the odds, though? Because Corey would have felt the guiltiest of all, but I never picked up even a whiff of that. The whole time that he and Jade were allegedly together, our marriage was as loving as it had ever been.

It was passionate, too. We had hot sex regularly, and it had only gotten hotter over the past half-decade once I had no other focal point. We were excellent travel partners. We rarely disagreed on anything significant, so there was no need to fight. Our biggest, most profound, nearly existential disagreement about having kids got settled. It wasn't in my favor, but I accepted that. We were aligned around the new goal: wanting only what we had.

And we had a lot. Like Alyssa said, we'd been role models to everyone else in our social circle. We were That Couple.

Thank God for Alyssa, here to set me straight. None of my other friends would want the job. I can tell they don't want to talk about Corey at all; they prefer not to think about how fragile life is.

"I'm not about to let anyone prey on you," she says. I can see that she's getting fired up. She loves a good fight, and it means everything that she's in my corner.

I smile. Emmanuel and Alyssa are pretty amazing teammates. Jade doesn't know what she's up against.

Alyssa takes her phone out of her Balenciaga purse. "What did you say Jade's last name was again?"

"Bastone."

I've already looked her up on social media, of course. I saw only what was public because I didn't know what she'd make of me following her. She's not on TikTok, though I would have expected she would have been given her age and her profession as a hairstylist.

She doesn't post publicly about Tai (unless that's a sign he's not really her son). She also doesn't post often, and when she does, there's not much personality or feeling behind it. My sense is that she feels she has to do it as self-promotion for her work at a salon called Angelica's.

"She's trash," Alyssa says definitively. "Did you see that salon?" She does a "Yikes!" face.

I feel another peculiar impulse to defend Jade. "It might not be high-end, but it looked reputable."

"It's in the Meatpacking District. Do you know how many other salons they're competing with? That website was bare bones. Maybe it's not even a real salon. It could be a front for money laundering or something."

"Really?"

"Maybe Jade put it up herself as a cover." Alyssa is looking at her phone again, scrolling. "These posts are just so plastic. It's like she's a bot."

"First you thought the pictures were AI-generated, now you think the woman herself is?" I laugh.

Alyssa doesn't laugh. Instead, she gazes into the middle distance speculatively. "Maybe Jade had a one-night stand with Corey and then became obsessed."

"I thought you were convinced she's a con woman."

"Oh, I am. Almost a hundred percent."

"Do you know something? Did Sean say something? If he did, you have to tell me."

"Don't panic." She touches my hand lightly. "I haven't heard anything, and if I did, I would absolutely tell you. I don't believe in patronizing women, letting them live in ignorance. You're stronger than you think."

I never thought I was weak, actually. She's the one who insinuated it earlier.

"Corey wouldn't be the first man to give in to a stupid impulse and then regret it later because he has a phenomenal wife at home. He might have slept with her a few times and gotten it out of his system. It confirmed that you're the one he wants, always. Then she became a stalker. You know, a fatal attraction."

"Do you really think that's what happened?" I far preferred the idea that they'd never been together at all.

"It could be that. We'll never know."

A stalker. A fatal attraction. That suggests violence, which makes my blood suddenly run cold. "The police said it was an accident. But do you think Jade could have hurt Corey?"

"It's not impossible," she says. "I can't believe you've never listened to true crime podcasts. I'm addicted. I'll send you my top ten list."

Like I need her true crime when I'm suddenly in the midst of my own.

Since Jade showed up, I've been ruminating about whether her story could be true, but now I'm realizing that might not be the most important question. The real question is, how dangerous is Jade?

I'd hate to pay off a mistress or a con woman, but I might have to for my own safety.

I told all the doormen that they are never to let anyone upstairs without getting my explicit permission—there are to be no more surprises—but Jade seems like one determined woman. She got to Corey, and now she'll get to me.

Seeing how disturbed I am, Alyssa starts rambling and rhapsodizing about my relationship with Corey, going on and on about how she only wishes Asshole showered her with the kind of attention and admiration that Corey had displayed toward me. She's petting my arm again. "You're the only one Corey loved."

She wants me to be reassured, so I pretend that I am.

But I've got this feeling like she might believe Jade more than she's letting on, or that she knows more than she's telling.

SIX

MAREN

I'm still here, Maren.
When can we talk?
We need to meet.
We need to finish our conversation.

Jade's been relentless all day. It's 3 p.m., and I finally turned the phone off an hour ago, but I keep imagining the ping of an incoming text.

I'm still tangled up in bed, thinking and rethinking. The blackout curtains are shut tight over the sliding glass doors. I have a balcony that overlooks Central Park in all its spring glory, and this is how I'm back to spending my days. It's not right. It's not fair.

But what's right and fair where Tai is concerned? I wish I didn't care. I wish I could be as selfish as Corey was.

As Corey might have been. I don't know anything for sure.

Well, I know one thing: If Tai is Corey's son, then Corey should have made sure to take care of him.

So why didn't he? Is it because Tai isn't Corey's son? Or because Corey was not at all the man I thought he was?

Jade is saying that since Corey didn't do what he should

have, the responsibility now falls to me. And maybe she's right, even if it's not fair. I don't want someone like her to be right. She was sleeping with my husband (probably). She's an immoral person telling me to do the moral thing, and frankly, that really pisses me off.

Then it comes to me, a way that I could take back some measure of control. Jade is asking—no, insisting—that we see each other again, but any appointment would essentially be on her terms. She'd be able to project the image she wants in order to support her story. Instead, I need to show up unannounced. If I catch her off guard, if I observe her natural habitat, I can see the truth with my own eyes.

Who is Jade? Is she the (other) woman Corey loved or some sad, pathetic stalker or a con artist? How dangerous is she?

I'm about to find out.

The idea is like a shot of adrenaline. I spring out of bed and into a long hot shower, thinking all the while about how to do my hair and makeup and what clothes to wear. What image do I want to project? The first time Jade and I met, I was in workout gear; the second, I'd dressed up. Overdressed, probably, out of insecurity. This time, I'll go for the midpoint: the kind of subdued makeup that takes twice as long; my hair in casual, tousled waves; jeans and a summery sweater that flatters my curves (I noticed she didn't have any curves herself, that her body was stick straight, in contrast with her hair, which was deliberately avant-garde frizzy).

It hurts, thinking that Corey might have engaged in a years-long affair with someone who's so diametrically opposed to me. But then, I also would have hated if he'd chosen someone too similar to me. Me, only better. Me, but younger. Me, but more fertile.

Who am I kidding, I'd hate it any which way. I'm not built for sharing.

When I picture Corey with Jade, the pain is searing, and I

want to kill him all over again; when I imagine her lying about him, I want to kill her. But beneath it all is this terrible sadness and desolation, the drumbeat of an old song: "I'm So Lonesome I Could Cry."

Only I haven't been crying. I wish I could because it's like having a sneeze that just won't come out. I would love the release, but instead, all these conflicting emotions are trapped inside, and there's no relief on the way.

But there is a sense of agency, finally. I'm taking matters into my own hands instead of just waiting for Jade's next move.

As I apply blush to the apples of my cheeks, I remind myself that if all else fails, I have a parachute. I could pull the rip cord at any time. Give Jade my money, which she seems to think of as Corey's money, and she'll go away.

She's not entirely wrong. Corey is the one who earned it. Maybe I don't need to be so attached to it.

She has a child to support, and I could help. It'd be a good deed, a bit of philanthropy. I gave away plenty of Corey's money while he was alive.

Maybe it's a bargain: I pay her, and she leaves me in peace. Whether she and Corey had a long-term affair or a one-night stand or they barely met or she's insane or a total con woman, I won't ever have to know. The uncertainty could work in my favor. It's like that paradox I learned about in college, how a cat is in a box, and it might be alive, or it might be dead; both are true until you open the box.

This could be a box I never have to open. Nothing has to change for me, if I don't want it to. I can just remind myself of what Alyssa said. Corey and I were That Couple. We can remain so forever, preserved in amber.

Yet through some sadomasochistic impulse, I find myself once again looking at the pictures that Jade sent, the ones of Tai and Corey. They have the same brown eyes, don't they?

But then, there are billions of brown eyes on the planet, and some are bound to be the same toffee as Corey's.

I've been dreaming of those eyes for months now. Missing Corey with a ferocious agony that I would have previously thought impossible. Since he died, I've spent most of my time polishing each memory until it shined, even though that made the suffering even more acute, and why?

I've needed Corey to be perfect. I've needed our life together to be perfect to justify how little I've done with my own.

I didn't work during our marriage because I was waiting to be a mother. Along the way, I became a bored housewife. But I didn't want to admit that. I thought I was supporting and nurturing the ambitions of an incredible husband whose love and devotion were boundless.

Was that a lie I was telling myself? How much did I have to overlook while Corey was alive in order to believe it?

If Jade's story is true, there must have been clues, and I missed every one of them. I mean, we're talking about six years and a second family.

I think of how Alyssa sounded yesterday, how certain she'd tried to be about Corey's fidelity, but she'd waffled, hadn't she? She'd gone from 100 percent to *almost* 100 percent. Between impossible and nearly impossible lies a vast chasm.

Her line that's looping in my head? *It could be that we'll never know.*

I can't live with that. I have to know.

Besides, I don't think it'll be as simple as paying Jade off, either. Emotions aside, that plan works only if Jade is of sound mind. If she's after more than money—if she wants revenge, say, because Corey was my husband and not hers—then the most ironclad contract won't really protect me. She'll know that I can be intimidated and that there's more money where that came from.

Besides, if she is a con woman, doesn't she need to be stopped before she does this to some other unsuspecting widow?

Crime shouldn't pay. And I'm not some damsel in distress, waiting for a man to save me.

I'm no one's easy mark.

SEVEN
MAREN

By the time I look up Jade Bastone's address, which is disturbingly easy to find online, it's somehow almost four-thirty. Emmanuel and I are going to be stuck in rush hour traffic. What a coincidence, Emmanuel and Jade both living in Bushwick.

After he drives me all the way out there, I decide that I'll arrange for a car service or take the subway back. I wouldn't make him do the extra round trip and miss dinner with his family. I'm sure he'll try to convince me to join them, but I just can't face Zauna. He must have told her what's going on.

I'd already felt small in her presence, listening to all she's dealing with as a teacher, seeing her interact with her own kids. It'll be much worse now. I don't have a career, and I'm not a mother, so my only accomplishment was my marriage, and now it turns out…

It hasn't turned out yet. I don't know anything for sure.

When I get into the car with Emmanuel and tell him Jade's address, he doesn't seem surprised. But then, he's a professional. He's frequently understated and he doesn't ask extra questions. Sometimes it feels a little awkward to me, the slight lines—the fault lines—that delineate employer/employee from friends. In some regards, I'm always calling the shots even when I don't want to be. When it would be sweet relief to tell my partner, "You pick." I really miss that.

"You've never been to that address before, have you?" I ask. "I mean, you never took Corey to Jade's?" He shakes his head as he pulls out into traffic. "She's not expecting me."

"Ah, an ambush," he says. "The element of surprise equals the upper hand."

"I hope so."

"What's your plan?"

I stare out the windshield at the line of brake lights. This is going to take an hour, if not longer. "I just need to see what's really going on. Who she really is."

"She might feel the same way about you. Remember, you only know what you've heard about each other from Corey."

"I never heard anything about her." I stare at him. "Do you think it's true? That she really was Corey's mistress and he told her all about me?"

"I assume so. Women don't generally lie about the father of their children."

My mood goes dark, and we lapse into silence. We slowly traverse the long stretch on FDR Drive south and then move through the Brooklyn-Battery Tunnel, under the mouth of the East River.

Did Corey do this trek all the time when he told me he was working late? It never even occurred to me to doubt him or check up on him. He always came home to me, every night. But no matter how late it was, he always showered before climbing into bed. Was he washing away the smell of Jade? Or the baby scent of Tai?

Since Emmanuel wasn't doing the driving, Corey probably took Uber (he hated the subway). I wonder if I could get access to Corey's Uber account, if I could somehow guess the password. Or maybe I could appeal to some kindly supervisor who would take pity on me?

So mortifying, just like the rest of this experience. Everyone must be thinking how stupid I am.

Unless I'm not. Unless Jade is a stone-cold liar. Or even a stone-cold killer.

I feel a ripple of fear. I might be walking right into the belly of the beast, unarmed. Maybe I should ask Emmanuel to come inside with me, just in case?

He's pulling up and stopping beside a row of rundown brick buildings set close together. The first floor of every building is commercial, with awnings for a Chinese restaurant, a florist, a pawnshop, and jewelry repair. Halfway up the block, I see a few homeless squatters. I know Bushwick is gentrifying, and now the crime rate isn't that much higher than the other Brooklyn neighborhoods, but there's still plenty of crime. I've always been concerned about Emmanuel's daughters' safety, worried that they could easily become victims walking to and from school. So while this isn't total squalor, I can't imagine Corey would let his child grow up in these circumstances.

There it is. I have my proof. Jade must be lying.

I'm considering whether I even need to get out of the car when there's a knock on the window. I startle as I realize it's Jade.

I roll down the window.

"Thanks for coming," she says with a smile, as if I'm here at her invitation. "Come on up. I can make us some tea. Or I have Angel's Envy."

Angel's Envy. That's Corey's bourbon of choice.

I feel faint, and that's when I notice Tai. He's holding Jade's hand, and he steps closer to the car. "You're Mommy's friend," he says. He must recognize me from the other day, and maybe that's why he doesn't seem nearly as shy. I'm not a stranger anymore.

"Come inside?" Jade says. "Please?"

She looks so young and hopeful that while all I want is to tell Emmanuel to step on it, to get me out of here, instead I find myself nodding. There's no turning back.

EIGHT
JADE

Well, well, well. What have we here?

Tai noticed the town car before I did, and it nearly broke my heart when he said excitedly, "That's Daddy's!" Ah, the magical thinking of childhood. It's been hard convincing Tai that even though Daddy will live in our hearts forever, he'll never walk through the front door again or idle by the curb.

No, that's not Daddy's anymore. It's Maren's. Everything belongs to her now.

My eyes narrow as I stare at the back of her pampered head. I feel my feet aching in my three-inch heels. I've easily walked a mile today in between subway rides. And sure, I could wear cutesy little kitten heels like the ones Maren had on at the bagel shop the other day, but I'm a hellcat. I'm in stilettos, though they're murder on your feet and your calves, especially when you're standing all day, cutting hair. I'd give them up if I could, but then I wouldn't be me, which is kind of how I felt about Corey.

Maren had better be done holding out on me. I'm running out of patience (not to mention funds).

Her responses to my texts have been brief, unrevealing, and monotonous: *I need time.*

I don't have time.

Angelica, the salon owner, gave notice that she's raising the rent on my workstation, and it's due in a week. She's also been on my ass about having more cancellations and selling less product than some of the other stylists, implying that my chair would be better rented out to someone with a work ethic more like her apprentice Sophie. I wanted to tell her to fuck off, then thought better of it. I'm not exactly sought-after these days.

When I was first starting out in the field almost ten years ago, I was full of fire. My salon was an up-and-comer, and so was I. We were styling models for shows at New York Fashion Week. My social media was on point.

I can't entirely blame motherhood for the change. Hairstyling is a burnout field. An expensive field. It costs money to make money. That's what I was told at the outset, and over the years, I've incurred a load of debt paying for additional training and certifications, keeping up with the latest new techniques. Contractors don't get benefits, but kids need health and dental insurance.

I'm putting all my energy into my retirement plan. Her name is Maren.

At the bagel shop, she'd been absurdly polite, like that was going to deter me. I hate that phony bullshit, the kind that's supposed to connote class and good breeding. Give me authenticity any day. I can take it.

She'd looked a lot different than when I surprised her at her apartment that first day. Her ash-blonde hair had been blown out, and she was in full makeup and an expensive rose-gold silk blouse. She wasn't dripping in diamonds, that would have been gauche, so they were tasteful, and everywhere: on her wrists, neck, ears. She glittered like a constellation in the night sky, and her style screamed Upper East Side, though we were in a coffee and bagel place in Times Square surrounded by tourists. That was where she'd picked to meet, and the reason was obvious. She didn't want anyone she knew to see or hear us.

I could understand that. I'm not a monster, even if she thinks otherwise. I mean, I never set out to blow up her life. If Corey were still alive, she would never have had to know about Tai or me. I kind of like it in the shadows.

But the fact is, Corey's dead. Nothing I say or do will change that. Another fact is that she's been left with everything, which is blatantly unfair. They had a shallow marriage. He couldn't be his full self with her, and they barely saw each other. He was either working or with me (while telling her he was working). How much is really different for her now that he's dead?

Meanwhile, I've lost my soulmate. My son lost his father.

She sat across from me, dressed like that, waving her money in my face. She might think she's better than me, but I'm not easily intimidated. Corey loved that about me, by the way, how I was tough, always giving him shit. We laughed all the time.

Maren had been staring down at the crumb-laden Formica table as I went into my spiel. I couldn't quite read her expression, maybe because expertly injected fillers made her face slightly immobile. Or could she really be that repressed?

It doesn't matter. I don't want to know her. I just want my money. Tai's money. Which she has yet to cough up, despite the abundant evidence I offered that Tai is Corey's son.

Sometimes her eyes lifted to meet mine. They're a dark blue-gray, like the ocean during a storm. Spectacular. She must get compliments all the time, like I do. Corey wasn't an ass or a tit man; he was an eye guy.

When I told her that he said good things about her all the time, I could tell she thought I was lying. But I wasn't. I just was never threatened by her. I'd never want a marriage that's so sanitized and careful, like it exists under glass. Corey and I were real. Sure, we fought sometimes, but I knew all of him. He didn't have to put on airs or pretend. With me, he could be his entire self and feel accepted. With Maren, he had to curate.

He never said that. But I could read between the lines.

To tell her the whole truth would have been cruel, not to mention inefficient. I intend to take the money and run. I deserve it. I'm raising Corey's child, which makes me every bit as legitimate as Maren is. More legitimate, really. Tai is what's left of Corey. Tai is Corey's blood and his legacy.

I'll only beat that drum if she makes this hard. I'm hoping she won't. Over the years, Corey's told me many times, in many different ways, just how tenderhearted, generous, and charitable Maren is.

But that's not the Maren I've seen so far.

Maybe her heart got calloused after Corey died. Sorry about that, but everyone has to face the world's brutality sometime, and I don't entirely mind being Maren's reality check. I'm no sadist, but Corey obviously babied her way too much. Maybe it was penance for never having made babies with her?

Whatever, that's her problem. I've got enough of my own, and Maren's going to be the solution.

All she has to do is make a deal, and I'm gone. I don't want to be entangled with her any more than she wants to tangle with me. I was trying to get that across to her in the bagel shop, but she wanted to turn it around on me, pretend I'm some crazy woman. I'm saner than she is.

It rankles, though, how she looked right past me, toward the street, the same way she had in her apartment, like even wallpaper's more interesting. Like I'm nothing.

I've felt that too much in my life.

I had to take a few minutes to compose myself then. I'm proud that I was able to do that because I have a tendency to let impulse override rationality.

It had felt like a game of chicken, and I hadn't wanted to

swerve; I'd wanted to turn the wheel and go right into her. But I couldn't afford a fiery collision, not when Tai's future is at stake.

Maren was supposed to be sweet. Kind and compassionate, that's what Corey always said. She should want to do the right thing, which is to provide for Tai.

But there might have been levels on which Corey never knew Maren. He kept her sheltered. It makes me wonder what she would have done if he'd tried to come clean and tell her about me. You never know what'll come out of somebody until their back is against the wall.

Maren's fighting to protect the status quo, to believe in the life she thought she had with Corey. She's defending the safe little world that she's inhabited, the one that Corey built for her. It's not my fault that it was built on sand. If it hadn't been me, it would have been someone else.

No, that's not true. The other woman always wants to think she's special, but I actually was. Corey had never cheated on Maren before, only he couldn't resist me. What started out as bomb sex became so much more. I wouldn't trade a moment we spent together, even the wretched ones. Not for anything.

I don't just mean because of Tai, though obviously he's part of it. But the love Corey and I shared was bigger than procreation. It's the reason Tai is the amazing kid he is.

If Maren wants to make this a battle, that's on her. I'm fighting for Tai, so I have to win.

I did lie a little, though. I told her I skipped the funeral. Actually, I slipped in late and slipped out early and sat in the back. It wasn't the party I would have thrown; this was no celebration of life. It was staid and boring and, occasionally, accidentally, hilarious. Finance bros think they're immortal, and they have no idea how to give a eulogy.

Somewhere in the bagel shop confrontation, I had a realization: I wasn't 100 percent there for the money; I'd also like validation. I want acknowledgment that Corey and I were real. A tree fell in the forest, but nobody heard it. We spent the bulk of our relationship hiding out in my apartment and now I want to be out in the light. Maybe it's too little, too late, but it's something.

We existed. We loved. I still love. Wherever he is, he still loves me.

He probably still loves Maren, too. I never said he couldn't. People don't own each other, though Maren can't understand that. She needs Corey to have been all hers. She's provincial like that.

She probably looks down on me, thinks Corey wouldn't have loved someone so different from her. But Corey craved variety. Who doesn't?

Maren, that's who. She wanted predictability and security. But I wanted something else. Something more. And Corey and I found that in each other.

The thing about Maren is that she wants me to be crazy, or for my relationship with Corey to have been sordid or pathetic. But it wasn't. It's an abundant and generous love.

If I have to, I can make myself someone she really, really wants to be done with. I've got bills to pay, and, as I've made clear, I'm not going anywhere.

She might have thought she could turn the tables by showing up here unannounced, but I'm way more adaptable than she is. I can work any situation.

I've got home court advantage. I've heard all about her while she's heard nothing about me. I know her weaknesses and vulnerabilities, while to her, I'm an unknown quantity.

Sorry, Corey, your wife's about to find out who she's dealing with.

Because if there can be only one woman left standing, it'll be me.

NINE

MAREN

I'm still sitting in the town car, window rolled down, trying to seem cool and calm. But inside, I'm panicking.

Emmanuel turns to me with a tender expression. "Maren?" he asks softly. "What do you want to do?"

Jade is watching me expectantly. I don't want her to see me cower. And I can't look at Tai. He's too perfect. It would be like staring into a solar eclipse.

There are tears in my eyes, which I keep focused on Emmanuel. "I should go with them," I say, though a part of me wants him to talk me out of it. I initiated this, and now I want an escape hatch.

I'll just give her some money. She could clearly use it. I don't need to know any more than that, do I?

But I'm so close to the truth. How will I feel later if I chicken out?

"Are you sure?" Emmanuel says. "I can take you home."

"No, you can't. This is your neighborhood. Go home to your family." That clinches it. I can't be that selfish. Or that cowardly. I have some self-respect left.

As I reach for the door handle, Jade rewards me with a brilliant smile.

That feels like a red flag. Somehow, even when I employed the element of surprise, I wound up playing right into her hands.

But Tai is smiling, too, and it's spellbinding.

Guess there's no turning back now.

TEN
JADE

As I let myself, Maren, and Tai into the apartment, I'm surprised to find that I'm overcome with a level of self-consciousness that I haven't experienced since I was a teenager. Meanwhile, Tai is chattering madly, like he often does after he leaves my mother's house. He's hungry for the attention he didn't get all day.

I suspect that Mom is sitting him in front of a screen practically the whole time. That she doesn't even take him out to the park anymore. That what she really finds so exasperating about dealing with him is that he actually wants to engage. He's eager for her company, especially since losing his father.

Eager for anyone's company. Just look at him, tugging at Maren's hand, asking her what her favorite color is.

I can't blame my mother. She just doesn't have much to give. Her last chemo treatment was nine months ago and she's still not up to full strength. She's probably depressed, too. Since Corey's gone, I know the feeling.

I'm not gone, he tells me. *I'm right here.*

I like to talk to him in my head; I like to think he's talking back. *Be nice, Jade.*

I can't always control what he says. That's the thing about us: We weren't trying to control each other. Ours was a different kind of love. The true kind.

I'll do my best, I promise him. But it's really up to Maren. This is going to happen. So does she want to make it easy or hard?

I'm not in the greatest mood. I should have been walking up my street three hours later, urging my sleepy boy on during the walk home from the subway at 9 p.m. But my mother's texts had been unceasing, so I finally had to cancel my remaining clients, despite how much I need the money, despite how much I don't need to alienate current clients or create negative word of mouth.

But maybe it was serendipity, because now I can get Maren to take pity on me. In fact, pity is written all over her face.

It's probably not just the mess—the unwashed dishes, the couch piled with pillows and blankets because Tai loves making forts, the clutter and the dust bunnies because I haven't vacuumed in weeks—but the general shoddiness of the place as well as my belongings. Everything in here is of much lower quality than anything Maren would ever own. It's all either thrift store or off-brand, ripped up and colored on by a rambunctious little boy.

When Corey was first coming around, my apartment had been bohemian and vintage. All the street finds had felt like a mark of authenticity, a distinction from his mannered Upper East Side existence with Maren. He liked it dirty.

The thing about edgy, though, is the actual sharp edges. Babyproofing and childproofing eradicated my personality.

Now Maren is looking around at the walls like she can't find the words.

"Tai loves color," I say, half defiantly and half sheepishly.

Maybe a year ago, on a boring Saturday, Tai and I had the idea to paint every wall a different color. Sure, we're renters, but why should owners have all the fun? The only rules I gave Tai were no pastels and no matching. Each wall had to be distinct from the others. We went to a paint store and got dozens of slips of paper with all the different hues and shades and we laid them out on the living room floor. Tai spent hours deciding.

We painted the one wall of the galley kitchen in the blue of a cloudless sky on a perfectly sunny day. I gave Tai his own mini-roller and brush so he could do segments, too. He begged me not to go over them with my own roller later. He wanted them to be all his. The living room/dining room is deep yellow, fuchsia, violet, and kelly green.

We didn't tell Corey beforehand, just let him come over and discover it. He laughed in this delighted way, like he was a kid himself. I needed a little extra money that month to cover it, but he didn't mind.

With Corey, I never felt embarrassed about the way Tai and I lived or what we could afford, even though I knew his other apartment had been carefully decorated by an interior designer, good taste affirmed by a high price tag. That's the world Maren still inhabits.

I can tell she's feeling sorry for me. Only she shouldn't. Because I would never choose to live her life, and I'm the one who gets to raise Corey's child.

I set that very child up with an iPad inside his fort so that Maren and I can talk at the nearby kitchen table (everything's nearby, it's a very small two-bedroom), and I assume that this looks like terrible parenting to someone like Maren. But that's because someone like Maren would always have square footage and help.

"We'll need to talk quietly," I say as I clear the kitchen table. "Do you want something to drink?"

"No, thank you." She's stiff and visibly uncomfortable. But at least she's dressed in jeans this time, not trying to show me up like at the bagel shop.

"I appreciate you coming all this way." I wait for her to take the reins. Several awkward moments pass. "Are you sure you don't want that bourbon now?"

"Angel's Envy," she says slowly, like she's processing. "Isn't that hundreds of dollars a bottle?"

"Corey left it here." But then, she's already figured that out. She must have been hoping against hope that I'm a liar. Now the converse is sinking in, painfully.

I turn to look at Tai to make sure that he's thoroughly caught up in his video. Maren does the same, her gaze lingering longer than seems necessary.

"You have his bourbon. Do you have anything else of his?" She's whispering, but I suspect it's not only because of Tai. She can't bear to hear her own words and face what they mean.

"I have some of his clothes." I'm whispering, too. "Do you want to see them? Or smell them?" What I mean is, *Do you need more evidence or can we move on to the negotiation phase?* I'm reasonable; I'm not out to bleed her dry. From what I know of Corey's finances, there's more than enough to go around.

Maren knows very little of Corey's finances, or at least, she didn't used to. Corey made it sound like her ignorance was a sort of charming quirk, that it went to show she was still just a sweet, simple girl from Utah.

Bullshit. It's the ultimate sign of privilege to not have to know, to never worry, to just turn on the spigot and let the money gush out, someone else's money that you get to call yours. And now it really is all hers, which I truly resent.

I'm not remotely charmed by Maren's babe-in-the-woods act. I find it tremendously irritating. Insulting even. Because while Maren's been skating, just gliding along the ice, I've been scrapping.

Still am.

But I paste a sympathetic look on my face because I see that

Maren is feeling sorry for herself, imagining Corey's clothes spending all eternity here, in my shitty apartment.

"A smell is like a fingerprint," she says mournfully. "You can fake a lot of things but not that."

"I'm not faking anything, I swear to you. You want me to bring out his clothes?"

Our eyes meet, and I can see that she's giving up. She finally knows that I'm telling the truth. All the fight in her is gone in an instant, and while I'm grateful for that, poised as I am on the cusp of victory, I'm still a human being. So now I get to take pity on her.

"I'm sorry I fell in love with your husband," I say in a hushed tone. "It wasn't my plan or intention. It wasn't his, either."

"If he hadn't died, would he have hidden you away forever?"

"Probably. I didn't make any demands, and we didn't talk about the future. We just enjoyed the present."

She stares at me, stupefied. "I don't understand that. You had a child. You have a child." Her volume has increased slightly, and she looks fearfully over at Tai to make sure he hasn't heard. I do, too. He's still engrossed in his screen. She lowers her voice. "Didn't you think Tai deserved better than a part-time father?"

"Better a part-time father who's happy to be around than a full-time father who's been coerced." I'm trying not to sound defensive, though I feel it. "Corey chose to be in our lives."

I can tell what she's thinking: that she never would have accepted an arrangement like mine or allowed it for her child. But she doesn't know anything about me. I didn't allow it; I chose it, actively.

"No one has to stay, no matter what vow they take or paper they sign," I say tightly.

"Life is unpredictable, that's for sure." She's looking down at the large rock on her engagement ring, half-dazed.

"I could have taken Corey to court, established paternity, and had guaranteed child support. But our bond was worth so much more than that, you know?"

She doesn't answer, just keeps staring at her diamond. It's like she's doing self-hypnosis.

"Since I can't have Corey and Tai doesn't get to have his father, yes, I'd like financial security." My indignation is rising. "You have an apartment that's way too big for one person. You have a house in the Hamptons. You have Emmanuel to drive you around."

No response. I feel like shaking her. Why hasn't she surrendered yet?

"I need a settlement," I say. "It doesn't have to be monthly child support. In fact, a onetime payment would probably be best for everyone."

"You didn't want Corey's money, but now you want mine?"

"You loved Corey." I'm fighting for calm. "I loved Corey. Corey loved Tai, and I'm the one who's raising him. That's why I have to swallow my pride and appeal to your sense of fairness and decency. Corey told me that it's strong."

"My husband gave me a character reference. To his mistress." She shakes her head. "I don't know what world I've stumbled into."

"And I don't know how many more times I can apologize. Let's make this easier on everyone, okay?"

When she looks over, her eyes are bone-dry and very, very cold. A chill goes through me.

Because I know some people like it hard.

ELEVEN

MAREN

"Oh, hi!" I say breathlessly. I wouldn't have expected to quite literally bump into Sean on the street in the middle of a workday. What's he doing in the West Village when his firm is located a stone's throw from Wall Street?

After our collision, he reached out an arm to steady me and now he pulls back, fixing me with a huge smile. Suspiciously huge—the kind you plaster across your face when you've just gotten caught where you shouldn't be.

To be fair, I do have infidelity on the brain after my visit to Jade's apartment last night.

I have to face the truth. The pictures are real. Angel's Envy is real. The life that Corey shared with Jade—and with his son—was as real as the one that he and I had.

He had another family, and he lied about them for years, right to my face. I don't even want to think about how many times he must have told me he was at work and gone to be with them.

Maybe he didn't consider them his other family. Maybe they were his one and only. What was I to him, really?

I'm his beneficiary.

I suppose Corey proved my primacy (and assuaged his guilt) by leaving me practically everything. According to his will, his parents' and sister's mortgages will be paid off, but the rest of his estate goes to me, including millions in investment accounts plus real estate and the two-million-dollar life insurance payout. There's no paperwork about Jade and Tai, which means that I'm in the clear. I have no fiscal obligation to them.

But I do have a moral obligation, and I've decided to start fulfilling it immediately.

That's why I'm here in the West Village, exiting a boutique toy store. The proprietor is a woodworker and she hand-makes intricate puzzles, play sets, and even old-fashioned rocking chairs. I'll visit FAO Schwarz, Lego, Disney, and all the rest of the major players, but I wanted to start out supporting a local artisan.

The reason I was able to make it out of bed this morning when I should have been demolished by the news?

Tai. He needs me.

The first time we met, he'd been so reserved, like he didn't want to be there at all. But last night, he started talking to me right away, almost as if he'd been waiting for me to show back up.

Like recognizes like. Tai's lonely, too, just like I am. He lost his father, and I lost my husband. We need each other.

I'd been too stunned and preoccupied last night to properly respond to Tai's bids for attention, but now I will, tenfold. Jade settled him on that couch, and he was so instantly and creepily absorbed in the computer that it was like no one else was even in the room. So unhealthy. It made me wonder how often Jade lets a video game do her work for her.

Tai needs to be engaged with people and activities, and I'm in a position to provide for much more than his material needs.

That's what got me out of bed today, full of purpose. Crazy as it sounds, I feel almost... happy.

Sean and I step to the edge of the pavement so that other pedestrians can stream by. We're on a classic West Village street, charming and tree-lined with brick façades and striped awnings. But I'm paying it no mind. All my attention is on Sean. I owe it to Alyssa to do a little investigating.

"So why are you here?" I ask, my expression pleasant and my tone neutral.

He doesn't squirm exactly. Maybe he's being totally normal when he says, "Just finished a business breakfast meeting," but who calls it a "business breakfast meeting"? He's either behaving very suspiciously, or I'm very paranoid.

Sean is a hulking man, built like a linebacker who's let himself go, though Alyssa says he works out five days a week. Is he *really* at the gym, though?

He probably is. He probably does exercise hard; he just lives harder. At parties I've seen how much he eats and drinks. Alyssa says he would have loved Roman times, all those bacchanals. "He's a hedonist with very little restraint," she once said, with an affectionate eye roll.

She's never once called him a cheater, though. Alyssa seems so sharp-eyed, but she could have the same wifely blind spot that I did.

"Does Alyssa know where you are?" I say.

"Always." He holds up his phone. "Tracking app. I guess you never used one?"

Ouch. So apparently, Alyssa told him about Jade. (I've never known the precise inner workings of their marriage, what she shares and what she holds back.) Or had he known already? He and Corey weren't the closest of friends, but they were friends. They'd been colleagues for years in a business that requires copious shmoozing.

Alyssa says that Sean can't keep a secret from her. So if he'd known about Jade, then she would have, too, and there's no way she would have sat on that information.

Sean is smiling as if he hasn't just shivved me. And maybe he didn't mean to. Sean's never really been an asshole to me. He's also never struck me as the brightest bulb. He's got family money and connections, and his success screams nepo baby.

"I never tracked Corey," I say. It hadn't even crossed my mind.

"He was a good guy," Sean says.

So maybe Alyssa has kept him in the dark. Well, I'm not about to enlighten him. I'm trying to decide how to respond when we're interrupted by Emmanuel. He's come out of the toy store laden with packages.

"Sean, this is Emmanuel," I say. "Emmanuel, this is—"

"Emmanuel and I go way back!" Sean grins. "Good to see you! You been doing some shopping?"

Emmanuel looks at me deferentially.

"I have some birthday parties coming up for my friends' children," I lie. I mean, I have to. Alyssa doesn't know my plan yet, and I know she won't approve.

Sean raises an eyebrow slightly. "A lot of kids. Or a lot of parties?"

"Both." I laugh, trying to make it sound airy. Trying to sound like I have nothing to hide.

"I miss your house," Sean says. "In Southampton. So cute." I don't think he means "cute" as an insult, though I'm well aware that his Southampton house is at least twice the size. "You make it out there lately?"

"Not since—" I'm about to say, "Corey died," but then I clam up. "It's only April."

"April's the best month! Traffic's light on the Montauk Highway. You should get away."

He's right, the Montauk Highway is only two lanes and it's a congested nightmare all summer. But why is Sean so eager to get me out of town?

I wonder if this is how it's going to be from now on, with me questioning every man's intentions.

"You threw great parties," Sean says. "You were the best hostess of all of them." "All of them" meaning the finance wives. Again, he doesn't even know he's being insulting, that he's diminishing me to just the function I served for Corey.

I feel Emmanuel stiffen beside me. He doesn't like what Sean's just said, either. "I'll go put these in the car," he tells me. Then to Sean, without a smile, "Enjoy the rest of your day."

"You, too, man," Sean says.

I wish Emmanuel hadn't left me here with Sean, who seems in no rush to hurry off. Emmanuel's been by my side through so many hard moments. Right after Corey's death, Emmanuel was the one who accompanied me to Monarch Financial and to the estate attorney. He was my note taker and my emotional support.

I was a wreck already, and it had been strangely destabilizing, learning just how much Corey had left to me, how wealthy we actually were. How wealthy I am now, singularly. There are accounts that I hadn't been aware of, seeing as Corey managed everything and paid every bill. It made sense to us at the time, seeing as he's a seasoned professional, but it also meant that once he was gone, I was adrift.

When they say you don't know what you don't know... well, how right they are.

Last night, Jade enumerated the things I had that she presumably wanted (money, two homes, a driver, etc.) and all I could think was, *I have nothing. You have everything. Just look at that little boy over there.*

My heart goes out to Tai, who doesn't have a father anymore. But Corey's money isn't Corey. Nothing I do will bring Tai's dad back to him. And honestly? I hate the idea of subsidizing Jade. She made her choices, which included sleeping with another woman's husband—my husband—for years.

Yet I also hate the way Tai is living. That apartment was a shambles, and that neighborhood...

I could change Tai's life, if I wanted.

Do I want?

I'm fairly certain I do, but it won't be with a blank check. Jade is the kind of woman who clearly needs supervision. She makes poor choices. She didn't even put Corey's name on Tai's birth certificate! Didn't insist on child support! I would never have made those kinds of mistakes.

But then, I've obviously made plenty of my own.

"You threw so many awesome parties in that house," Sean says.

I feel myself stiffen. Was that all I was to Corey, his cruise director? The one who kept up appearances and held down the fort while he went off with Jade and Tai?

As a young girl growing up in Utah, I'd heard of the Hamptons but knew little about it. I hadn't realized that it's not one place; it's about twenty different towns and villages along the eastern end of Long Island, each with its own vibe.

Corey bought a gorgeous three-bedroom in Southampton near Coopers Beach, one of the best beaches in the country. It has a traditional exterior, gray and shingled with leaded lattice windows, giving it the feel of a British manor. The living room was made for entertaining, with high ceilings and favorable light. Corey and I were both struck by the beauty of the millwork: open wood beams and trim, ornate crown moldings, elegant wainscoting on the walls, and an oak bar. There's no dining room, which I appreciated because it meant no dinner parties, only cocktail parties.

The kitchen is large, too, perfect for the caterers we always hired for hors d'oeuvres and tray passing. The custom cabinetry is the perfect shade of teal—understated yet distinctive—with a built-in matching banquette that seats six. There are double doors onto the deck, which then opens onto the backyard. The pool is surrounded by high hedges for a feeling of serene privacy.

I've always loved that house, but I'm a little afraid to go back, with what I now know. From now on, will everything feel tainted?

I thought we were happy. But maybe it was nothing but artifice.

Otherwise, why would he want Jade to be the mother of his child and not me? Had Jade's pregnancy been accidental, when I'd always been so intentional?

WHY NOT ME???!!!

We bought the Southampton house six months after Corey told me he didn't want to try for a family anymore. By that point, Jade must have already been pregnant.

She got his baby, and I got a house. Did he really think that was a fair trade to make on my behalf?

I would have given anything—given up anything—to be a mom. But Corey took the choice away from me.

I never got mad when Corey had to work late (which was often, and maybe he wasn't even working late, he might have been with Jade and Tai). I acted as his little wifey and hostess extraordinaire, and I never complained.

When I think about all the things I overlooked, all the ways I minimized and downplayed my own feelings in order to preserve my goodwill toward Corey, I want to scream. Goodwill? More like good riddance.

I'm entering into a whole new mourning period, entirely different from the one I've been in for the past five months. I have to grieve for the life and the man I thought I had, for my own innocence, because how could I have been so blind? How will I ever be able to trust myself or anyone else ever again?

I remember how hard I worked to enable Corey's success

and to project the right image, how I decked out the Hamptons house for the finance bro parties.

Wives were hostesses and window dressing. All the men (there were no women at the VP level and higher) drank to excess on a regular basis. That's not the shame. The shame is in drinking to the point of alcohol poisoning. After a night out with clients, Corey had returned to his office. That's where his body was discovered in the morning.

A double life. Two women who loved him. And in the end, he died alone in his office, choking on his own vomit.

I remember talking to a therapist soon after, how we had a whole session about my paranoia (that's what she gently labeled it). I kept saying there's no way that Corey would have been so irresponsible, no way he would have left me alone, not when he loved me so much. There had to be someone else involved. What I meant was, there must have been signs of foul play that the police had missed. Corey must have been taken from me; he would never have made such a stupid mistake and given up the life he had with me. It just wasn't him.

Eventually, the therapist convinced me that people make mistakes. They have accidents. I wanted a villain I could blame and an investigation that would distract me from the pain. "But in the end," she said, "the only way out is through. You have to accept the truth and feel everything."

Back then, if I'd learned someone had hurt Corey, I would have wanted to punish them to the fullest extent of the law. I'd have wanted them to suffer. But now...

He didn't love me. He couldn't have, not with how he treated me. I wasn't his partner; I was just an accessory.

Is it possible that Corey only kept me around as long as he did because I fit in with the finance wives, because I was the "best hostess," like Sean just said? If all had been equal, would Corey have chosen Jade over me? Did she have his heart while I was being used and manipulated to further his career?

I used to skip meals the day of our cocktail parties. I was just so nervous, wanting to do well by Corey, to come through for him. Part of it was that I could tell he was nervous, too, even as he reassured me. He came from a lower-middle-class family in Pittsburgh. It wasn't until he went to NYU and majored in business that he saw how the other half lived, and he wanted to be one of them. And I was determined to help him in every way I could.

What an idiot I was. For all I know, Corey and Jade used to laugh at my stupidity as part of their pillow talk. Or had it been foreplay?

Angry tears fill my eyes. I guess good girls really do finish last.

"Are you okay?" Sean says. He looks concerned as he moves closer. I still can't tell whether he already knows about Jade or if he's assuming this is just me being a fragile widow.

I guess it doesn't matter what he knows. It only matters that I do. It only matters what I do next.

"I'm going to be okay," I say.

I'm not usually at this proximity to Sean, and maybe that's what unearths a memory that I must have buried. It used to be so easy for me to go into denial, to dismiss anything that ran counter to my high opinion of Corey. It could be that the truth was right in front of my face the whole time, and I'd chosen to remain willfully blind.

Just months before Corey died, we hosted a party in Southampton. I'd been circulating, making sure everyone had what they needed, that they were all having fun. Corey had just kissed my cheek and told me how beautiful I looked, how perfectly it had all come together, how proud he was to be with me. I was feeling so good that I allowed myself a few canapes and a glass of champagne. Two glasses, actually, in rapid succession.

My fizzy head allowed for reasonable doubt, and I seized

upon it. Because I had yoked myself fully to Corey, because I had given up the possibility of having children. He was everything.

I never even told Corey what I overheard. Didn't ask him a single question.

Sean had been talking to another finance bro, someone relatively new whose name I couldn't recall, and I paused just a second when I heard them mention Corey. They weren't loud, but they were louder than they thought. They were drunk already and thus indiscreet, not even looking around to see who might be listening.

"You think it'll catch up with him?" the new one asked.

"I don't know," Sean said. "He's slick, you know? And everyone likes him. Fuck, I like him. He's been my buddy since I started."

"What are we going to do anyway, report an ethics violation?" the new bro laughed.

Sean didn't. "It would hurt him pretty bad if it got out."

"It probably won't get out. But I've heard this isn't the first time, that he's done it before."

"Makes sense. There are no isolated instances."

As their conversation moved on, so did I. I told myself there's a reason Alyssa calls him Asshole.

I even let myself wonder if I'd misheard Corey's name. Told myself that even if they had been talking about Corey, the bros were a catty bunch, even though no one applies that adjective to men.

Had Sean been talking about Jade that night? Maybe. I'd assumed it was something business-related, seeing as it had never once crossed my mind that Corey would be unfaithful.

Cheating isn't such a big deal in that crowd. But what about having a child with another woman? If some of Corey's more conservative bosses had found out about Tai, it might have been a problem.

There are no isolated instances. As in, Corey might have had more women? More children?

Meanwhile, I'd done nothing. Said nothing. Just put my hands over my ears and hummed.

I was so stupid.

So blind.

So trusting.

I can never make that mistake again.

Corey had a child, and I never will. The injustice feels like something I might never recover from. I can't get back what Corey's stolen from me.

Technically, Tai is a bastard. But in truth, Corey was.

Tai is not his father, though. He's not his mother, either. And seeing as I'm in control of all Corey's money, I could be quite influential in Tai's future.

One way or another, I was always meant to know Corey's son.

TWELVE
JADE

Since we exited the subway, Tai's been looking around curiously. He has an excellent memory, so I'm sure he realizes we've been here before. He's intrigued by the pedestrians, like the old dowager who's wearing a fur coat to walk her tiny dog. We're definitely not in Bushwick anymore.

Tai huddles a little closer to me. He's always been afraid of dogs, though I don't know why. He's never been attacked, never even been growled at. But despite the lack of any overt displays of aggression, he's deemed them unpredictable, a potential threat.

Which is pretty much how I'm feeling about Maren. I'm dreading this visit to her apartment, whereas I'd been eager and adrenalized the first time.

It was on my terms then; I'm on her turf now. The commanding tone of her text had made that clear. Tai and I have been summoned: *Come this Sunday at 10 a.m. I need to get to know Corey's son.*

She *needs* to know Tai? What does that even mean?

I'd been hoping that after she showed up at my apartment,

she'd come to her senses and call her lawyer to draw up the papers. I'd hoped this would soon be over, but instead, it feels like it's just beginning.

Or maybe this visit is a formality, like an interview before a job offer. It's the prerequisite to a financial settlement, and Maren's just doing her due diligence.

The sidewalks are more sparsely populated than what Tai and I are used to in our neighborhood, and we can easily have an entire conversation while walking without having to raise our voices. I don't need to hold his hand, but I'm doing it anyway. I'm probably holding on a little too tightly.

I hate that Tai's mixed up in this. I should have gone to see Maren without him that first time, only I'd assumed that seeing him once would be enough; she would have known I was legitimate, and she'd never want to see either of us again. I wish I'd planned better for all the contingencies, realized that maybe Corey didn't know his wife as well as he'd thought. Now I have to be more strategic.

"Who is she, Mommy, really?" he asks. "Why are we seeing her again?" Sometimes he's eerily smart. Mommy's little mind reader.

"Remember what I told you the first time we came here? That Maren had been a good friend of Daddy's, and I was giving her the chance to meet you? Well, now she wants the chance to get to know you a little more."

"She seemed mad. Both times."

"She definitely wasn't mad at you," I say. "You have nothing to worry about."

We're still moving, less than a block away now. Tai doesn't respond, and with a glance down, I confirm that he's confused but trying to work it out.

"She was mad at you," he finally says.

"A little," I allow. "I probably should have called first. Some people don't like when you just show up at their door. This time, she invited us. She's going to be happy to see you."

"Okay," he says, but he still sounds uncertain and a little nervous. He might be mirroring me.

I'm extremely uncomfortable at the thought of being inside Maren's apartment—Corey's old apartment—and at having to watch Maren interact with Tai. I want our worlds to collide as little as possible. I've always felt that way and, fortunately, so did Corey.

But there was no way I could refuse this invitation, not if I want to activate Maren's empathy/sympathy and secure ongoing financial support. After today, we should never have to see each other again.

"Best behavior, all right?" I say to Tai. "Maren was a very important person to Daddy, so I want to see good manners. Lots of 'please' and 'thank you.'"

"Okay."

I'm grossing myself out, but it's true, Maren is important. So much hinges on the impression that Tai makes today. Still, I feel like I'm pimping my son out. But it's only this one time, and he'll never even remember it. Soon Maren will be a distant memory.

I announce myself to Javier, the doorman, who isn't smiling this time. "You're expected," he says, gesturing toward the elevator right past the gilded lobby.

Tai remembers this elevator. He loves all the gold and looking up at our reflection in the mirrored ceiling. "Can I push the button?" he asks excitedly, just like he did last time.

We're propelled upward. Then as Tai and I head down the hall, I almost trip, my heels getting caught in the thicket of incredibly plush carpet. Tai is trailing behind, that earlier nervousness more pronounced now.

"It's okay," I urge him on. "Remember, she's excited to hang out with you."

He picks up his pace slightly, but I can still sense his foreboding. I feel it, too, as I force myself to knock on the door.

Maren opens it almost instantly. It seems that I was telling the truth: She really can't wait to meet Tai. She's smiling down at him with enormous warmth, ignoring me completely.

"Come in!" she says, throwing the door open wide. "We're going to have so much fun!" This is addressed to Tai, though she finally glances over at me and says, "Thanks for bringing him."

As Tai and I enter, I nearly gasp. The other day, Maren had angled her body so that I couldn't see inside, but now I'm taking in the full splendor of the apartment. Not only have I never been inside before, I've refused to even look it up on Zillow, believing in the separation of church and state.

While the apartment is shockingly pristine and beautiful, it's also imposing. All white walls, of course, though you just know some consultant was paid an ungodly amount to make sure they're the "right whites"—not too bright or harsh or dim, can't have ivory when only cloud will do. The furniture is all silver, gray, taupe, or brown. Color—true personality—would be seen as an offense.

It must have been like living in an *Architectural Digest* spread. I can't imagine the Corey I knew loving this place, or loving Maren, for that matter.

No wonder Corey loved my place. He needed the respite of chaos.

Tai and I take our shoes off in the white marble foyer with the twenty-foot ceilings and massive chandelier. "This way," Maren says, and we follow her into the living room, which is undeniably spectacular.

There are four large windows overlooking a densely wooded part of Central Park. You can see the cityscape beyond, including the Met Museum. The ceiling is coffered and trimmed in gold leaf; the floor is white marble dotted with expensive rugs. The built-in bookshelves feature carefully curated volumes arranged by color, with a number of picture frames that are currently face down. I wonder if Maren has had them like that ever since I showed up, or if it's something she's doing today because of Tai's visit.

Tai's eyes have lit up and he's run over to the enormous glass coffee table, which is covered with toys, puzzles, and games. Others are arrayed on the nearby rug.

It's all wooden and obviously pricey, with no plastic in sight. There are multicolored blocks, magnetic blocks, and number and letter blocks. Puzzles of all types, a stacking game, kids' Jenga, old-school Tinkertoys with rods, connectors, and spools, a pegboard, another pegboard with spinning gears, toys to practice threading and lacing, a full pretend play cooking set, memory games, card games, a real porcelain tea set, and an entire rack of elaborate costumes for dress-up. There's an art area with a child-sized easel set up, and a musical instrument section with a large xylophone, ukulele, tambourine, cymbals, and maracas. Maren's laid out some train tracks that Tai could build onto if he so chose. I notice there's nothing messy—no Play-Doh, slime, or paint.

My chest and stomach tighten simultaneously. Would she really do all this for one visit?

"What's this?" Tai says to Maren, pointing to a curved piece of wood.

"That's called a wobble board," she says. "It's for balance. Go ahead, stand on it." He doesn't move, just watches her tentatively. "Everything in here is for you."

"Really?" His eyes grow wide; she nods encouragingly. She's watching him with what can best be described as a sense of enchantment while he carefully steps on the board. Then he begins shifting his weight from side to side, laughing at the motion. She beams at him, and he smiles back.

When he steps off the board, she sits down on the floor beside the coffee table. She starts building with the blocks, and he joins in. I hover awkwardly before taking a seat on the sectional.

She's still barely looked at me; she only has eyes for Tai. It's unsettling how captivated she seems. How territorial. I feel as if I'm somehow invading their space, like they're the mother-and-son duo.

She asks him, "What's this?" again and again, and he answers correctly every time. He knows all his letters and numbers. She oohs and aahs, which sounds annoying and phony to my ears, but he has a different reaction. I see how puffed up and proud he is.

I guess she's good with kids, Corey. You always said she would be. Of course Tai likes her. Would she really have bought out FAO Schwarz for one visit?

As I'm watching Maren spoil Tai, my worst fears are realized. This is not ending. Not at all. Maren's just getting started.

She's not going to give me Corey's money; she's going to use it to seduce my son.

See, this is the kind of mother she would have been, I silently rage at Corey. *The kind who has to buy her children's affection!*

Or I could be reading this whole situation wrong. She might have owned all this stuff already. She might keep it around for her kids' friends and she's just telling Tai it's all his. Or she could have jumped the gun and bought it all way back, when she and Corey were still trying to have a family. No need to panic or jump to conclusions. One and done, that's my motto.

"I have to go poop!" Tai announces, standing up and grabbing his butt in the way that I've told him many times not to do.

But Maren acts like it's utterly charming. She glances at me. "Is he able to go by himself?"

"I can go by myself," he says. "I like to do it. I can wipe and everything."

Maren laughs. "Well, I'll show him the way, then."

"Shout out if you need us," I tell Tai. He doesn't answer;

he's taken Maren's hand and they're walking back toward the foyer together.

When she returns, she says, "I was going to wait outside the door, but he told me not to." She takes a seat on the floor again, looking up at me on her couch. "He's so smart! And so independent!"

"Sometimes." I want to burst her bubble, quick.

"He really is something else." She sounds admiring as she looks back in what I assume is the direction of the bathroom. "But could I just ask—" She hesitates for a second before deciding to plunge ahead. "Was Tai conceived on purpose?"

"Wow," I say. "That's a pretty offensive question."

"It's just something that I've been wondering about. You probably would, too, in my position."

"Tai was very much wanted." I can tell she's not entirely convinced. "If you're not going to believe my answers, why ask the questions?"

"I'm not trying to make this antagonistic." Her tone is dulcet. "If you and I are going to have a relationship—"

"We're not." I can't help myself; I'm losing patience fast.

"Well, I'm sorry to hear that. Sorry you feel that way." She looks truly disappointed. But what on earth was she expecting?

"I've been honest with you from the start. I approached you because it's in the best interest of my son. Corey's son. You *can* tell that Tai is Corey's son, right? It's pretty obvious."

"Yes."

I feel a sense of relief. "So can we just get this done? Work out a settlement, you move on with your life, I move on with mine?"

She starts fussing with the games, and I can see that I've upset her. And maybe that's the best tactic at this point. I don't want her thinking this is a budding friendship.

Sorry, Corey. I've got to throw you under the bus.

"Corey betrayed you," I say. "I wouldn't think that you'd want any reminders of that around."

I assume she's more upset now since she's moving the toys and games even faster. Otherwise, her face gives nothing away.

"I encouraged Corey to tell you about me so we could have been out in the open, but he didn't want to do it." It's not entirely true, but where has the truth gotten me so far?

"He knew that if he told me, I'd leave," she says. "I wouldn't put up with that kind of bullshit." It's a not-so-veiled insult. But she doesn't know how much I called the shots, and I'm not about to tell her.

"Corey and I were really similar in some respects. I understood him in ways that you couldn't be expected to. I mean, he didn't expect you to. He kept certain parts of himself from you for your own good."

"He told you that?" I can see I'm getting under her skin. Good. She needs to want me out of her life; she should be willing to pay to restore her peace of mind.

"He really loved you, Maren. He wanted to protect you."

"From what?"

"From his darker aspects. But happy as he and I were, he never once talked about leaving you. I never would have asked him to. Because I get that love is—"

"Please don't tell me what love is." She squeezes her eyes shut. Good. If she doesn't want to see me anymore, there's a real easy fix.

"You can love more than one person, and it doesn't have to conflict. Because you're different parts of yourself with different partners. There were ways he behaved around me that he couldn't around you, and vice versa. I accepted that. With you, he was his most conventional. With me, he was... someone else."

"Who?"

"I don't know how to answer that. He wasn't wild, exactly, but sort of free, maybe?"

"I never chained him up," she says. "I like monogamy, and I don't think there's anything wrong with that."

"There's not. For you. But I wasn't looking for anything serious. I didn't expect to fall in love, and once I did, I still didn't think it needed to be serious. Why make it heavy? Shouldn't love be light and fun and buoyant and beautiful?"

I can see that she doesn't get it. Not at all. But then, she doesn't have to. Corey did.

"Corey was a complicated man," I say, "but he liked being simple around you."

"Complicated how? Simple how?"

"Anger is the only emotion that's socially acceptable for men. They're not allowed to be sad, you know?"

"Corey wasn't angry. Or sad. Not around me."

"Exactly. Because he couldn't be. He knew you couldn't handle it. There was a lot of pressure on him to be the perfect husband."

"I never said he had to be perfect!"

"You were the perfect wife, that's how he saw you, and he felt like he had to live up to that. That meant concealing certain things. With me, Corey never had to hide." This should really inflame her. She should be hating him right about now.

Sorry, Corey. She left me no choice. You left me no choice.

She and Corey were repressed together. That state of being is no good for anyone. I sometimes thought the reason he needed me as much as he did was because I was the antidote to their toxic love story.

"You think my marriage was a sham," she says slowly. "And I guess you're right. He was lying to me for years, raising a child with you instead of having one with me. Even though I wanted to be a mother more than anything, I didn't even fight him on it. I just let him have his way."

Despite myself, I feel a little sorry for her. Could I show her compassion while slipping in the knife at the same time? "He took some of the best years of your life." She doesn't answer, but she's obviously troubled. "Corey needed both of us, you know? To balance him out."

Tai has always had some constipation issues, but really? It's almost like he knows that I need this extra time with Maren, like he's my accomplice.

We're sitting quietly when Tai comes back looking triumphant. He's always proud after a poop, crowing about how well he wiped, and this time is no exception.

Maren immediately shifts back into her saccharine voice. I hope that she's going to say it's getting late and thank us for coming, but instead she tells Tai that they should go through the games and pick another.

She lays out all the cards for a memory game on top of an ottoman. As she and Tai start to play, she's cooing over how well he's doing. When it's her turn, I suspect she's making mistakes on purpose so he'll win.

"He's actually a really good loser," I say.

"He's so good at this," she responds. "He's got me on the ropes!" She smiles at Tai.

Corey wouldn't have approved of her behavior at all. He believed strongly that you never just let kids win. What Corey used to do was assign himself some kind of handicap so that it was a fair fight. He trained Tai to respond to a loss by saying, "I'll get you next time!"

Recalling that, picturing the two of them at our kitchen table, I'm hit with a wave of sadness.

"We should be going soon," I say.

Maren's face falls. How long did she think we'd stay? And how can she even want to be in Tai's presence, after what Corey did to her?

"One last activity," I say to Tai, though I'm really talking to Maren. "Then we're going to say thank you so much and goodbye."

"What do you want to do?" Maren asks him. "Pick anything. The world's your oyster."

"What's an oyster?"

"I'll tell you next time. Go ahead and look around."

I could feel that's where this was heading since I first saw all the loot, but the confirmation still hits hard. Because how am I going to get us out of this? She's holding all the cards right now, and I have a strong suspicion that she knows it. Maybe she enjoys seeing the mistress squirm.

Tai does as instructed, surveying the room until finally his eyes linger on the music area. "Be in my band!" he says. He starts distributing instruments. I get the maracas and Maren has the tambourine. He debates between the xylophone and the ukulele.

"You can play all of them," Maren says. "They're all for you."

He chooses the ukulele. "Play, Mommy!" he instructs, and I do. "Play!" He points at Maren. I can see he's not sure what to call her. She starts tapping the tambourine against her wrist, and then he joins in with the ukulele. It's an atonal mess, but he looks so joyous. So does Maren. I shake my maracas and wonder how soon we can make our getaway.

When the song's over, Maren asks me, her voice soft and almost dreamy, "Could I please read him a book before you go?"

I feel sick, but I can only nod.

Maren brings out a stack of books and spreads them on the floor. "Which one should we read?" she says. Tai points. "You know, I was hoping you'd pick that." They smile at each other. It's so sweet and poignant, and I'm entirely boxed out. But the fact is, he's going home with me.

She takes a seat far away from me on the sectional and instead of sitting next to her, he climbs right onto her lap. I can see the cover of the book he's chosen: *I Love You to the Moon and Back*.

It's a board book, one that he would have outgrown except that it's the one that used to be his and Corey's favorite. Corey wasn't there every night for tuck-ins, but when he was, that was a staple.

Tai doesn't even let me read that one anymore, it's been retired, but he'll let Maren?

I want to flee. I don't want to hear Maren reading, "I love our time together as we start each happy day!" After all, Corey was never there at the start of Tai's happy days. He was home in this apartment, waking up next to Maren.

How could you, Corey? You didn't take care of us at all. You just left us at her mercy.

I don't want to see Tai snuggled up against Maren, and I'm trying to block out the sound of her voice, speaking the words that Corey spoke. Tai is chorusing along with her. He knows every line by heart.

Maren looks over at me. "He's such a bright boy, isn't he?" Then she looks down at him in her lap and says with great affection, "Such a good, bright boy." He beams up at her.

I feel even sicker.

Finally, mercifully, the book ends. "It's time to go!" I say, standing up. "Tai, say—"

"Thank you!" he bursts out, swiveling his body around and giving Maren an exuberant hug.

"Oh, no," she says. "Thank *you*, Tai."

They cling to each other for far too long, but I decide not to interrupt. Let her have this, a goodbye gift from me to her. I'm going to find a way out of this mess.

Tai isn't usually this quick to warm up to new people, especially since he lost his dad, but then, Maren's the only person who's ever laid an entire toy store at his feet. She can donate them to some other children. All Tai needs from her is a settlement.

She says, "Tai, choose anything. But only one."

He looks elated, then somber as he attempts to make his best decision. He spins around slowly and lifts up various items to examine them. Finally, he selects the ukulele.

"Good choice," Maren says, smiling at him tenderly. "The rest will still be here waiting for the next time you visit."

Next time?

Over my dead body.

THIRTEEN
MAREN

My phone had been muted the whole time Tai was here. I wanted to give him my full attention. Now I see that Alyssa's sent a series of texts.

Thinking of you!

Lunch? Dinner? Best of all, cocktails? She's added the martini glass and highball glass emojis.

I'm throwing a party on Saturday. Come. Bring a plus-one.

I laugh out loud at that last message as I imagine taking Tai with me. It's a laugh of actual mirth. I feel so light, almost drunk, in the wake of his visit.

I have a purpose again. Or finally.

Jade only wants my money, but Tai wants me. It's apparent how hungry he is for emotional connection and intellectual stimulation. I can't wait to provide those things. I wonder if Corey used to, and now that he's gone, there's a vacancy in Tai's life that I'd love to fill.

I'm also happy to pay for enrichment that Jade can't afford. But if she thinks she can show up in my apartment and lecture me on the true nature of love and then leave with a settlement check, she's in for a rude awakening.

What struck me in our conversation was how young she is. She might be streetwise, but she's painfully naïve. It's obvious that she's proud of her relationship with Corey. She thinks they had some great love story.

Somehow Corey convinced her that being the mistress was better than being the wife. She spent her time waiting around and putting up with his anger outbursts and listening to him talk about how perfect I was, yet she thought that was the superior role because she was getting all of him.

Meanwhile, he never even slept at her apartment. Who did he come home to every night? Me. Who was he with every weekend? Me.

He never set up regular child support, didn't create any sort of trust for Tai or put Jade in his will. He let them keep on living in that shitty apartment. Yet Jade sat rhapsodizing about him in my living room with the multimillion-dollar view.

When is she going to figure out that she's spent the last six years subsisting on table scraps and calling them filet mignon?

I feel sorry for her. She's not mentally ill, but she is deluded.

I know Alyssa would have some worse names for Jade. I don't want to hear them right now. I'm in too good of a mood.

Sean must not have mentioned running into me outside the toy store. If he had, Alyssa would have wanted to know whose kid's party I was going to and why she hadn't been invited. But then, I never told Alyssa about seeing Sean. Does that mean Asshole and I are colluding?

I don't think he's cheating, but I do think Alyssa underestimates his capacity for deceit. I get it, though, why Sean might want to hide some things from a person as opinionated as she is.

I mean, I'm doing it right now. Can't let Alyssa rain on this particular parade.

You know what's strange? While I was focusing on Tai, I forgot all about Corey. For that brief period, there was no pain or confusion or anger; it was pure pleasure.

I adore Alyssa, but I doubt she'd understand. She doesn't seem to be into her own kids. How could she fathom how deeply attached I feel to Tai after just a few hours?

It might be unusual, but I'm not doing anything wrong. Actually, this is the most right anything has felt since Corey died. Tai is Corey's son, which means I've got a new and wonderful nephew.

The conversation with Jade was surprisingly healing. It's time to accept that I didn't know my husband at all. The real Corey was a terrible, selfish person who'd lie to his wife and shortchange his son. How could he have thought that arrangement was good enough for me or for Tai? Really, he should have left me to be with Jade and Tai full-time. He should have owned his choices and responsibilities. But he was a thoroughly dishonorable, disreputable person.

For the first time, I am truly happy that he's out of my life. Happy that he's ashes.

Corey manipulated Jade, and he manipulated me, too. He pretended to be loving, thoughtful, and kind; he encouraged me to do as much volunteering as I wanted in order to feel fulfilled. He said that the helping professions I was drawn to (social work, teaching, nursing) were burnout jobs. I would have been overworked and underpaid, with nothing left in the tank for him at the end of the day.

I'd assumed he was looking out for me, but no, Corey only cared about himself. He was keeping me at his beck and call. He wanted a traditional marriage, with a wife who stayed home and ran his social calendar, who nurtured his business prospects. I was the mother of his career.

Now that I can see Corey for who and what he was, I don't have to think about him at all. I have all the answers I need. Corey's the past; Tai is the future.

Today couldn't have gone any better. Tai is the sweetest, smartest little boy I could have dreamed up. I'm smiling now just thinking of him and how he nestled against me when we were reading. I can still feel his warmth, am still breathing in his scent.

I have a lot more to offer than just money. Jade might not see that now, but she will.

I'll start by giving her a thousand dollars, enough for her to settle some bills. That should tide her over.

I spent my life with Corey overplanning, and look where that got me. I'm not trying to see too far out anymore. I'm flying by the seat of my pants for the first time, and I can't wait to see what happens next.

I'm in the best mood I've been in since before Corey died. Or maybe even before that. I was unhappy and I didn't even know it. I never let myself feel it.

But I feel everything now.

FOURTEEN
JADE

"Hello?" I call out. I need my mother's help. I can't open the door to her apartment because my arms are full of the three Amazon boxes from her lobby.

My mother's apartment used to be her mother's. In lieu of intergenerational wealth, Mom's the unicorn with actual rent control, not just rent stabilization like me. She also has the same peeling wallpaper and battle-scarred wood floors as the generation before, seeing as her landlord has no financial incentive to update or upgrade anything.

I love my mother, I truly don't know what I'd do without her, but I wish I didn't have to keep smothering her in appreciation for the two days of every week that she watches her grandson. Yet I can barely afford the other three days of preschool.

Why didn't you want me to be more secure, Corey?

I know the answer. He hadn't looked far enough ahead, hadn't predicted his fate. None of us can tell the future, even if people like Maren want to pretend otherwise.

It's my fault as much as his. I never pressed. We were both acting like we'd live forever.

Mom's acting that way, too, spending every penny of her

fixed income on utter crap as if that'll lift her out of the pit in which she's found herself. But I can't exactly stage an intervention. She's my mother; I'm not hers. And it's not like I'm some paragon of mental health. Sometimes I'm hanging on by a thread.

She's your mom, though, Corey says. *You should at least try.*

Her excessive spending isn't my business, I tell Corey.

Maybe it's not even excessive, I can imagine him answering. He was always quick to defend her. I think he felt sorry for her, and that's why he gave her lavish Christmas gifts. Not anywhere close to as lavish as what he gave Emmanuel, but still.

Who knows what Maren is giving Emmanuel now? Enough to buy his silence, apparently. His complicity.

I bet he accompanied her on the toy-spending spree and didn't say a negative word. He probably complimented her on her generosity and good taste. Fucking enabler. Did it occur to either of them how insulting it was, treating Tai like a charity case? Or how plain weird it was to shower the mistress's son with gifts? Though they weren't gifts, since she intends to keep them at her apartment for him. That means they're more like bribes.

But back to Mom. She's not doing well, anyone can see that, and she doesn't take pleasure in any of the garbage that's begun littering every surface. There's barely any room for Tai to play, or even for people to walk. In her advanced age, she's becoming a hoarder, though isn't a hoarder someone who hangs on to, like, old newspaper clippings and Tupperware from thirty years before? This junk is all new.

"Hello!" I say, even louder. I could just put down the boxes and then open the door, but I'm feeling stubborn. And irritated. And exhausted. It's been a long day, though I had one client cancellation in addition to two empty slots. Somehow, too many free hours take more out of me than working constantly. It represents time I could be spending with Tai and money I could be making. Money I need, since Maren's hoarding hers.

I set down the boxes, open the door, and step inside. No wonder Mom couldn't hear me, when the TV is on at that volume. She's watching CNN, which I don't appreciate because the world stresses her out, and these programs can give Tai strange ideas since he can't understand what he's seeing. I've asked her repeatedly not to watch the news in his presence. Did she forget? Or is she being passive-aggressive because she resents taking care of my kid?

It hurts because that kid happens to be her grandchild, and he's fully awesome. Maren could see that; why can't my mother?

Every time I drop him off, I tell him to be good, but I really hope she's listening. Be a good grandmother. Take some interest in this happy, curious boy.

Not that he's looking very happy or curious now. He's sitting on the floor, playing listlessly with an aged plastic puzzle (nothing like the beautiful craftsmanship of Maren's wooden puzzles). Normally, he runs over to greet me, but today, he just looks up with glassy eyes.

Something is definitely wrong.

This sense is confirmed when my mother realizes I'm here and leaps to her feet with an overly broad smile. "Oh, Jackie!" she says. I gave up years ago on having her call me Jade. Much as I hate "Jackie"—and "Jacqueline"—that's who I'll always be to her. "How was your day?"

She starts flitting around the apartment like a hummingbird. Usually, she just stays on the couch while I collect Tai and thank her for another day of substandard childcare.

"My day sucked. What about yours?" I go over to Tai and plant a kiss on the top of his head.

"Hi, Mommy," he says. He sounds tired. Lackluster.

I look quizzically at my mom, who is full of a simpering

sympathy for my tough day. She's offering to make me something to eat, which she *never* does. "What's going on, Mom?"

The air whooshes out of her manic balloon. "There was a tiny accident." She starts to ramble, an excruciating windup that involves detailing the toppings on a frozen pizza and finally ends with a hot sheet pan that just *barely* grazed Tai's arm and—

"Show me, please," I say to Tai. I unzip his hoodie and he shrugs out of it.

There's a raised pink horizontal burn on his upper arm that's beginning to crust and blister. No wonder he seems so lethargic. He's in pain. Or maybe he's been overmedicated? She anesthetized him so she wouldn't have to hear him whine and then she could watch TV in peace?

At this point, I wouldn't put anything past her. She burned my son!

Accidents happen, Corey is trying to tell me, but I'm too upset to listen. Too incensed. Because of course accidents happen, but this one shouldn't have.

"Oh, Tai." I take his face in my hands. "I'm so sorry, baby. Does it hurt?"

"Not really."

I advance on my mother. "You left him alone with a hot pan?" I don't pause for an answer because the answer is right there, on his arm. It might not hurt right this second, but it probably will again. He may very well scar. "What is wrong with you?"

"Don't yell at me. I already feel terrible." Her mouth turns down, and she looks a hundred years old, and I believe her. She feels terrible all the time. I know she worries about me, too. She can see that I'm struggling and wishes she could help more, but she can barely take care of herself. Even if she quit her shopping addiction, she wouldn't have the means to come to my rescue.

Besides, she shouldn't have to. I'm a grown woman. I should

be able to take care of myself and my child without needing handouts from my mother, or from anyone else.

Tai was burned on Mom's watch, but it's my fault.

"I know you didn't do it on purpose." I soften my tone. "Did you already give him Tylenol for the pain?" It pains me, just thinking of it. Tai must have been crying, and that's part of his overly placid demeanor now. Crying takes a lot out of a person.

I should know, I had a long bout myself last night after the trip to Maren's. Angry, helpless tears. I can keep strategizing, but at the end of the day, I can't make her do anything. She has all the power.

"Yes, I gave him Tylenol," Mom says.

"*Children's* Tylenol?"

"Of course." She gives me a slightly sharp look. "I looked on the internet and did everything you're supposed to for a second-degree burn, which is the most common kind. People get these all the time, Jackie."

"What did you do for him, exactly? What's the treatment?"

"I ran his arm under cool water for more than five minutes, and I put on antibiotic cream. I didn't have the right kind of bandages, I only had Band-Aids and no gauze, so I couldn't cover it."

"But it's supposed to be covered?"

"Yes."

In other words, she didn't do everything she was supposed to. "Why didn't you go to the store and buy gauze?"

"I thought you'd be here soon enough. It's just a small burn."

"But you're supposed to keep it covered!" I remember something about the importance of keeping it moist and preventing infection.

"Only for the first few days."

I'm trying not to go off on her. She's right, it's not a large burn, but he is a small boy. She should have taken care of him.

She should have made sure there wasn't a hot sheet pan sticking out where he could graze it, and she should have bought gauze. There's a pharmacy two blocks away!

"What time did this happen?" I ask, fighting for calm.

"Three hours ago, maybe? He'll need more Tylenol soon."

So his burn should have been covered for the past three hours. I know it's not the end of the world, but what's going to happen the next time she should be watching him and isn't? When he needs medical attention, and she can't be bothered?

I'm not only upset with Mom; I'm upset with me. Because I've been overlooking my mother's increasing negligence, not saying anything when she parked him in front of the TV for hours, but now it's escalated, and I haven't devoted any time to figuring out alternate arrangements. That's because I can't afford to make any changes, not until Maren comes through for us.

Meanwhile, I can't be around more because I can't afford to work any less. I'm already behind on my rent. If we were evicted, where would we go? We already have rent stabilization. I can't imagine what we could get that's cheaper. We'd have to move into my mother's already cramped apartment; Tai and I would share her tiny spare room. Or we'd have to move out of New York entirely and start over somewhere cheaper.

I can't do that. I'm a New Yorker, born and bred. This is who I am. This is where I have to be.

The fact is, even without deliberately cutting back, my client list has been dwindling. I don't keep up with social media or networking. I don't have the time or energy to do the kinds of things that might attract new clients. After Corey died, I couldn't work for a while and lost some of my clients. It didn't improve my standing with Angelica, either. Her apprentice, Sophie, is the apple of her eye, so Angelica gives Sophie all the overflow referrals.

I need to find another childcare provider for two days a

week. How much would that cost? My finances are already stressed to the max. And how would Tai handle it? It would mean introducing him to someone new and disrupting his routines. He doesn't usually warm up very quickly to new people, with the notable exception of Maren.

I will not lose it on Mom, though. She didn't cause any of these problems, and she's barely keeping her own head above water.

"We should go," I say, resigned. I turn to Tai. "Come on, sweetie." He gets to his feet silently. Has he said a single word since I arrived?

My poor baby.

I give my mom a hug and tell her it's all right, it'll be all right, because she's looking so distressed. As Tai and I head home—which is fortunately just a quick walk—I'm reeling. Something has to give, that's obvious, but I don't have the bandwidth right now to figure out what it should be.

Once home, Tai gets a second wind. He races to get his ukulele and settles on the couch. "I want to play for real," he says. "Play a real song for Maren."

Give me strength. "Come on, Tai. You need to get ready for bed."

"When can we go back, Mommy? To see Maren? I want to do my wobble board. I want her to read me stories."

I don't like that he's thinking of it as his wobble board, but then, she set it up that way. She kept emphasizing that those toys were all for him. No wonder he's fantasizing. I can't take it personally, even though I'm feeling so raw right now that everything is personal. It's all falling apart.

I let Tai play a little because he's had a rough day of his own. I serve him Tylenol with a cup of orange juice while he plucks away at the strings. Then I clean his burn and put on ointment, wrapping it in gauze. He makes a few whimpering noises but doesn't protest.

Once he's in his pajamas and tucked into bed, neither of us is in the mood for a story. I kiss him and tell him how very much I love him. As I'm turning off the light, he says, "So when can we see Maren?"

"I don't know. Let's talk about it tomorrow."

"Do you think she wants to see me again?"

I'm glad it's dark so he can't see my face. "I'm sure she does." Then I hurriedly add, "Good night," and shut his door. No more talking tonight.

I collapse on the couch. I hope he doesn't get out of bed because I truly don't know what I have left to give. And I hate for him to see me cry.

What am I going to do, Corey?

As if in answer, I hear the incoming text. I check my phone, and it's Maren: *I've been thinking of you and Tai. I'd like to help. Let me transfer you a thousand dollars.*

I could almost believe Corey put her up to it, that this was his way of proving she's the good person he always claimed she was. She's going to be my guardian angel after all.

But with a guardian angel, there are no strings attached, and that's clearly not the case with Maren since she's texted again: *When will I be seeing Tai next?*

This should be the answer to a prayer. I need money, and Maren's got plenty more to give. If she keeps spending time with Tai, she'll want to invest in him. And he's already said he wants to see her, too.

But four-year-olds don't know what's actually good for them, do they? They touch hot pans and they get burned.

I've got a very bad feeling about this, and no other options.

FIFTEEN

MAREN

"I have to admit, I was surprised to hear about this life change," Emmanuel says as he pulls away from the curb.

I laugh gaily. "Life change?"

"I didn't think you'd want a regular babysitting gig at—"

"Do not say 'at your age'!" But I'm still smiling. "I prefer the term *nanny*. No, I really don't. Maybe *childcare professional*? Okay, *babysitter*'s fine."

"So it's going to be every Wednesday and Saturday?"

I nod, then realize he can't see me since his eyes are on the road. "Yes, every Wednesday and Saturday. But we only have to do it like this one time, with you coming from Bushwick to get me, then us driving together back to Bushwick to get Tai. In the future, you can just pick Tai up on your way and take him back with you when you go home. But I thought I should be there for the first pickup. I can introduce you to Jade and Tai."

He doesn't answer; he's concentrating on the traffic.

"Tai could not be more lovable." Jade, though—I don't know quite how to describe her. It's not like she's unpleasant or rude, at least not intentionally. On the subject of Corey, she can be pretty condescending. She seems to think she's the authority on my former husband.

I've come to grips with the fact that he was a narcissistic sociopath. He used me, and he used Jade. He obviously had no conscience or empathy, and I can't blame myself for falling for it. I didn't know people that deceitful and predatory existed in real life. I also can't blame Jade for still being under his spell, though my stint in the cult of Corey is well and truly over.

"You seem much better," Emmanuel observes.

"I don't just seem it," I say. All the misery of the past six months has evaporated; all the churning of the past ten days has stilled. This must be why people get addicted to painkillers, though I don't need drugs. I have Tai.

I know I don't *have* him, per se. I just mean that he's out there, and he needs me. With Corey gone, there's an opening for another loving person in his life, and I'm thrilled to accept the position.

I guess I didn't just accept it; I sort of insisted upon it. But it's for Tai's own good, and it'll save Jade money, and I'm super excited. Everyone wins.

It all came together a couple of days ago at the Sloomoo Institute, a.k.a. the slime museum. It wouldn't have been my first choice of activity, but Jade said she'd been meaning to take him for ages and would I mind meeting them there? Of course I instantly said yes and paid for the tickets.

We wore plastic ponchos and shower caps, and it turned out to be great silly fun. Doing things I never would have otherwise done is one of the reasons I always wanted to be a mom. The day would have been perfect except for how downcast Jade seemed. She'd been wearing all black again, a loose t-shirt and leggings. She's got such a pretty face, but she's way too skeletal.

I spied a bandage on Tai's arm. When I asked about it, he said it was a burn he'd gotten at his grandmother's house.

Jade looked uneasy with the subject. "He's an active kid, and unfortunately, sometimes he's going to get hurt."

"Grandma was watching TV," Tai piped in. "She watches TV a lot." He looked longingly at the cisterns of slime. "Can I go play?" Jade nodded, and we watched him join a group of kids.

Now I was the uneasy one. Should I ask more questions? It sounded like Grandma had been negligent, and as a result, Tai had gotten injured. But maybe I'd misunderstood?

Jade recognized the expression on my face. "Listen, Maren, I can see that you care about Tai, and I appreciate your concern. But it's unnecessary. I love my son very much, and I would never let anything happen to him."

"I know you love him," I said gently. "But something did happen." I overlooked so much in my marriage; I'm not going to stand idly by anymore. If questions need to be asked, then I'll ask them. I used to be all about adaptation, but now I'm going to be about action.

Jade dropped her eyes. "We all have scars from childhood, right?" It made me wonder what had gone on for her. "My mom's a recent breast cancer survivor. She went through chemo, and she's never really recovered her energy."

"I'm so sorry."

"It's okay, she's improving, but right now, two days of childcare is a lot for her." Jade paused. "The truth is, Tai could use a new caregiver and money's tight. I appreciate the thousand dollars, I really do, but have you given any more thought to a settlement from Corey's estate?"

I felt a surge of excitement. "I'll do it."

"You'll have a settlement drawn up?" Jade looked relieved but a little wary, like it might be too good to be true.

"No, even better. I'll watch Tai. Free of charge." She seemed taken aback. "Please. I really want to help."

We went back and forth for a few minutes. She kept saying

she couldn't ask that of me, it's too much, and I kept reassuring her that it would be my pleasure. Eventually, she relented.

"It feels so good to be needed," I tell Emmanuel now, almost dancing in my seat.

"Are you sure you want this much responsibility, though?" he responds. "Twice a week, for eight hours?"

"There's nothing I'd rather do." I look out the windshield. "I'll be curious to see what you think about Tai since you have more direct experience with kids than I do. You're raising a certified genius." Blessing is eleven, and she's following her own advanced curriculum. This year, she's taking high school biology. It helps to have a dynamic mother who teaches at the same public school. "I'm not saying that Tai is at Blessing's level, but he seems really bright to me."

"I'm sure you're right."

"I know Zauna's done a great job advocating for Blessing, but do you think that exceptional kids are, in general, better served by private schools?"

Emmanuel does an exaggeratedly furtive glance around. "Don't let Zauna hear you say that."

"Just between you and me, if money were no object and Zauna wasn't a public school teacher, what would you have wanted for your girls?"

"But money is always an object."

"Imagine it isn't."

"My imagination doesn't stretch that far."

I feel slightly frustrated. He must know what I'm asking. Zauna has often talked about her struggles, how the resources aren't meeting the students' academic or mental health needs, and that nearly all teachers are overwhelmed, if not entirely burned out. The system needs an overhaul, and it's not going to get it by the time Tai is ready for kindergarten.

"Okay, yes," Emmanuel says. "If things were different, I would have put the girls in private school."

I can tell that's a big admission for him. He's a deeply loyal person.

"Thank you," I say, appreciating his candor. "So I should talk to Jade about private school, then. Maybe Tai could get a scholarship, but if not, I have the means."

Emmanuel raises an eyebrow. "You've met this boy how many times, and now you're thinking of spending a million dollars to educate him?"

I can understand Emmanuel's skepticism but decide to ignore it. "He's Corey's son." Though this isn't really about Corey anymore.

I always wanted to help people in a hands-on way, but Corey dissuaded me. He acted like it was somehow beneath me to be of service to others, which I can now see is a tremendously flawed and selfish way to approach life. Which makes sense, because he was a tremendously flawed and selfish man.

I had the ring. I had a beautiful home—two beautiful homes —and yet I was still a second-class citizen. My world was organized around Corey's well-being. I served his ambitions. But now I have my own.

I've spoken to Bernard, the estate attorney. He assured me that since Jade has no proof of paternity, she's got no claim on Corey's estate; whatever I choose to give is solely at my discretion. Corey made no provisions for Jade and Tai, so now I have all the power. But unlike Corey, I intend to use it wisely.

The car is slowing to a stop, and I break out into a smile. I want to clap my hands like a kid myself. "We're here!"

SIXTEEN

JADE

"Jade and Tai, this is Emmanuel. Emmanuel, meet Jade and Tai!" Maren is doing the introductions with a flourish on the street in front of my building. She looks positively giddy.

"I've heard so much about you that I feel like I know you already!" I say to Emmanuel, a little pointedly.

"I can't say the same, though I'm pleased to meet you now." Emmanuel's eyes crinkle genially. He's a good liar. I'll give him that.

"Hi," Tai says. He looks down at the ground and then squints up at Emmanuel. "You're tall."

Emmanuel laughs. "So are you! How old are you? Ten?"

"I'm four."

"You don't say!" Emmanuel smiles at Tai, and then turns toward Maren, waiting for her cue. It's a reminder that no matter how much Maren and Corey talk up Emmanuel, he's not really family. He's the help.

Deep down, he must know that. No wonder he wasn't willing to speak truth to power on Tai's behalf.

"It's good to see you, Jade," Maren says with a warmth that I can't quite believe.

"I appreciate you doing this," I say, "but it's only a trial run. If it's not your thing—"

"It'll be my thing." She grins at Tai; he grins back at her. "I've got a fantastic day planned. I was so excited I could barely sleep!"

I try to catch Emmanuel's eye—he must realize how bizarre this is—but he's watching Maren. He seems a little nervous. Nervous for her, or for himself? He might be worried that he'll be found out, that Maren will realize he's known about Corey and me the whole time.

I give Tai a hug, which feels strangely performative. Maybe it's because Maren is a disconcerting combination of soft with Tai and sharp-eyed toward me. I think about how she acted about Tai's burn the other day, the way she interrogated him and then me, as if it were any of her business. She made me feel like having my mother continue to babysit would be tantamount to child abuse. That's how we wound up here, with her taking over Mom's role.

Was Maren truly worried about Tai, or had she just manipulated the whole situation to her own advantage?

She'd manipulated that whole day, really. I hadn't wanted to get together with her again, but she wouldn't let up so I tried to pick someplace she'd loathe. From everything I'd heard from Corey, everything I'd seen at her immaculate apartment, I assumed that a slime museum would be her worst nightmare. It seemed like just the kind of activity that would make her prissy stomach churn. She likes a clean and orderly life, and that's incompatible with a four-year-old. I wanted to puncture her fantasy bubble ASAP.

It backfired. She was delighted by Tai's delight, and then after she found out about the burn, she saw her chance to embed herself more firmly in our lives, and she seized it, with both hands. My polite objections fell on deaf ears. She essentially appointed herself Tai's babysitter, put me on the spot, insisted on an answer right then, and how could I say no?

Maren's life is entirely empty, and she wants to fill it with Tai.

Only how could anyone want to devote herself to her dead husband's child, a boy she didn't even know existed until two weeks ago?

That's why I hadn't seen this coming. Because it's nuts. Maren's nuts.

And she's got me in a vise. She knows that what I really want is a settlement and instead she's making me offer after offer that I can't refuse, no matter how much I want to. I'm stuck kissing her feet over a thousand dollars when she's sitting on millions.

I hate fakeness. That's part of why I could never have been Corey's wife. Being the mistress does have its advantages, though in my case, none of them were financial. Still, I would never have traded positions with Maren. I never wanted what she had, contrary to what she may think.

But she wants what I have. I see how she looks at Tai with such fervent emotion, her expression downright covetous.

"You have everything you need in your backpack, okay?" I say to Tai. He nods. Then I look at Maren. "His lunch and snacks are in there."

"We're going out for lunch," she says. "I picked someplace special."

"You don't have to—"

"I want to." Her tone is firm. "Emmanuel, could you please get Tai into the car seat? I just need a minute with Jade."

Ugh.

"Bye, baby," I say to Tai, planting a kiss on the top of his head.

"Be good?" He sounds questioning, is probably wondering why I'm not saying that when I always do.

It's because I don't want him to be good at all. I'm hoping for public tantrums all over Manhattan and huge messes all over Maren's pristine apartment. Then she'll realize what a terrible idea this is. She can cut me a check, and we'll be free of each other, the way nature intended.

"Of course," I say, "be good." I smooth the hair back from his forehead. I feel a certain ache in letting him go that I never feel when I'm taking him to preschool or to my mother's. "I love you."

Emmanuel takes the backpack and gets Tai situated. Once the doors are closed and Maren and I are alone on the pavement, she beams at me. "This is going to be so much fun! Should I text you photos of our adventures?"

No, no, no! "That would be great. Thank you again for doing this." Insult to injury: Maren insisted on being Tai's babysitter, wouldn't take no for an answer, and is once again waiting for gratitude.

"You're so welcome. Have a good day at work!" Then she pulls open the back door and gets in next to Tai. "Wave to Mommy!" she tells him, and now they're both waving goodbye.

I wave back, wearing a pasted-on smile.

You fucked us, Corey. Why couldn't you have thought about Tai and me just a little? Would it have been so hard to put a bank account or an investment account in your son's name? To start a college fund? Maren would never have had to know.

Corey told me that Maren's never been privy to their true finances; she never even inquired.

Sometimes going to college makes you dumber. More insulated. I didn't go, so I had to stay savvy and depend on myself.

Corey's really only confirmed what I already knew. If you want something done right, you have to do it yourself.

It's on me to take care of Maren, once and for all.

SEVENTEEN

MAREN

Was it my imagination, or was Jade a bit chilly?

She was probably just in a rush to get to work. Plus, this is a pretty unorthodox situation. It couldn't have been easy for her to fire her mother.

I turn my attention toward Tai. He and I are sitting together in the back seat, and he's peering curiously out the windows, and then at Emmanuel in the front. I have the sense that Tai hasn't spent much time in cars. I know Jade doesn't have one.

"Is Emmanuel your train conductor?" Tai asks.

It takes me a second to figure out what he's saying. What a mind that boy has! He must not know the words *driver* or *chauffer,* so he's making a connection to what he does know, which is that a train conductor drives the train.

Emmanuel laughs. "Yes," he says. "Maren, please call me that from now on."

"Emmanuel is my driver, and one of my best friends," I say to Tai. "He's amazing. He knows every street. He can take us anywhere."

"Wow," Tai says. "To the moon and back?" He's so clever,

referencing the book we read together in my apartment. But then I see his face is serious.

"Anywhere in the city," I amend. "Anywhere in New York." Tai nods, looking a little less impressed. He's painfully adorable. "Our job is to decide where we want to go first."

"I'm hungry," Tai says.

"Didn't you eat breakfast?" He shakes his head no. "I'd made lunch reservations, but we can go now. Emmanuel, could you drive us to the restaurant, please?"

I'm a little disappointed because this disrupts my morning plan to take Tai on the ferry to Governors Island. I'd move it later, but Jade said Tai really needs his afternoon nap.

Well, there will be other times. I'm not going anywhere.

The car ride to Midtown goes fast—not in terms of traffic, but in company. The first time I ever saw Tai, I mistakenly thought he was shy. It turns out that once he's comfortable, he's a veritable chatterbox. He has lots to say about his preschool teachers, the other kids, and what they're learning. It's obvious to me that he'd love greater challenges.

I need to talk to Jade about getting his private school applications in ASAP. He's already years late, honestly, but I know some influential people from the charity circuit.

Emmanuel pulls up in front of the hotel. Tai and I will be going to the restaurant, which is on the top floor, high above the city, offering panoramic views of the skyline. It's so close to the Empire State Building that it feels like you could reach out and touch it. I bet Tai's never seen anything like it.

But first, we have to get there, which means riding up in the glass elevator. He loves pushing the button for us and asks if he can push the buttons for everyone else. As we ascend, he keeps spinning around, emitting sounds of amazement. I feel like Willy Wonka, like I'm getting to open up a magical new world for a special little boy.

We're led to a banquette that is upholstered in a sumptuous

royal blue fabric. Tai is entranced by the wall of windows, smashing his face flat against the glass before looking back at me with his mouth wide and gaping. "Look, Maren!"

"I know. It's beautiful, right?"

"That building is *right there*!"

"It's the Empire State Building. When people come to New York from other places, they often want to visit that building. They ride up in the elevator for a hundred floors."

"A hundred?" He settles into the banquette and fixes on me with rapt attention. "Then what happens?"

"Well, then they can go outside and look at the whole city."

"People come from other places to look?" It sounds like he thinks people are hopelessly stupid. I start laughing.

"Maybe they should be bungee jumping instead." I try to explain bungee jumping, and he seems amazed at first before losing interest and returning to the window for more face smashing.

I should tell him to get off the glass, he's leaving fingerprints and faceprints, and it's probably less than sanitary, but I don't want to limit him. I'm reveling in his exuberance.

After all these months, I feel as if I've been shocked with a defibrillator. All these years, even. Ever since Corey told me that we wouldn't be having a child, I've been the walking dead. I just didn't realize it until now.

Tai doesn't have much in the way of table manners, but he's a quick study. He's interested in learning what the different forks are for and how to use a cloth napkin. He's even willing to try new foods. Since it's a small-plates restaurant, I order dish after dish. He takes a bite of everything, enjoying more than I would have expected, though half the time, he assumes an expression of almost comical disgust. Seeing that I'm amused, he clowns more, which means he knows how to read a room. So he has emotional intelligence, too.

We keep making up games, and he's always ready to play,

though sometimes he gets a bit antsy and wants to go to the window or wander through the restaurant. Still, he's a good listener, and I can corral him quickly. All credit to Jade for raising such a wonderful young man.

I'll never give Corey credit for anything again.

Tai's favorite game is where we compete to spot a certain color or shape. He legitimately beats me half the time; I let him win the other half.

"You're so bad at this!" he chortles.

"I know, I am! You're going to have to start letting me win."

"No," he says, suddenly serious. "Daddy says never do that."

"Oh." Does that mean Corey beat his own son, routinely? I always knew how much Corey hated to lose, but that's just pathetic.

We go back to the game as we wait for Tai's gelato sundae to arrive. He makes it through maybe a quarter of it before he's groaning melodramatically. I've been taking photos throughout the meal but decide to commemorate the grand finale with a video.

I send a few more photos to Jade and then a text to Emmanuel to let him know we're almost through. By the time I've paid the bill and we've taken the glass elevator down to street level, the town car is idling at the curb.

Jade hasn't responded to any of the photos yet, but she's probably just been busy with clients.

Tai and I get into the back seat. Emmanuel turns around and asks, "Did you have fun?" He looks from me to Tai and back to me.

"Yeeeees!" Tai is bouncing up and down, bouncing all around. I've been at kids' birthday parties after the cake, so I'm somewhat familiar with the sugar-high phase.

"Yeeeees!" I echo, laughing.

"Glad to see it," Emmanuel says, meeting my eyes. "Would you like help getting him buckled in, Maren?"

"No, I've got it." I turn to Tai. "We can do this together, right? You can sit still for me while I get you buckled?"

He nods, still bouncing. As I keep my gaze locked on him, he settles down and gets into the seat. I like how close we are and am almost sorry when I hear the click.

"Let's do a video for your mom," I say. "You can tell her what you saw and what you ate and how much fun we had. Okay?"

"Okay."

Emmanuel starts driving, and I start recording. Tai is mostly able to do the descriptions himself though I add a few asides, like that the big building was the Empire State. "Tell her you love her," I say in a stage whisper.

"Love you!" he sings out.

I send it off to Jade. I imagine that it's a little nerve-wracking the first time your child goes with someone new. Hopefully, I've set her mind at ease. She can see that I'm taking excellent care of him.

After the sugar high comes the crash. I knew that, but I didn't expect it to be quite so sudden or so total. Tai's already fast asleep.

I wish he weren't in his car seat, that I could have him dozing against me. Someday. Maybe even today, if he'll let me tuck him in before his nap.

In the rearview mirror, I catch Emmanuel watching me as I watch Tai. Is his brow furrowed? Surely he can see how well this day is going. How much better I'm doing now that Tai's on the scene.

As we pull up to my building, I gently rouse Tai. When he wakes up, there's a feral edge to him, as if he's been caged for hours instead of catnapping for minutes.

I'm a little thrown by it. It seems like Tai should go to a

playground and burn off some of the energy, but we don't really know each other. What if he's too hyper to listen? What if he starts running toward the street and won't stop when I call his name? What if...?

I don't even know all the worst-case scenarios. I've never been a mom, or even a real babysitter. I like kids, and they generally like me, but I'm not exactly experienced.

"Could you come with us to the playground?" I ask Emmanuel.

His eyes widen. He's a cautious man, not the type to suddenly assume responsibility for another woman's child. But I know how good he is with his own kids, who are precocious and energetic. A lot like Tai, come to think of it.

"Please?" I say.

He nods with only a touch of reluctance. I'm flooded with relief.

Emmanuel parks the car in the lot beneath the building. Tai and I hold hands as we emerge into the sunlight.

"Central Park has playgrounds, right?" I ask.

"Only about twenty of them," Emmanuel answers, with a wink.

"Lead the way," I say, and he does. Within a few minutes of walking, we're in a leafy area with three kinds of monkey bars, tunnels, sandboxes, swing sets, slides, and climbing structures for kids of varying ages. Tai looks thrilled.

"Do we stay close to him?" I say to Emmanuel. "Or do we give him some freedom? Should he go meet other kids?"

Emmanuel gives me a reassuring smile. "He's only four, and we're new to him. We stay close."

I smile back, grateful to have him by my side.

Tai wants to partake of everything and seems to like having an audience. We stay for well over an hour, and while I can imagine how it might become tedious, especially with the constant praise that Tai is seeking, it's never boring for me. On the contrary, it's exhilarating, and I have the sense that Emmanuel feels similarly. He confides that his children have reached the ages where they're the opposite of Tai, that what they want most is for him to look away. They want their independence, and the approval of their peers is of much greater value than his.

"Even Blessing?" I ask. She's only eleven.

"It's true, that saying about how when it comes to raising children, the days are long and the years are short."

"I wish this day would never end." I give Emmanuel a blissful smile. This is what I used to imagine it would be like to parent with Corey.

Emmanuel and I watch Tai working his way across the monkey bars, his face knotted in concentration. When he gets to the end, I explode into applause, and he beams over at me.

Tai is at this phenomenal age where he wants Jade with him all the time, and she's missing it. Corey could easily have paid her entire rent every month so that she could have worked fewer hours and had more time with Tai. Was Corey just too selfish or greedy? Maybe it never even occurred to him because he was too consumed with his own needs to think of anyone else's.

What I really don't understand is why Jade put up with that arrangement. She gives off this aura of strength, but that's obviously just a façade since she let a man call all the shots. Or could there be more to the story of Jade and Corey?

All I know is, I'm on Tai's team now, and I'm going to make sure he has everything he needs and more.

EIGHTEEN
JADE

Today was AMAZING!!! You're raising an incredible little boy!

I want to throw my phone across the bedroom, but I can't afford a cracked screen. It's after ten at night, and Maren still won't leave me alone. Doesn't she have any actual friends she can text?

It took forever to get Tai settled. He went on and on about his time with Maren and Emmanuel. He said he loved them.

"That's great, baby," I murmured, smoothing down his covers, gritting my teeth.

I had to humor him because none of this is his fault. He's not even five years old. How's he supposed to defend against Maren's love bombing? But the last thing I want to do right now is humor her.

I can't stop thinking about him, Maren rhapsodizes. *Thinking about his potential.*

I want to tell her that my son's potential is none of her concern, but I can't risk alienating her, not until papers are signed. I just have to figure out how to move her in that direction, and fast. I don't know how much more of this I'll be able to tolerate. *Thanks again! Good night!*

She refuses to take a hint, sending me yet another photo from the playground.

As if I haven't already seen enough. I immediately deleted that video from the town car, where Maren coached Tai into sharing all about the outrageously expensive restaurant they'd gone to, rubbing my nose in it. She's showing me just what money can do for a kid, while continuing to keep Corey's all to herself. It's the first time I've thought that Maren might be a little bit cruel, though her sadistic tendencies are likely subconscious.

I wish I could forget that video. But the ending, with her pushing Tai to say he loved me? That was the cherry on top of the $32 gelato sundae.

Yes, I looked up the menu. I saw the photo of all those plates on the table with just a few bites taken from each. I bet she spent close to a thousand dollars—the same as she gave me—on that one meal.

It's enough to make my blood boil.

Tai's so bright. I really don't think the local public schools will be adequately stimulating.

There are some decent charter schools but I think private is the way to go.

Of course she does. If Tai had been her kid, she probably would have been applying when he was *in utero*.

But he's not hers, he's mine.

It's never too early, or too late, she says. *Not if you know the right people.*

As in, her kind of people? No, thanks.

I need her money, not her research. Not her contacts. I hate all that shit, and Corey knew it. He respected it about me.

How could he stand this woman? How could he have built a life with her?

Maren's just as shallow as I always suspected when I read between the lines of Corey's stories. I always sensed that her vaunted kindness and generosity were only skin deep, that she's more about image than true feeling, that her charity work was just a way to meet the "right people." Beneath the surface, what's really going on?

I'm a little bit afraid to find out. A little bit afraid to piss her off. Women who don't have anything left to lose can be dangerous, and that's pretty much the definition of Maren.

It doesn't have to be Manhattan. There are some great private schools in Brooklyn. Does she really think my hesitation is about geography?

It's about territory, and I don't want to cede any to her.

I head for the kitchen, opening the cabinet and removing a box of Oreos. I stuff one in my mouth grimly.

He might be able to qualify for scholarships. Have you ever had any testing done? She's relentless.

Like IQ testing? I eat another Oreo.

Educational testing. I'm sure it would prove what's so obvious.

How much does that cost?

I don't know. We could work something out. If he doesn't qualify for a scholarship, we might be able to work something out on tuition, too.

Work something out. What an ominous phrase, used twice in one text.

She needs to get a fucking hobby because my son isn't it.

I'm his mother; I get to decide what's best for him. I believe in public school where he'd meet all sorts of people and not just the "right kind."

But what am I going to do now? I literally can't afford to insult Maren. We're two women who would never be friends, no matter how we'd met, but I need for us to remain friendly. It's rough, though, with how she's treating me. She's the babysitter who wants to run the show.

It's increasingly obvious: she thinks she's better than me, just because she's richer.

It's not like she earned any of her money. Really, she was Corey's leech. Meanwhile, I've put in the work. I've been improving myself forever, since I was born Jacqueline Bastone. Jade's my own creation. I'm a self-made woman, and Corey loved that.

But the fact is, he loved Maren, too, who had everything handed to her on a silver platter. Corey told me she graduated from college without any student loans. First her parents paid her way, and then Corey did.

I didn't go to college, unless you count a few semesters of a predatory online school that's since gone bankrupt. Yet I'm still stuck paying off the loans. I didn't get a degree, only debt, but I learned a lot about how to protect myself next time. I'm always learning because, for people like me, life is a struggle and a constant teacher. When we make mistakes, we pay for them. We don't have a safety net. There are no golden parachutes.

Maren is a climber. She believes in people accumulating and hoarding wealth, power, and advantages for themselves and their friends.

Now she's telling me that she wants to make Tai in her image. She's going to spend two full days a week indoctrinating him and will try to coerce me into sending him to a fancy private school that'll finish the job. If she has her way, he'll become an elite and leave me behind.

I went to public school, I text.

I did, too. Don't you want more for Tai, though? Isn't that what parenthood is all about, giving our kids what we didn't get?

Parenthood is about a lot of things. She's in no position to know that, is she? Those who can't do, teach. Those who can't teach, Google and dispense unsolicited advice.

Let's talk more about this soon. I'm going to send you a link with some educational toys. Smart as he is, you still need to feed that. You want to give Tai every advantage.

No, she does. She's confusing the two of us, something Corey never did. He appreciated our differences.

The toys aren't just for academic development. They're for his emotional health, too. They can help him with his grief.

What does she know about his grief? They spent one day together.

I've been researching. Kids that young can look okay, but on the inside, they're not. He's probably been affected in ways you can't see. The symptoms can show up years later.

I'm on it, I say. *You don't have to worry.*

Has he seen a therapist?

No. I don't feel the need to soften it when she is so out of bounds. Just, no.

I can find a child grief specialist for you. And I'm happy to pay. As long as it's her idea, she's happy to pay. I'm too angry to answer.

Bubbles appear to indicate that she's typing, then they disappear. Now she's typing again. *There's no shame in accepting help now and then.*

The gall. The condescension.

I will get my hands on that money, pronto. I'm going to give Tai what I never had, and I won't have the slightest shame about what it'll take.

NINETEEN
MAREN

I'm a lucky woman.

I can't believe I'm feeling that, after everything, but it's true. I'm tired of thinking negatively, ruminating on what kind of man Corey turned out to be or how stupid I was or how deeply and profoundly he betrayed me or all the ways he destroyed my life.

Because my life isn't destroyed. His is. Corey's the one who's out of chances. When you think about it, he got his punishment by dying young. God's already dealt with him.

Meanwhile, I have an opportunity gleaming before me, the opportunity to create opportunities for the sweetest, smartest little boy I could have ever hoped to meet. Corey brought Tai and me together, and the two of us have our whole lives ahead of us.

Tai is wonderfully consuming. It's not just about the time we spend together but about researching schools, therapists, and activities, plus shopping for him. I've also been reading child development and parenting books, including ones about childhood grief.

I'm hoping that Jade and I can meet up sometime soon. I

could be an excellent resource, if she's open to it. Her texts have been curt, but some people are just like that by text. I barely know her, though I'd like to change that. Since I'm going to play a significant role in Tai's life, I need a relationship with her, too.

I do worry sometimes that I'm coming on too strong, that maybe she feels like I'm overstepping. I just don't want to waste any time. I already missed the first years of his life, and other kids have been on lists for private schools since their mothers were undergoing IVF. Why shouldn't Tai get to have all those same advantages?

Corey must have been too cheap or too self-involved. Maybe he just plain didn't care what happened to Tai. But I do, desperately.

Hopefully Jade will feel my good intentions. Right now, I'm focusing on Tai, cementing my relationship with him, making sure he has loads of fun. I thought I knew New York so well, though I've never tried to see it through the eyes of a child before, or rather, through the activity schedule of a child.

Central Park is right across the street from me, and it's full of overlooked gems, like the Swedish Cottage Marionette Theatre. As Emmanuel mentioned, there are at least twenty playgrounds, with different themes and specialties. I've never even been out on the lake before! Weather permitting, Tai and I can rent paddleboats this Wednesday.

Then there's the New York Botanical Garden, Bronx Zoo, Wave Hill, One World Observatory, Queens County Farm Museum, live music at Washington Square Park, Audubon for birdwatching, Roosevelt Island Tram, Museum of Illusions, Madame Tussauds... I've begun compiling a list of all the best ice cream parlors in the city. Serendipity 3 is a no-brainer, but there are a ton of little mom-and-pops, too. Tai loves ice cream. And at mealtimes, I'll make sure he eats his vegetables to balance out the treats.

I'm taking him to the Strand for sure. It's got, what, two

million volumes and hosts children's readings often. Kids need loads of books around, and I didn't see any in Jade's apartment, though admittedly, I hadn't looked very closely. There'd been other things on my mind. Back then, I was still hoping against hope that Jade was lying about Corey. Now I'm glad she wasn't.

What a difference a few weeks can make.

I've started to be more social again, texting with some of the finance wives, the ones who have kids about Tai's age and are deeply involved with them. That means that I don't bother Alyssa (or her two nannies). Alyssa would see through my AFAFs; she'd know I'm not really asking for a friend. And I already know what she thinks about Jade. Alyssa is incredibly loyal and incredibly stubborn. She doesn't change her initial impressions easily.

But I know that babysitting Tai is the greatest idea I've ever had. I can expose him to all sorts of things that Jade doesn't have the time or money to provide.

She texted to ask how I'd feel about setting up a trust that she could use for his education, therapy, and other expenses. It's not a terrible idea. But the thing about a trust is that it relies on trust.

To be honest, I have some concerns about her judgment and decision-making. Look at the arrangement she had with Corey. It's not that I think Jade would ever try to hurt Tai; I'm sure she's doing the best she can. But she does make some questionable choices.

My phone rings, lifting me out of the internet rabbit hole. "Hi, Alyssa!"

"Well, you sound perky!" As does she. Perk with just the slightest hint of snark. That's her brand. "I'm in your neighborhood. Do you have time for a quick drink?"

"I wish I did." I try to infuse my voice with regret. It's not that I don't want to see her, but I'm cozy in my bed, wearing silk pajamas, a glass of wine on my nightstand. I'm going to eat popcorn for dinner since there's no man to cook for. It all feels delicious and decadent. "Sorry, I'm heading out in a bit."

"Right," Alyssa drawls. I get the sense that she doesn't quite believe me. "Do you have a minute to catch up, before you go?"

"Sure."

"So how are you, really? You haven't been responding to my texts." She sounds slightly reproving.

"I've responded to most of them."

"But you haven't gone into any detail. You said you believe the affair happened and that Corey really has a son." I know Alyssa still has her doubts. "I can't even imagine how horrible you must feel. Have you taken to your bed again, like you did when Corey first... you know?"

"When he first died. You can say the word." I haven't "taken to my bed"; I've reclaimed it. I sleep in the middle now, splayed out like a starfish. "I'm doing really well. Like I said in my texts."

"But you haven't told me how that's possible. I mean, what have you been up to?"

I take a big swig of wine and brace myself. "I've been babysitting."

"Babysitting who?"

"Corey's son, Tai. Two days a week. I love his company, and Jade could really use the help, being a single mother."

There's a long silence. "That is a profoundly awful idea," she says.

"Then why is it making me so happy?"

"All I'm going to say—and then we can drop the subject—is that you're playing with fire."

"Noted. So what's going on with you?"

"Okay, just one more thing. Need I remind you that Jade is a single mother because she fucked your husband *for years*?"

"I'm not forgetting anything. But this isn't about Corey

anymore, or about Jade. If you met Tai, you'd see. He's just the best."

"Because he reminds you of Corey?"

"Absolutely not," I say with distaste. "So what's up with you? How's Asshole?"

"We'll get to that, but I just need to say one final thing. Pretend you've asked for my advice. Pretend you're asking for a friend."

Of course, the other finance wives told Alyssa I've been in touch. Nothing gets past her, and she wants to remind me of that.

"Be careful," she says. "You're dabbling in the dark arts, my dear."

TWENTY
JADE

"Thanks for watching Tai," I say. "I know it's last minute."

"Hi, Grandma!" Tai trills.

"Hey there." Mom already sounds weary as Tai runs past her and into the apartment. "So you said you're working only a few hours?"

"I'll be back by three o'clock. Four, at the latest." I agreed to fill in for Sophie, who's sick, which means that I have to charge her junior stylist rates, but I'm still grateful for the extra cash.

Maren hasn't given me an answer about setting up the trust, even though I pitched it right at her sweet spot, saying it could be used for private school and therapy. Once she's out of our lives, I'll do whatever I want with that money. But she's being cagey. Her last text on the subject read: *It's not a no. I'm still thinking. Maybe I'll talk to the estate lawyer.*

Maybe? What is she thinking about at this point—the best way to string me along and keep the upper hand? The best way to punish me? Because this is starting to feel like water torture.

Mom and I are still in the doorway. I can hear that she's already got the Disney Channel turned on, and Tai has settled himself in the spot where he spends most of his time with her.

On one level, I know that Maren is a definite upgrade from my mother's caregiving (if you can even call it that). Maren will always give Tai her undivided attention.

Which is part of my problem. It's the ick factor. She's the betrayed spouse. She should want Tai and me to stay far, far away.

Other problems? I don't want her indulging Tai's every whim, spoiling him like milk. And I definitely don't want her interference. I didn't want Corey's, either. That's why the arrangement worked so well for both of us. I made all the major decisions, and he could occasionally act as a sounding board or a bank, but mostly, I was on my own. I was in control.

These days, I'm feeling increasingly out of it.

"I have good news," I tell Mom. "The other babysitter is working out so you don't have to watch Tai on Wednesdays and Saturdays anymore."

There it is, the expression I didn't want to see on Mom's face. Pure relief. "That's probably better for everyone," she says. "I'm just so tired these days."

"I know, Mom. I'm not mad at you." I probably shouldn't be mad at Maren, either. She's doing me a favor, helping me. No, helping herself to my son. It feels predatory somehow.

"Someone must be giving you a really good deal," Mom says.

Yes, it's a really good deal with the devil. "Maren's doing it for free."

There's a long silence. Mom's mouth opens slackly, and then she says, "You know, I can still do it. I can watch him."

"We both know it's gotten to be too much." Her reaction is freaking me out a little. I'd hoped that I was overreacting to Maren's offer, that I was being unnecessarily territorial. But it must be a legitimately bad idea if my mother is prepared to report for duty again.

"No, I can do it. I just started taking a new vitamin."

I'm touched by her gesture, but it won't work. I can't take this away from Maren, not when Maren believes my mother is a danger to Tai. And maybe she's right. Look at his arm. I can't take the chance that something worse will happen next time.

"Thanks, Mom. But Tai's really excited. Maren is, too. She keeps texting with ideas for all these little adventures they can have." Little adventures with exorbitant price tags.

Mom lowers her voice. "Does Tai know who Maren really is?" Meaning, does Tai know that Maren was his dad's wife?

"No, and Maren would never tell him. She's not my type of person, but she's a good person. That's what Corey always said."

"But you don't like her." I haven't said that directly, but a mother knows.

"I need to get to work."

"Jackie, you must be able to see how messed up this is. The wife and the mistress are never supposed to meet. For sure, the wife isn't supposed to become the mistress's babysitter."

"I don't do things the usual way. You've always known that about me." I force a smile, like this is even slightly funny.

"You don't want this. She does. Which means it's going to be a train wreck." She often seems so checked out that I forget how well she knows me, and how prescient she can be.

When I was growing up, she could sense a storm brewing inside my father from miles away and a lot of the time, she was able to get me out of harm's way. I spent a lot of time in our neighbors' apartments. Mom did her best to protect me, and she took the brunt of the violence. What's crazy, though, is that Dad died twelve years ago, and she still misses him.

I would never miss a man who'd abused me. Corey didn't live in my apartment, but our home was full of love. Tai has never known the type of fear that I experienced as a child. I've made sure of that.

"I can handle it, Mom," I say. Just like I've handled everything else life has thrown at me. I'll always keep Tai safe.

She shakes her head. "You say that now, but this woman... Tread lightly, okay, Jackie?"

I feel annoyed. Who is she to question me? I'm stronger than she's ever been.

Sure, growing up, I made some bad choices. Sometimes people got hurt. But I'm a mother now. I get what's at stake.

"I'm handling it," I say. She's still shaking her head.

Irritation and anxiety are rising like twin flames. She's giving voice to my deepest fears. I don't want Maren to be Tai's babysitter, but I'm powerless. Which is the worst thing I can ever be.

"This is a mistake," she says. "Stop this now, or you're going to regret it. Everyone will."

"I have to go." I plant a kiss on her cheek. "And be good!" I call out to Tai, hoping I'll be able to keep following that advice myself.

* * *

"I was in the neighborhood and happened to see you in here. You're still open, right?" The ombre blonde with the red lips sticks her head into the salon as I'm sweeping up my last client's hair. You can just tell she doesn't usually take no for an answer.

"Sorry," I say. "I should have locked the door. I'm finished for the day."

She does a little pout, which I guess I'm supposed to find cute. When I'm visibly unmoved, she converts it to a smile. "Are you sure you don't have time for just one consultation? We can make this quick. Quick and painless!"

She's wearing a floor-length skirt covered in feathers and some sort of cape. It looks couture. Her skin is eerily prepubescent. It seems like she's wandered into the wrong neighborhood, or onto the wrong stage. She has a dramatic quality that I dislike instantly.

But I like money a whole lot, especially these days. Getting in with a rich bitch and her friends would be a very good idea. This woman's pumping out queen bee vibes.

"Come in," I say. I direct her to my chair and hurriedly sweep the rest of the hair. She takes a seat without a thank you; she must expect that people will make time for her. Ask, and ye shall receive. That's what I've been trying to do with Maren, unsuccessfully. Maybe it only works when you already have everything. I've heard that the richest people rarely pay; they get comped.

I glance over at my consult in the mirror and see that she's watching me, her eyes narrowed, all trace of the earlier ingratiation gone.

"Do we know each other?" I ask. Because now the queen bee is radiating hate.

"I don't think so. I mean, you'd remember me." There's an edge of contempt in her voice as she picks lint off her cape. I have the sense that to her, I'm very much like that lint.

"What were you thinking of doing with your hair?" I say. Fortunately, she doesn't seem to want to be in my company any more than I want to be in hers. This really will be quick, though I'm not so sure about painless.

"What do you think I should do?" Her voice is icy. It's like she's daring me to insult her, or impress her.

"How long have you had this particular look? Because it's great on you—" it is, though ombre strikes me as a touch dated for someone who's otherwise so fashion forward—"but I'd like to gauge your appetite for change."

She looks amused. "My appetite for change?"

"Yes." What exactly is her problem? Why is she here, if she just wants to mock me? "Maybe we could go bronde—you know, a seamless blend of brown and blonde—or if you want to stay blonde, we could go for babylights—"

"Babylights?" She arches her eyebrow.

"They're more subtle than regular highlights and spaced closer together—"

"I know what a babylight is, obviously." What I don't know is why she keeps interrupting me, or how long I have to put up with this rudeness. "Do you have a baby?"

"I have a son." The last thing I'm going to do is talk to this woman about Tai. "I'm sorry, I didn't get your name?"

"Amelia."

"I'm Jade. So if you wanted a less drastic change, you could do sombre." I go to touch her hair, wanting to check the health, and she jerks her head away like I might be contaminated. I've had nasty customers before, but she is another level. "Sombre is a softer ombre. More blended than what you have now. More low maintenance."

"Do I look low maintenance to you?"

I stare at her in the mirror stonily. It's been a very long week, and I've just about had it with this woman. She'd better get out of my chair, fast.

"You know what I call a supposedly low-maintenance woman?" Amelia pauses, her eyes drilling into mine. "A liar."

"This isn't going to work out. I'm not the stylist for you." I've had to say that only a handful of times in my career, and every time, it's been a pleasure. A true statement of independence.

She laughs in haughty disbelief.

I walk over to the door and open it. "Thanks for stopping by," I say. "Have a great rest of your day."

She stands up slowly. Approaches me slowly. Sizes me up slowly, her eyes moving from the top of my head to the very tips of my shoes. From her expression, I've been found wanting.

I steel myself for the insult, but she doesn't say anything, just walks past me. The silence is even more degrading.

What the fuck was that?

Well, it doesn't matter. It's not like I'll ever see that particular rich bitch again.

TWENTY-ONE
MAREN

It's been a fantastic few weeks. I've got a new lease on life, and I'm not taking anything for granted anymore.

It's hard to convey just how much I adore Tai and our adventures together. So far, we've visited the New York City Fire Museum, the best dim sum restaurant in Chinatown, the Museum of Ice Cream (followed by Serendipity 3 to share a sundae), Rockaway Beach, Sugar Hill Children's Museum of Art & Storytelling, and Hudson River Park. He loved it all. I always knew I'd take to parenting like a fish to water.

For the past three weeks, I've stayed out of Jade's way, and I get the sense she's doing the same with me. Emmanuel acts as our go-between. He picks up Tai in the morning and drops him off at the end of the day, trading reports back and forth. So far, Jade hasn't tried to impose any limits, which I appreciate. Tai and I make our own rules.

He's just so engaging, and up for anything. Within reason, of course. I understand I'm dealing with a four-year-old. His stubby little legs can only carry him so far and so fast.

I love tucking him in for his afternoon naps. Sometimes he's too tired for a story, but at other times, he can't get enough of them. I've amassed a library on the little blue bookshelf that I asked Emmanuel to put together in Tai's room. It used to be the guest room but now it belongs to Tai, totally. Just like my heart.

Too sappy?

While I only see him those two days, the uplift is lasting. I get to daydream, plan, research, and shop all week long.

Yesterday, I asked him to call me "Aunt Maren." He did it, unhesitatingly. Happily, which is how he does nearly everything. Looking at him, you'd never guess that his father recently died. Maybe that's because Corey was more like an occasional visitor.

Tai lost his father, but he's gained an aunt, someone who's faithful and reliable. He traded up, in my humble opinion. I sent Jade another thousand dollars earlier this week, just because.

Tai can benefit from having a mother and an aunt with resources. I've got so many ideas. Too many to be contained in just two days a week.

> *Hi, Jade! Hope you're doing well. What do you think about me getting subscriptions to a few of the children's theaters in the city? It'd be great to expose Tai to the arts. I know he'd love it. But some of those are outside of my babysitting days. Would you mind if I saw him other times, too?*

I probably won't get an answer for hours, but I understand. She has to work. She can't text while there's a client in her chair.

What I don't understand is when she doesn't respond to photos and videos at all. Doesn't she care how her son spends his days? Doesn't she like seeing his joy? It takes only a second to "heart" a photo or send an emoji.

I've asked Jade if we could talk on the phone or meet up, but she's always saying how tired she is, and that she prefers to text. I try not to judge since I don't know what it's like to work full-time and be a single parent. But then, that's why I'm trying to be here for her, to ease the burden, yet her communication is often so terse.

I shouldn't read into it. I'm sure she really is exhausted.

In a lot of ways, Jade is a good mom. But a great mom would want her child to have every opportunity. A great mom would at least be willing to have a conversation with me about private schools.

I don't have an ulterior motive; I only want what's best for Tai. My impression? He's not getting much out of that preschool of his. It sounds more like group babysitting. I could provide a whole lot more stimulation myself, while also taking him to enrichment classes so he'll get to socialize with kids his age. Sometime soon, when Jade and I are on more solid footing, I'll talk to her about an extra day or two. I can highlight all the money she'll save.

Jade doesn't seem to realize how good she has it, dealing with me. How many other women could learn that their dead husband had a long-term mistress and a child and then step up like I have?

Not that this is about me; it's about Tai.

He deserves the world, and if I can give it to him, then Jade should be on board. Any great mom would.

TWENTY-TWO

JADE

Hi, Maren! I really need to think about the children's theater subscriptions. I get so little time with Tai as it is. If the shows are on Sunday or Monday, that'll be a problem.

The real problem is, he's my son, not hers! I expose him, she doesn't!

She's changing him, I can feel it. On my most recent day off, Tai was insufferable, rejecting every one of my ideas. All day long, he kept comparing the toys and games at our apartment to the ones at Maren's. Guess which are superior?

It was a little triggering for me, to be honest. I grew up with a father who was volatile and impossible to please. With Corey, I was never submitting myself for his approval; I could make him happy while being entirely myself. It probably helped that it was part-time.

When I have my few minutes alone with Emmanuel in the morning and evening, I try to subtly pump him for information. I'm getting the sense that Maren pretty much never tells Tai no. How am I supposed to compete with that? I've never been a pushover; I'm never going to be Cool Mom (except insofar as

I'm innately cool). But now I feel like I have to woo back my own son.

I've been hinting to Emmanuel that Maren's obsession with Tai is not normal. He might very well agree, but what can he do? He's on her payroll. He has to tell her what she wants to hear.

Tai's now calling her "Aunt Maren." At that, even Emmanuel gave me a sympathetic look. He must know that Maren's gone too far. But who's going to stop her?

I need to talk to you, I text Emmanuel. *I know you live close by. Tai's asleep. Can you stop over?*

I can see that he's read the text, but he doesn't respond for a long while. Then, finally: *I don't think this is appropriate.*

I'm not trying to fuck you, Emmanuel. I need your help.

He doesn't answer. Have I offended his delicate sensibilities? Ridiculous. Maren's behavior is the most offensive of all, taking liberties with someone else's child, but somehow he's giving her a pass?

I add, *It's not like Maren will know you were here. She wouldn't be caught dead in our hood.*

Other parts of Brooklyn, like Park Slope, sure. But never Bushwick. She'd assume it's rife with crime. Personally, I love the grit. I love street art and murals, second-hand stores, and international food that's authentic and affordable. Unlike more gentrified areas, Bushwick is eclectic and vibrant in ways that someone like Maren couldn't begin to appreciate.

Corey loved it here. It's where we spent most of our time, where we could be incognito. Just another couple, another family.

Corey would want you to help me, I type. *He'd want you to help his son.*

Nothing.

I'd imagined Emmanuel would be more open to my pleas, that he'd want to do the right thing. Corey always talked about what an upstanding guy Emmanuel was. But then, Corey might not have been the best judge of character. Think how he used to talk about Maren.

Emmanuel and I didn't see each other much while Corey was alive, yet on those rare occasions, Emmanuel seemed warm enough toward me. I assumed that he could see how happy I made Corey, how in love we were.

Or had that just been an act, a way to suck up and stay in his employer's good graces? Corey thought they were true friends, but maybe Emmanuel is wilier than he seems. I'd been shocked to learn how large Emmanuel's Christmas bonuses were. I'd teased, "Wow, where's my Christmas bonus?" Corey laughed, but I wasn't entirely kidding. Corey doled out small amounts to me each month; it would have been nice to receive a lump sum in December and breathe easier all year long.

I get it, though. Corey didn't want to feel like his lover was on his payroll. I didn't want to cheapen what we had, either.

You don't know Maren. Interesting how Emmanuel is texting back to defend her honor. *She's been in Bushwick plenty. She's had dinner at my house. My wife and I introduced Maren and Corey to a number of local restaurants.*

Wow, that was practically a novel. When Emmanuel defends someone, he *really* defends her.

I'm surprised and mildly hurt. Why didn't Corey ever tell me that he was bringing Maren here? We told each other everything.

This isn't about Maren, I write. *It's about Corey's money. Once Maren pays up, I'll be able to afford childcare. She shouldn't be Tai's babysitter. You know how weird that is.*

I'll take his non-answer as agreement.

Corey told me that Maren has a lot of respect for you as a family man. Maybe you could nudge her toward creating a trust for Tai?

Still nothing.

You know how hard it is to make ends meet when you're raising a kid in the city. All I want is a fair settlement. I met with a lawyer. He said that since I never established proof of paternity, I can't win a claim against the estate. So I need Maren to do the right thing.

You saw a lawyer about suing Maren?

I can practically feel the frost through the phone. *This is about Corey's estate. I just want what Tai's entitled to.*

But is he entitled? When Corey never made any arrangements?

Emmanuel must be parroting Maren. Doesn't he have a mind—and a spine—of his own? He's acting all powerless, but I know that he's more than just an employee. Corey said that Emmanuel was like family to him and to Maren.

Can't you please talk to Maren? She'd listen to you.

Another long pause. *I don't think that's my place.*
Someday, Maren will thank you. Since he seems to be all about Maren, might as well go this route. *Her conscience will thank you.*

Maren's conscience is clear. Yours should be another matter.

Is he serious right now? He's judging me? Did he judge

Corey, too, or is he unable to judge the people who sign his checks—first Corey and now Maren? I never took a vow to love, honor, and cherish anyone.

I feel a flare of anger. While Corey was alive, Emmanuel kept me a secret from Maren, so he's not exactly pure as driven snow, either. But I can't afford to call him out when I need him in my corner. I need to elicit pity or kinship from him. So I take a deep breath and compose a novel of my own.

> *Maren doesn't know what it's like to claw your way through life, to have to fight for everything you get. To have to fight for everything you give to your children. I understand that. Don't you?*

Emmanuel and I are two hardworking people who've had to struggle, and now we want life to be sweeter and easier for our kids. Maren's different. She can't imagine life on the margins.

Maren has suffered, Emmanuel texts. *I won't let her suffer any more.*

I hadn't anticipated the intensity of his attachment to Maren. I should have, though. Corey was like that, too. Overly protective of Maren, acting like she's some kind of delicate flower at risk of being trampled.

Maren is kind, Emmanuel continues. *She's generous. Every year, she gives thousands to my girls' college funds. She talks about setting up educational trusts. Because of Maren, my youngest daughter will be able to go to medical school.*

A sequel to his earlier novel. When it comes to Maren, it seems he can't help himself. But then, no wonder he's so enamored of her if she's sending his daughter to medical school.

Or is he enamored for other reasons? Is it possible that Emmanuel and Maren are having an affair? Maren as mistress—that would be a sweet irony.

But none of my business. Unless Emmanuel and Maren make it my business.

Don't you think Tai deserves an educational trust, too? Can't you talk to her about his future?

I'm sorry. This is between you and Maren.

In other words, I'm on my own. Maybe he thinks that Tai is some kind of threat to his daughters, that there isn't enough to go around. It's all just so enraging.

Did you hear that, Corey? AUNT FUCKING MAREN???!!!

I can picture Corey saying, S*top shouting!* He hated when I got shrill. I hated it, too, but these are desperate times.

STOP DEFENDING HER! This is indefensible! I had your baby, and now your wife wants to take over. All those nudges about private schools, how she thinks she knows more about my son's "potential" than I do.

He's our son, Jade, not just yours. You used to forget that.

This isn't the time to rehash old arguments. Maren is coming for our kid.

How do you know? You and Maren have barely spoken over the past three weeks. You're not even giving her a chance. Tai's having the time of his life.

It's so easy for her to be the fun aunt when she doesn't have to work like I do. She doesn't have to scrimp and save and scrabble. She doesn't have to say no. She doesn't have to parent.

Why am I even defending myself to Corey? The truth is, I'm entirely alone in this. He's a figment of my imagination, not a partner. And Maren's putting me in a tremendously awkward position since I do want Tai to have amazing experiences; I just don't want them to be with Aunt Maren.

They should be with me. Or they should have been with Corey. Ideally, with Corey and me, both of his parents.

I've become acutely, painfully aware of not only how much Corey is missing out on now, but of how much he would have missed out on even if he'd lived, if he'd continued to divide his life in the way he did. Sure, Tai adored Corey; sure, we had lots of great times as a family in the apartment or out in the neighborhood under cover of darkness. But Tai should have been able to walk proudly in the sunshine with both his parents.

We'd been on borrowed time, since at a certain point, Tai would have started asking questions. When would he have realized his father had another life, that he was married to a woman who wasn't me? How could I have explained we weren't second-class citizens?

I've started wondering what would have happened if my hand had been forced by Tai, if I saw that he needed me to stand up for our rights. If I'd told Corey that he needed to make a choice: it's Maren or me.

Sometimes I'm a little bit glad I never had to find out his answer.

But I can't keep avoiding Maren; I have to force her hand. Emmanuel's made it clear he won't help.

Time for plan C.

TWENTY-THREE

MAREN

"I can't remember the last time I ate at a real deli," I say, biting into my corned beef sandwich.

"I was really craving some matzo ball soup, with latkes." Emmanuel dips his latke in the soup. "Laugh all you want. It's the only way to eat it."

"You've become a true New Yorker." I smile at him fondly. "Not that I'm the one to bestow any titles. I mean, this is my home, but you can't take the Utah out of the girl." I spear a forkful of sauerkraut. "You have to try this. It's just beyond."

"I'm not much for fermentation."

I laugh again. "I never knew that about you!"

"I'm a man of mystery." He dabs at his mouth with the paper napkin in a way that's almost hilariously dainty. He's my gentle giant.

"I'm so grateful for you, man of mystery."

His brow furrows. "I have to talk to you about something, Maren. That's why I suggested going out to lunch. I didn't want to do it in the car."

Or in my apartment, since he's never fully comfortable there. Come to think of it, he's not comfortable now.

"You thought we should have this conversation when we're surrounded by photos of Catskills comedians." I'm needling him, hoping he'll give me a smile. No such luck. I feel a twinge of nerves. "What is it? Is it about Zauna or the girls?"

"It's actually about Jade and Tai."

"Oh." I set down my sandwich as my nervousness intensifies. He spends all that time alone with Tai during their drives to and from Bushwick, and he also sees Jade during the pickups and drop-offs. What has he seen? What's he heard?

"You know I'm always looking out for you," he says.

"Yes. I trust you implicitly."

"As a driver, my job is to see nothing and say nothing. I'm not paid to make observations. I'm paid to shut my mouth and be discreet. But as a friend, as someone who cares about you very much, I have to speak up."

"Of course. I always want to know what you think."

"I've loved seeing you so happy these past weeks, and I know Tai has a lot to do with that. But I worry that maybe it's too much."

"What's too much?"

"The time you spend with him. The way you focus on him. It's almost like"—he averts his eyes, and I can see just how stressful this is for him—"you're obsessed with the boy."

"It's not an obsession. It's more of a calling. If things had been different, I'd have been a teacher or a social worker, someone who worked with kids. I'd have been a mother."

"But Maren"—now he looks truly pained—"you're not his mother. Jade is."

"I know that! Don't you think I know that?"

"Sometimes I'm not sure." He pushes both his plates away. "You're trying to give advice and make decisions. Like about his education."

"Did Jade tell you that?" I can see that he doesn't want to

answer, which means yes. "If she's bothered, she should be telling me directly. She shouldn't be getting you involved."

"She's afraid of you."

"Well, that's silly! I've been nothing but gracious to her."

"Until you do a settlement or a trust, she's having to beg for crumbs. Surely you can see how that might feel to her. It feels perilous, like you have all the power."

I want to ask him whose side he's on, but he's already told me unequivocally that it's mine. I've always known how empathetic he is, and Jade can seem like such a waif. She's a hundred pounds soaking wet.

Alyssa's coming at this from a very different perspective. She's worried that I'm too involved with Jade. "You have to get away from that woman," she told me the other day. "I don't trust her at all."

"I'm not even around her," I said. "We text, rarely. We haven't had a conversation in weeks."

"I don't trust her," she repeated.

"Based on what?" A thought hit me like a meteor. "Did Sean tell you something?" As in, had Corey told Sean about Jade while he was still alive, and Sean finally shared it with Alyssa? Or—worst of all—has Alyssa known all along and she's been playing dumb? Whether it's to protect my feelings or for any other motive, I won't have it. I'm not going to allow anyone in my orbit to lie to me ever again.

"Asshole knows nothing. But I know Jade's type, Maren. She's an operator who's used to getting what she wants. She must have been manipulating the shit out of Corey for years."

If that's true, how come she's so broke? Why didn't he leave her any money in his will or even set up a secret bank account? It seems far more likely that the manipulation went in the other direction.

"Mark my words," Alyssa said ominously. "If you push her too far, she'll snap."

I was reminded that Alyssa doesn't watch only true crime. She's also addicted to a whole spate of shows with names like *When First Wives Kill*. Which meant I'd take her assessment with a grain of salt.

"I don't push Jade," I said. "My relationship isn't with her. It's with Tai."

"Don't you get it? They're a package deal. You can't have Tai without Jade."

In a strange way, Emmanuel and Alyssa are saying the same thing. Jade and Tai are inextricably linked, which means Jade and I are inextricably linked. Jade can't be removed from the equation. Since she can't be cut out, she needs to be invited in.

I want more time with Tai, and I'll have to go through Jade to get it.

"I appreciate what you're saying," I tell Emmanuel. "But you don't have to worry. I know just how to fix this."

TWENTY-FOUR
JADE

You have off Sun and Mon, so let's take a little vacation!

You, me, and Tai at the Hamptons house. What do you say?

I really want to get to know you better, seeing as we're going to be in each other's lives for a long time.

The last text in Maren's barrage is followed by five insipid emojis intended to communicate friendship and goodwill. But she's not fooling me. I know when I'm being strong-armed.

It's yet another summons, and this time, it's for a multiday extravaganza. How am I supposed to get out of this?

I can't.

So how am I going to use this trip to my advantage? I need to make this the last time that Tai and I have to endure Maren's company.

I'll be the houseguest from hell, one she's willing to pay off just so she never has to see me again.

She brought this on herself, Corey. It's not like I'm going to enjoy it.

Or maybe I will, just a little.

TWENTY-FIVE
MAREN

"There!" Tai says excitedly, pointing at the license plate in front of us. It's bumper-to-bumper traffic though it's 8 a.m. on a Sunday. "There's the J!"

"Good job!" I tell him. Do I always sound so high-pitched and phony when Tai and I play Spot the Letter? Or am I just feeling self-conscious because Jade is here, with Tai in his car seat between us?

I'm also aware of Emmanuel in a new way. I hope he can tell that his message from the deli has been received. There's certainly a role for Jade in our modern family dynamic; she's the mother.

The plan is to kill Jade with kindness, to win her over, so that she'll start to be more amenable to my suggestions. Sure, over the next couple of days, I'll get to spend more time with Tai, which is wonderful, but I'm playing the long game. I want more of him every week, and more of a seat at the table in terms of the decisions about his future.

So far, so good. Jade and Tai had been waiting outside their apartment with two enormous bags, which tells me that even though it's only for two nights, Jade didn't want to forget anything. I appreciate thoroughness and attention to detail. It means she cares. She's also been friendly and chattier than ever before. She must want a fresh start, too.

"Now we're up to K!" I announce.

It does feel a little strange to realize Emmanuel is listening in. While I trust him more than anyone, it's jarring to realize how indiscreet I've always been in his presence, acting as if he weren't a person with natural curiosity, opinions, and judgments.

Emmanuel and I grew truly close only after Corey's death. Sure, I used to have dinners with Corey and Emmanuel's family, but I also used to sit in the back of the car, talking to friends in person or on the phone. Over the years, Emmanuel must have gleaned my insecurities, fears, and dissatisfactions. He'd known the ins and outs of my marriage. He's a secret-keeper by trade. Yet somehow, the biggest secret—Jade and Tai—had escaped his notice.

It's a little troubling, thinking of how asleep at the wheel Emmanuel was when it came to Corey. If he didn't know about Jade, what else didn't he know about? Or what else hasn't he shared?

I refocus on Tai and notice Jade is doing the same. It's perfectly companionable. We're just two women with little in common except for our love of Tai. We used to love the same man, but now all I feel is indifference with just a splash of hate. Or is it hate with a splash of indifference? Depends on the time of day, really.

Mostly, Tai keeps me occupied, but thoughts of Corey do sneak in. Especially late at night in my apartment when there's no one next to me and no kids down the hall. That's when the longing and the regrets and the hatred hit hardest.

But there's no point thinking about any of that now, when I've got a full town car.

I lean forward and around Tai to make eye contact with

Jade. "Emmanuel was at the Southampton house all day yesterday childproofing," I say. "In case you were wondering, he already childproofed my apartment."

"That's great, thank you!" Jade seems so enthusiastic and grateful that I wonder if I've been misreading her all along. "Tai has a way of getting into everything. Don't you, little monkey?" She tickles him and he giggles.

"That hasn't been my experience, but I'll take your word for it," I say.

Jade turns more serious. "I do worry sometimes about his energy levels because of how boys are overdiagnosed with ADHD, especially in private schools where they don't want to deal with any kids who have even the smallest behavioral challenge. They don't have to. They can just kick them out and take any one of a hundred other kids off the wait list. The pressure's on the parents to solve the problem, and I definitely don't want Tai to wind up medicated."

"Of course not! He'd never need that!" I love that Tai's spirited. "He's never been a problem for me. Not in the slightest."

"There! K!" Tai points.

"Good job, monkey," Jade says. Then she looks back at me. "Tai's the most awesome kid, but he's not like the others, is he?"

I have no idea what she means, and I get the sense that I shouldn't ask, not in front of him. Is there something I'm missing? I feel a twinge of worry.

"Next game!" Tai says.

"See?" Jade says to me. "He can't make it through the whole alphabet. He gets bored too easily."

"I've never had that impression." But what do I really know? I've been reading my child development books, and it's sounded like Tai's on target, precocious even, but I don't have real-world experience with other kids.

There are things a real mother would see and know that I don't. I'm not a member of that club.

I look out the window, trying to quell the sadness and regain my exuberant mood.

This conversation's the first time I've ever heard Jade's reservations about private school expressed directly. Knowing her concern, I can make some subtle inquiries to the admissions counselors and get back to her.

Now we're really cruising. Tai falls asleep, and Jade and I share a smile over his car seat before we each look out of our own windows. Soon enough, we're pulling up into the driveway of the Southampton house.

"We're here!" I say brightly. "This is going to be so much fun!"

TWENTY-SIX
JADE

"We're here!" Maren exclaims. "This is going to be so much fun!"

Could she be any cheesier? Any more of a phony? Has it even crossed her mind that I haven't come of my own free will?

I've been coerced. But I won't be controlled.

"I'm sure it'll be great," I say, smiling. "Thanks so much for having us." For now, I have to be as much of a phony as she is. I'm her mirror image. In this case, imitation is the insincerest form of flattery.

The car ride went well, I think. She didn't seem suspicious when I started dropping breadcrumbs about Tai, ones that will eventually lead to the inevitable conclusion that she needs to create a trust for Tai. An irrevocable trust, so that she can't change her mind later. Then I won't be subject to her whims ever again.

Emmanuel insists on getting everyone's bags from the trunk and bringing them inside. I know this is his job and he takes pride in it, but I've always chafed at the idea of a servant class. I'm part of it, in my way. The service industry, by definition, serves. But some jobs shouldn't be jobs. Everyone should be humble enough to clean their own houses, in my humble opinion.

Just one of the many areas where Maren and I disagree.

I'd have preferred to carry my own bags, even if they are ridiculously large. I wanted a ton of stuff so that I could throw it all around Maren's impeccable house. She should experience Tai's messiness and what a handful he is, particularly when he's overstimulated, which he will be. The new environment will amp him up and maybe I'll let him have more sugar than usual. If he misses his afternoon nap, he's likely to have a meltdown or two. Then she can see that he's not always the angel baby she's made him out to be.

Maren has us take our shoes off by the door (of course) and wants to show us around (of course), and I realize that authenticity is going out the window. She wants me to ooh and aah and I have to comply.

It's just the kind of house I hate. It's as fake as she is. There are all these wooden design details that are supposed to give the place personality and character, but really, it's just new construction trying to look old. New money trying to look old and not fooling anyone. And don't get me started on that teal kitchen that's supposed to show she's whimsical. Please. This house has no heartbeat.

"Did you pick this color?" I say, looking around the kitchen in faux rapture. "I love it!"

She's eating it up. "I didn't pick the color, but in part, I picked the house because of it. I walked in and just said, 'Yes!' Corey felt the same way." The smile drops from her face. I can see that many of her cherished memories are like corrupted files.

I feel for her, a little. But I can't let that stop me.

Tai doesn't give a shit about decorative accents, or stroking Maren's ego. "Can we go swimming?" he asks her. "You promised!"

"He told me he can't swim, and that you can't either," she explains to me. "I said I'd teach him."

Without asking me? But then, I have no real reason to say no. I've been meaning to sign him up for lessons. It's true, I never learned to swim myself. Not for lack of trying on my mom's part. She took me to the Y every Saturday for a month, but to no avail. The instructors couldn't get me to put my head under the water. It's a primal fear that I've never overcome.

"I'm an excellent swimmer," Maren says. "We'll do it in the pool, not the ocean."

I don't have a good excuse. It's early June, but it's ninety degrees out. I look down at Tai, who is chomping at the bit. "Sure, let's do it." He breaks out into a huge smile.

"Let's get you into your swim trunks," I say. I'd brought them thinking that we'd mostly just be making sandcastles, which is what he and I spend the majority of our time doing when we're at the beach. When we get too hot, we dip our toes into the ocean, splash water on ourselves or each other, never going in too far. But Maren clearly has other ideas.

There are only three bedrooms upstairs—the primary, the guest, and one that's furnished as an office—so Tai and I are bunking together.

He's wriggling around and chattering away, oblivious to my opposing mood. Once he's in his trunks, he starts to run out. I call him back, saying that he needs sunscreen. He begins whining immediately. He hates the slimy sensation of sunscreen, and he hates being slowed down.

I hope Maren is close enough to hear this. "Don't fight me!" I say loudly. "You have to do this."

"I want to swim!"

"If you want to swim, you have to wear sunscreen."

He pouts. "Who says?"

"Who says?" I repeat, as if I'm broadcasting to the cheap seats. Hopefully Maren will hear this and start mistakenly coding him as an ADHD-addled brat. "I'm your mother and I say!" I shake up the sunscreen tube, squirting the goop into my hands.

He shimmies backward, forcing me to pursue him. It'd be great if he'd run downstairs and I had to chase him, but alas no. He stops and I'm able to finish quickly.

I start putting on my own swimsuit—I went with a maillot instead of a bikini (keep it modest, don't show up the hostess)—while Tai says impatiently, "Can I go?"

"No, we'll go—" I'm about to say, "together," but he's already yanked open the door. Seconds later, I hear him and Maren talking downstairs. She overenunciates in this way that I can't stand, every syllable dripping with adoration.

Once I'm suited up and sunscreened, I head downstairs myself. Emerging through the glass kitchen doors, I see that Tai and Maren are already in the pool. "I bought him a swim vest," she calls, "and we reviewed the rules. He knows not to run."

"Good luck," I say. "I've been trying to teach him that for years." I give a wry smile, taking a seat on a lounge chair that's already shaded by an umbrella.

I don't know anything about teaching kids to swim but I can tell Maren's doing it carefully, by the book. She's getting him acclimated to the water, and he's instantly taking to it. It makes me feel bad for not having exposed him sooner. But he's only been alive four years. We've been busy.

The moment stings since I used to have a fantasy that someday Corey would be the one teaching Tai to swim, that he would do what I couldn't. Now everything's on me, including getting Maren out of our lives.

How nuts is it that the role of swim instructor has gone to Corey's wife, and the setting is their Hamptons house?

I don't know how I got here, Corey, and I just want out.

I notice that in their few short weeks together, Maren and Tai have already developed a shorthand language. They have in-jokes and make each other laugh easily. She teasingly gets him to pay attention when his mind starts to wander.

It's all quite sweet, and the strength of their bond is evident. Should I really be interfering with that? Shouldn't I want more people to love my son?

But anyone watching would think Maren was Tai's mother, and that's a perversion. It's just wrong.

Wouldn't anyone think so?

Corey, don't you think so?

I can't look anymore. I take out my phone and start scrolling. After a few minutes, Maren interrupts. "Aren't you going to watch? Or maybe take pictures or a video? He's doing so well!"

There's no missing the underlying criticism. She doesn't approve of my parenting. She thinks she could do better.

I could do better, too, if I had two houses, a driver, no job, and tons of money. But she's in no rush to level the playing field, is she?

I smile at Tai. "You're doing great, baby!"

He smiles back. Wearing his swim vest, he's buoyant in more ways than one, kicking his legs. Maren is always within arm's reach. "Video of me and Aunt Maren!"

Now she's grinning. "Send it to me, okay?"

This is going to be a very long two days. But they'll be productive, I'll make sure of that.

* * *

Despite the extra dessert, Tai still went down for his afternoon nap without any fussing at all. I could stay in the room with him or go downstairs and start working on Aunt Maren.

There's no use in procrastinating, is there? The sooner she initiates a settlement or trust—I'm not picky, I'd take either—the sooner I can be free.

Maren's reclined on the sofa, reading a book. She looks only too happy to sit up and set it down. "Hi, Jade!"

I'm thrown by her warmth. Is it possible that she really just wants to get to know me better, like she said in her text? That she is, in fact, a good person who doesn't mean to be overbearing or undermining? That by cutting her off from Tai, I'm robbing my son of a relationship that could be emotionally rich instead of merely financially lucrative?

Maybe she does have a good heart, deep down, and if that's the case, it'll emerge over time. We'd work something out, and she could see Tai on occasion, at my discretion. But I want my share of Corey's estate first. Tai's share, I mean.

I take a seat in the chair opposite her. "I think you're right," I say, without preamble. "Tai is struggling with Corey's death."

"Oh." She looks surprised, and then downcast. "I didn't want to be right about that."

"You offered to pay for therapy, which was incredibly generous. But therapy's one hour a week with a stranger. That's not what Tai needs. He needs his mother. He needs me to be around more. If I could, I'd shorten my work hours."

"Why? What's wrong with him?" I'm not positive but I think I'm catching a note of suspicion or reluctance, like she's not so sure she wants me around my son more.

"He needs me, like I said. And I need the financial freedom to make these sorts of decisions, in his best interest." I'd prefer to hint at the settlement without saying it outright, let her fill in the blanks. "If Corey had known he was going to die—if he'd had cancer, for example—he would have empowered me to do that. He'd have set us up for life."

"Don't kid yourself. Corey didn't want to 'empower' anyone." When she says Corey's name, her disgust is apparent.

I try to stifle my annoyance. She's entitled to her feelings about Corey, but she shouldn't talk about things she knows nothing about. "You never got to see Corey with Tai. If you had, you'd know how much they loved each other. That's why Tai is so impacted by Corey's death."

"You told me a few weeks ago that he wasn't. You said Tai was doing great."

"I was wrong, and when I'm wrong, I can admit it." Can Maren? Or does she think she's infallible?

"So what sort of impact is Corey's death having on Tai?" I don't like the turn this conversation has taken. It feels like I'm supposed to prosecute my case, and she's the judge and jury.

"Lately there have been a lot of tantrums."

"Only lately? Corey's been dead for, what, seven months now?"

"Sometimes Tai acts out," I continue stubbornly. "He doesn't listen, and he can't be soothed." She's not going to push me off my script.

"I haven't seen any of that."

I was ready for this. "Tai's not going to show that side of himself to you. He's on his best behavior. Deep down, he's probably afraid he'll lose you, too. But with me, he can let it all out. He's secure. He knows I'm not going anywhere."

"I'm not going anywhere, either."

Is that a threat? I can't tell, as her face is entirely neutral. So often in our interactions, I've found her difficult to read, which has made it hard to prepare.

"I'll tell him that he doesn't have to hide anything from me," she says. "That I'm here for him, no matter what. He doesn't always have to be a good boy."

Was that a dig since she knows I tell him to "be good" when I drop him off with people? "He doesn't even know he's hiding anything. It's not like any of these feelings are conscious. At his age, he can't really talk about them; he has to act them out. That's why as soon as Emmanuel drops Tai off, Tai melts down."

"He does?" I can see Maren's concern.

No, he doesn't, but the truth isn't going to get this done. "The door shuts behind Emmanuel and it's like everything Tai's been holding in all day comes out in a rush. It's intense."

"I didn't know that," she says softly.

"How could you? I haven't been honest with you. I guess I wanted you to think everything was fine. For me, and for Tai."

"He seems that way around me. I mean, he's happy all the time."

"I hope he really does feel that happy. But it's not the whole story. What I worry about is Tai feeling like he has to put on a mask, that he has to be strong all the time. That's part of what killed Corey."

She blanches. "What do you mean?"

"I'm speaking metaphorically. It's the burden of masculinity, you know? How Corey couldn't show his full self to you."

"He could have." Her expression sours. "He chose not to."

"I'm not blaming you. It's more about society. Living up to a certain kind of male ideal. Corey felt like he had to be invulnerable and be the provider. I don't want that for Tai."

"Tai is nothing like Corey."

That's what she wants to think. She's clearly come to despise Corey, but I feel very differently. I love when I see Corey in Tai.

The fact that she has such negative feelings about Tai's father is another reason for me to get her out of our lives, pronto. At some point, those feelings will come out in Tai's presence.

"I didn't force Corey to lie for years," Maren says stiffly. "Society didn't force him to, either."

"You and I don't have to agree on everything. But I think we agree about wanting a healthy environment for Tai where he doesn't feel pressure to conform. That's why I need your help."

She's watching me closely. I'm hoping she'll say it, so I don't have to.

"Let's be real. That takes money. Money is choice. Money is

freedom. Can we please put Corey's money toward a good cause?"

Silence. But I'm not going to break it.

I will not be the one to break.

Finally, Maren speaks. "I hear what you're saying. I'll need to think it over."

I feel like exploding. That's the same line she's been giving me for the past six weeks! Did she even talk to the estate lawyer like she claimed she would?

"You've been thinking it over for a while," I say, and there's an edge to my voice that contrasts with the supposed vulnerability of the rest of the conversation.

Maren must pick up on that because she lifts an eyebrow just slightly. For her, that's a macro-expression.

"When do you think you'll reach a decision?" I ask, making my tone soft as well-worn leather.

"Soon." She stands up. "Thank you for sharing, Jade."

As she leaves the room, I want to kick myself. I'd started out so strong, like I was an Olympic gymnast executing this incredibly complicated vault in the air—three and a half twists, at least—only to land on my butt on the mat. Now I might be out of medal contention.

Or has she been toying with me all along, knowing that regardless of what I say, she has no intention of ever giving me a cut of Corey's estate?

I can't know what's going on in Maren's head, but there's still a lot of visit left. I'm going for the gold.

TWENTY-SEVEN
MAREN

I don't know what to think about Jade. Tai and I were having the greatest time swimming today, and I had to press her into taking any photos or a video. She seemed completely detached and never even got in the pool. I know I offered to be a babysitter, but it was strange being treated like one. Anyone watching would think I worked for her.

I'm trying to hold a positive view of Jade, but it's hard not to notice certain things.

Like now, over a dinner of delivery pizza in the kitchen banquette, she's barely saying a word to me or to Tai. He doesn't even seem to care because he's fixed on me. Transfixed by me.

"Flattering" doesn't fully express what that feels like. His mother is right here, but he's choosing me.

That might be because I'm choosing to talk to him. It's like Jade's emotionally MIA, outsourcing her responsibilities.

All day at the pool, I was the one teaching him water safety and swimming. Now at dinner, I'm the parent: finding conversational topics, reminding him not to talk with his mouth full, helping him resist the "zoomies" (our word for his desire to run around a room in circles like a frenetic puppy). Jade might as well not even be here.

Maybe she's depressed. It sure sounded like she's in over her head during our conversation earlier. She wants to think that all Tai's tantrums and meltdowns are a function of his grief over Corey and how safe he feels with her, but there could be other factors, like the way she interacts or fails to interact with him. I didn't even recognize the Tai I know from her description of him, and that seems telling.

What if he's melting down when he gets home because he's missing me already? Because he wanted to stay with Aunt Maren, since I'm present with him in a way she's not? A way she can't be, since she's too broken up over Corey?

Honestly, I don't know if having Jade around more in her current state would be good for Tai.

She's angling for guaranteed income from Corey's estate, and I can understand that, with how she's living. But I have misgivings about how she'd use the money. Would it really go to Tai? I don't know this woman, and emotionally she seems to be all over the map.

Not to mention, if she changes her work hours, I'd likely lose time with Tai instead of gaining more. That would be disastrous for him, given how attached he is to me. He needs the stability, consistency, and nurturing I provide. And I need him, too. I love him.

I don't think Jade's malicious. But she is erratic. If that's because she's consumed with grief over Corey, then I need to help her with that. I don't like to think or talk about Corey, but I have to get her to see the truth about him. The fiction is eating her alive.

As dinner grinds to a halt, she thanks me again for having them and says that Tai's had a long day and really needs to get to bed. She already gave him a bath earlier, which is something I would have loved to be part of, but I gave them their privacy. Now I'm about to be shut out of the bedtime ritual, too.

I shouldn't be bothered by that. After how inert she's been, I should be glad for Tai that she wants to do bedtime.

"I'll just stay here and clean up." I give Tai a hug and a kiss. "Sleep well, sweet prince."

"You want to come?" he asks. "To tuck me in?" I always tuck him in before his naps when I babysit.

"No, that's a job for your mom."

I wrap up the remaining pizza and put the plates in the dishwasher. It takes me a second to recognize the emotion I'm feeling. It's jealousy.

It's funny because I'm no longer remotely jealous of the relationship that Jade once shared with Corey. But I do envy the relationship she gets to have with Tai, that she's the one who gets to put him to bed every night. Did it even occur to her that she should be the one cleaning the kitchen and I should be the one getting to do the bedtime ritual, for one night only? It's like she has no empathy at all.

I head upstairs to my own room, and at that exact instant, Jade is exiting the guest bathroom. Impulsively, I say, "Could we go downstairs and have a drink?" This weekend is about getting to know Jade and having a fruitful collaboration. With Corey gone, our relationship is a little like co-parenting.

"Umm." She pauses, a long pause. "Okay. A drink sounds nice."

"Is he already asleep?" I ask, indicating the closed door to the guest bedroom. Maybe I could still read him one book?

"Out like a light. The day tired him out."

"Okay then," I say, hiding my disappointment. "Let's go downstairs."

In the living room, she takes a seat in the overstuffed chair just like she did earlier, curling up with her legs underneath her. She's waiting to be served. "Bourbon, please," she says. She doesn't say she wants Corey's brand, Angel's Envy, but I assume that's what she means.

"I don't have any. I poured it all out." I'm not even sure why I'm lying, but there's no taking it back now. "How about some wine?"

"That's fine."

I grab a bottle, open it, and pour us each a glass. Carrying them over, I sit down on the couch, choosing the end that's closest to her chair.

"How are you, Jade?" I ask. "I mean, really."

She's looking down into her glass uncertainly, and it's the first time I've thought of her as insecure rather than withholding. But maybe that's all this is. She's a young woman who's probably never lived anywhere outside of Bushwick. Corey and I got to travel a lot, but it's likely that she never did. You can be born and raised in New York and still be provincial.

"You and I have had a strange beginning," I say gently, "but I'd like to make things work."

Her eyes flick over to me. They're such a beautiful pale green that at times, it's almost disconcerting.

I ask what Tai was like as a baby and a younger child, encouraging her to share funny anecdotes. She relaxes, and we even laugh together. It's what I was hoping would come out of this trip.

"I never thought I'd be a mother," she says, and I'm instantly gutted. She got what I wanted, desperately, effortlessly, while still in her twenties. She could go on to have more kids. Tai would make a great big brother. "But when it's right, you just know."

"How could those particular circumstances have been right?" I say. "I'm not trying to judge, but I really don't understand."

She stands and goes to the bar, picks up the bottle of wine, and brings it back to where we've been sitting. She pours herself another glass and tops mine off.

"I love Corey so much," she says. I note the present tense. Somehow, by the end of this trip, I'll make it past. It'll be better for Tai—and for her—that way. "I would have had a baby only with someone I loved, who would stay out of my way."

"You're saying you liked having the father of your child go home to his wife?" I'm trying not to sound dubious, but it's absurd, like something a predatory older man convinced her of for his own benefit. I've only just come to terms myself with how brilliantly manipulative Corey was. He managed to persuade me that he was enough, that I didn't need a child!

But Jade is nodding, still utterly convinced. Even now, she's in Corey's thrall and under his thumb. "I only wanted him to give me money when I asked."

"So you had to ask, every month?" Doesn't she get how demeaning it all was?

"No." Her gorgeous eyes flash. It's the most alive she's looked since we arrived in Southampton. "I *told* him."

"You wouldn't have preferred if he just gave you a million dollars and said, 'Use this however you want'?"

"Then I would have owed him. It would have changed our entire relationship. He saw me as a strong, independent woman because I was one. I am one."

She's saying that she's not me. Ironic, seeing as she's been hounding me for handouts since we met.

"What about Tai?" I say. "Did you think that living in that apartment and barely getting by was good for him?"

"He has a mother who works hard. What's wrong with that?"

"Nothing's wrong." I don't get her at all. Maybe I never will. That could very well be how she feels about me, too.

We drink our wine in silence.

"What about other men?" I say. "Before Corey, I mean. You

were young when you met him. Was he the first person you were ever serious about?"

"I had other boyfriends."

"At the same time? When Corey was with me, I could imagine you might want company."

"No. I was faithful to Corey. I've told you that." She sounds annoyed, like she thinks I'm accusing her of something. Did she tell me that? I don't recall. Our early conversations are hazy from shock.

I'll just put us both out of our misery. There's one topic that I know will interest her.

"I thought about what you said earlier," I say. "About you wanting to spend more time with Tai."

She sits up straighter. This is the moment she's been waiting for this whole trip, hasn't it? She's never wanted to build a relationship. I'm an ATM to her, nothing more.

"I'd like to give you a lump sum that represents three months of your total expenses," I say. "Rent, food, entertainment, everything. Then you can take a three-month sabbatical, or just reduce your hours and stretch it out longer. You can decide what's best for Tai."

It's obvious that's not what she wanted to hear. She swills her wine, formulating a response. Finally, she says, "That's very kind of you, Maren. Really, you've been nothing but kind in an incredibly difficult situation."

I can feel the "but" coming.

"But this isn't about me having the summer off. It's about taking care of Tai for the next fourteen years."

I set down my wineglass, trying to squelch my frustration. They talk about the rich being entitled, but sometimes it's the other way around.

"Can we talk straight?" I say. "You and I are in the same boat. We were both screwed over by Corey, and we both love Tai."

She shakes her head ever so slightly. What part does she disagree with—the being screwed over, or the loving?

"Corey was a horrible human being, but he managed to produce a beautiful son. And I don't blame you for anything that happened. In fact, I want to go on record right now saying that I forgive you."

She stares down into her glass stonily. "Thank you."

"How old were you when you got together with Corey? Twenty-two? Twenty-three? You were practically a kid yourself."

"Could you excuse me?" Her voice sounds strangled as she sets down the glass and gets to her feet. "I think I heard Tai."

Poor Jade. Corey did a real number on her. It's been more than half a year since his death, and she doesn't know whether she's coming or going. She's still repeating his lies. The fact is, he controlled us both, employing different strategies to do it. The biggest lie of all was that he loved either of us.

I watch her dash up the stairs, answering an imaginary cry for help, when I think that she's the one who really needs help.

Jade's basically a good mother with a lot on her mind and on her plate. In the wake of Corey, she's doing the best she can.

But is she a great mother? Like I would be?

TWENTY-EIGHT
JADE

To my admittedly untrained eye, Coopers Beach is just a beach, though Maren made sure to inform me it's the very best in all of the Hamptons. I mean, sure, the sand is silky and clean, and the restrooms are clean, too. In the pale morning sunlight, the water is an appealing aqua, chilly but not frigid. Other than a few people walking their dogs, we have the place to ourselves.

Since Emmanuel's not here, Maren hired a car service. But of course she had to mention that as a resident, she could have parked for free while visitors have to pay $50. Fifty dollars! To visit a perfectly adequate expanse of sand bordered and overlooked by weatherbeaten mansions? I bet that if Corey were still alive, Maren would have one of those mansions in her sight; he said she loved movin' on up. He sang a little song about it from some sitcom that I was too young to have seen, and I trash-talked about his old-dude references.

I miss you, Corey. Wish you were here.

Maren came prepared with a massive pop-up sun tent and a deluxe sandcastle-building set. You could practically build a real house with that. It's got its own excavator. Tai's in heaven.

She was out building with him, but now she's stuck her head

inside the tent with the smile of a consummate hostess. Fake, in other words. "Just wanted to see how you're doing in here!"

"I'm doing great." I hold up the cheesy thriller that she'd recommended from her bookshelf. "I don't usually get a chance to read in my normal life. There's no time."

"Glad you're enjoying yourself!" Another toothy grin, and then I expect her to return to Tai. Instead, she tells him to move out in front of the tent so that he can stay in our line of sight. He does immediately.

His instant compliance tells me that I was onto something with what I said to Maren yesterday about how he needs to stay on his best behavior around her. He doesn't feel secure with Aunt Maren, nor should he. There's something manic in her ministrations. Desperate, like she wants to devour him.

The more time I spend with her, the more convinced I am that Maren is not to be trusted. She's the proverbial wolf in sheep's clothing. The viper in Ralph Lauren.

I'm still steaming over yesterday. I know I need to contain myself, to stay even-keeled and stick to my strategy, but it's not going to be easy. I barely slept last night, due to the rage.

I can't believe there's still no settlement on the table, just that lowball offer of three months' expenses. Worse, though, was how patronizing she'd been. She's obviously made peace with my existence by deciding that my relationship with Corey was a farce like hers.

At breakfast, I said little since I wasn't sure I could turn in a skillful performance of the type that Maren has mastered. I'm no good at being a phony.

Now she's coming into the tent and settling in beside me. We're both facing out toward Tai, who's dutifully bringing his buckets over, resettling himself.

With reluctance, I set my book aside.

"I'm not sure our fresh start went so well," she says. "Last night, I meant to kill the elephant in the room, but it didn't seem to work."

Is that her attempt at an apology? I don't know that Maren is capable of a true mea culpa since she never thinks she's wrong.

What I do know is, this is not a conversation that I wish to have, and Maren doesn't seem to care, even though I'm sure she can read a room. Or, in this case, a tent.

She really is a wolf, and I'm prey. She doesn't care what I want or what Tai needs. It's all about her.

"We have more in common than you think," she says. "We're both Corey's victims, and we can both—"

"I'm sure you mean well." I'm actually not sure of that at all, though I'm sure *she* thinks she means well. "But you had a different relationship with Corey than I did."

"I hate him," she says. "You can't begin to fathom how much I hate him."

There it is. The unvarnished truth, for once.

Maren's obsession with Tai is the flip side of her obsession with Corey. She's in love with Tai; she's in hate with Corey. It's an emotional house of cards that can easily come crashing down. I'm not going to let my son be collateral damage.

"Corey might not have set out to destroy my life or my potential"—oh how she loves that word *potential*—"but that makes what he did even worse. He didn't give a thought to what he was taking away from me."

I glance outside to see if Tai is giving an indication that he can hear this. I kind of wish he was because then I'd have an excuse to cut her off.

"Corey couldn't love, because love means thinking about someone else. Caring about them more than yourself. Corey loved Corey. Period." I can feel how much she's embracing and relishing her hatred. She's not a person accustomed to indulging such ugly emotions. Now that she's getting a taste, she wants more.

"I can see why you feel that way," I say. It's a feeble response, which is probably why she doesn't register it, just returns to her rant.

"Corey was an awful human being. He used people for his own ends; he took advantage of their blind trust. When I say 'people,' I mean you and me, Jade. We both got played."

"I'm sorry, but I don't agree." And I'm not really sorry, either.

"You don't want to see it." She does a strange, twisted sort of smile as she gazes out toward the water. "If I were you, I wouldn't want to see it, either. Corey's blood runs through your son's veins."

"You need to stop this," I say, my voice shaking with anger. We're in treacherous territory, but nothing in her body language demonstrates awareness of that. Does she think she's untouchable?

Her expression is pitying. "You're still loyal to him. You and Corey and your great love." I can hear the implied air quotes around *great love*. "But it's not your fault. He was an expert manipulator, telling each of us what we wanted to hear."

"He told me plenty of things that I didn't want to hear. But I love him anyway." She has no idea what Corey said to me, and she never will.

"Don't you get it? That's how he played you. By telling you what you didn't want to hear, he was proving you were closer to him than I was. He made you think you were his number one. But *he* was his number one, always. *He played you*."

If circumstances were different, I'd haul off and punch her dead in the face, I really would. Because who is she to reduce Corey to a villain, me to a victim, and our love to a lie?

Maren is the manipulative one, not Corey. Somehow he never realized it. She's just that good. And that bad.

Corey was always honest with me, and she's trying to defame him. She wants to distort and taint the relationship. But I'm not going to let her succeed. She will not win.

Now that I've spent more time with Maren, now that we really have gotten to know each other better, I'm more determined than ever to keep Tai out of her clutches.

To do that, I need to stay cool and stick to the plan. Keep appealing to her higher nature.

"What you and I really have in common is Tai," I say. "I can see how much you care for him. Will you please help us? Help him?"

"I told you weeks ago that I'd pay for Tai's therapy," she says. "But he's going to take his emotional cues from you. Have you done any therapy yourself? I'd be happy to pick up the tab."

Unbelievable. "Have you done any therapy?"

"I did in the beginning, when Corey first died."

"Have you gone back since you found out about Tai and me? Because it seems like you need to process." *Process* seems like the kind of word Maren would really like.

"No, I'm in a good place."

"I'm in a good place, too," I say. It's a lie, but that's not because of Corey; it's because of Maren and what she's putting me through.

She won't commit to a permanent settlement and instead wants to hold on to the purse strings and dole out small sums. She's grinding me under her heel while I have to keep begging and then praising her for benevolence. It's a total mindfuck.

Maren thinks I'm fooling myself about who Corey was, while Maren is fooling herself about who she actually is.

"I want you and Tai to be healthy and strong," she says. "Maybe the two of you could go to therapy together. It could be that some small changes in parenting—"

"Let me guess, you'd be happy to pay for that." I stand up. "I'm going to play with my son now."

She continues talking as if I haven't spoken. "When you showed up, it upended my entire world. I had to give up the false narrative I'd crafted over many years about my perfect life with my perfect husband. And you know what? I'm so glad that I did. Now I can live honestly. I want the same for you."

I keep my eyes on Tai's back, willing him to turn around and come in here. To need something.

"I get it," she says, with a grotesquely compassionate expression. "No one likes to look in the mirror and see a dupe staring back at them."

Rage is coursing through me. How dare she? I'm not some naïve bumpkin. Where she was starry-eyed, I was clear. She was the dupe, not me.

I don't think Maren is actually evil, but she is misguided. If my life had suddenly been torn asunder, I'd probably be mad, too. But there's something sick about Maren. She's determined to control my narrative, and my parenting, too. She wants to send Tai and me to therapy when she's the one who needs professional help.

"I'm overheating," I say. "I should go cool off."

As I step out onto the sand, Tai gets up and runs over. "Where are you going?" he says.

"In the water."

"Can I go with?"

I shake my head. I need to be alone. Alone with Corey. I have to tell him what Maren is doing to me and how off base she is. I need my imaginary Corey to reassure me.

Our love was never perfect—perish the thought—because it was bigger and better than that. It was messy, chaotic, and incredible. It can't be replaced or reproduced. We were one of a kind.

I'm not going to let Maren ruin it for her own gain.

My toes have just barely touched the Atlantic when Tai

races up behind me, throwing his arms around my legs. "I want to go in with you!"

"Not with Aunt Maren?"

"With you!" he reiterates, and I feel a rush of gratitude, followed quickly by shame. *How did I get here, Corey?* "Why are you crying, Mommy?"

"I didn't know that I was." I reach down to clasp his hand in mine. "Yes, Tai. We go together."

TWENTY-NINE

MAREN

It's our second and final night, which is bittersweet. I'm sad that my concentrated time with Tai is coming to a close, but I'm more than ready to say goodbye to Jade. I don't know that I've made any headway with her, but Lord knows I've tried. I'll tell that to Emmanuel, too, when he picks us all up tomorrow morning.

Jade's impossible. She's so sensitive that I haven't even floated the idea of increasing the babysitting schedule. I might just have to figure out some way around her. I hate thinking of Tai's mother as an impediment to his well-being, but what other conclusion can I draw?

Still, I'd like to end the trip on a good note. That doesn't seem like a lot to ask, but with Jade, you never know.

She basically stomped out of the tent earlier, and while I can understand it on one level (I'm telling her a truth she doesn't want to hear), I also feel like she should act like an adult, especially when her son is nearby. She's supposed to be his role model.

Admitting that she was Corey's victim must go against her whole self-concept. She can't stand sounding and looking weak since she's streetwise, or whatever. She'd probably be better than I am at taking down a mugger on the subway, but she was no better at spotting a sociopath. She mated with a sociopath! That has to be hard to face.

I'm backing off since she obviously doesn't want to hear it from me. She needs to come to the realization herself. Pointing it out just makes her angry, and that definitely wasn't part of my objective for this trip.

It's not always easy to control myself, though. She can really get under my skin with how preachy she gets about the PURE LOVE that she and Corey shared. I mean, has she forgotten that's my husband she's talking about? I'm putting in all this effort to empathize with her but she's not extending me the same courtesy.

I can hear Alyssa's voice in my head: *She was fucking your husband FOR SIX YEARS! What are you doing barbecuing her dinner?*

Trying to barbecue her dinner. I can't get the damned grill to work.

I have a platter of Kobe beef steak skewers and veggie skewers next to me (Tai was so cute and careful in helping me load the cubes while Jade took yet more personal time), only the grill won't seem to cooperate. It's massive, commercial-grade stainless steel, with almost 2,000 square inches of cooking surface. There are multiple cast-iron burners, searing burners, infrared burners, and two different rotisseries with three-speed motors. All that power, and infuriatingly (and mortifyingly), it won't turn on.

Did Corey really leave me with a broken grill on top of every other indignity?

He was the only one who used the grill. It was a point of pride for him, a manly exhibition of mastery. He never cooked indoors.

God, he was such a cliché. How did I never notice it when he was alive? If only I had, then…

No sense in dwelling on that. My only crime was trusting the wrong man. Jade's crime was bigger. She was committing adultery, with full awareness. Even so, I extended the olive branch, which only seemed to annoy her.

So after this getaway, I'm done. I can tell Emmanuel that I gave it my best shot, the old college try. Jade simply wasn't receptive. To her, I'm Corey's widow and Tai's babysitter and nothing more. At least now I know where I stand.

I have to tread lightly. Jade's volatile, and she could turn on me at any moment. Good thing she can't afford any other childcare or she might have fired me already from my volunteer position.

Not that it's about money, but does she even realize how much I spend every time I see Tai? New York City adventures don't come cheap. I'm invested in him, but I sometimes get the sense that she wishes she could dispense with me entirely.

Why does she seem to dislike me? Has she forgotten that I'm not the other woman? She was.

Or maybe it's that she doesn't like me being the other woman in Tai's life. She could feel threatened by how attached Tai and I are to each other. The thing is, it doesn't have to be a competition. He can have us both, if Jade allows it. She's the one who pretends to be so open-minded, talking about how expansive and inclusive love can be.

What a hypocrite.

Despite the cooling evening air and the breeze, I'm starting to sweat, even though there's no reason for me to be embarrassed. So what, I don't know how to work the grill. Or so what, it's broken. That's Corey's fault, not mine; only Jade will find a way to render him blameless.

Pulling open the glass doors and walking into the kitchen, I see Tai and Jade at the kitchen table in the banquette. I have to admit, they look pretty sweet, their heads close as they fit together pieces of a Mickey Mouse puzzle. Jade brought it with them from home, along with a ton of other toys, games, and clothes, which have been scattered on every surface throughout every common area. For future visits, when it's just Tai and me, I'll make sure he cleans up one thing before moving on to the next.

"The grill's not working," I say.

"Your oven works, doesn't it?" Jade says, not looking up. "We can just make everything in the oven. Google something like 'sheet pan skewers,' and you'll be good to go."

Is she really sitting in my kitchen, finally playing with her kid, issuing directives to me on how to make them dinner?

I've been the one taking care of Tai the majority of the time, which is my pleasure, but still. I'm also in charge of the meal planning, grocery delivery, and food prep. I've been doing all the dishes. I know she's strapped for cash, so I didn't expect her to offer to pay for anything, but she could have at least cleaned up after herself and Tai. Worst of all, when I offered her three months' worth of expenses, she acted insulted.

Glowering silently, I look up "sheet pan skewers" and follow the directions. Neither Jade nor Tai pay me a bit of attention. I set a timer on my phone and head for the living room. I need to be alone to calm down.

When the timer goes off, I return to the kitchen, forcing a smile. "The food's done," I announce, to no reaction. They're still totally engrossed in their puzzle. "Should we eat outside, so we don't have to mess up the puzzle?"

"Good idea," Jade says. Then she and Tai let me fix plates for them.

As we eat by the pool, I continue to stew. Without me to engage them, dinner is brief and quiet. I sit back so that Jade is the one to cut Tai's meat for him, though she can't be bothered to coach him on his manners. I'm keeping my mouth shut.

When we've all finished eating, Jade stands up, stacks the plates, and then asks Tai to open the glass door for her. I wonder if she'll finally load the dishwasher. She's been a terrible houseguest, leaving dishes in the sink for me to do, as well as toys, clothes, and wet towels all over the house.

Tai hasn't gotten up from the table. "I want dessert!"

"You don't need any more sugar," she says. "We should go to bed early. You have preschool in the morning."

So now she's moderating his sugar? No wonder he acts out with her. Kids need consistency.

"Sugar!" he says.

"No, Tai." She jerks her chin in the direction of the house. "Get the door for me, please."

"Sugar! Sugar! Sugar!" He's chanting it, loud enough for the neighbors to hear, if they were around. But these are all weekend homes and summer homes, so it's just us.

"No, Tai," Jade says again, with a note of warning.

It's obviously the wrong approach. You don't engage in power struggles with overtired four-year-olds. She could be distracting or defusing the situation, but instead, she's escalating it.

"Sugar!" he shouts at her viciously.

I've never seen this side of him. He'd never talk to me like that, but then, I wouldn't be repeating, "No, Tai," over and over.

In one second, he's up on his feet, incensed, and in the next, he's down on the ground, pounding his fists and crying.

She looks over at me meaningfully as if to say, "See?" It's a meltdown, just as she'd described, only she had left out her own part in the interaction. She provoked him.

I kneel beside him. "Tai," I say gently, "we need to go inside now."

I touch his back lightly. He doesn't push me off, and as I leave it there and say his name with great tenderness, I feel him give way. His little body goes limp. He's exhausted.

Oh, my sweet, tormented boy. Jade's right, he needs help. But I don't agree that the prescription is more time with her. They trigger each other, that's apparent.

"Can I take you inside?" I ask. He looks over at me with that beautiful tear-stained face and nods. I pick him up and start to carry him toward the house. "Could you open the door, please?" I say to Jade.

She sets down the plates and does it, without a word. Maybe she feels like I've interfered, but what was I supposed to do? The situation was spiraling.

"Could I put him to bed?" I use a deferential tone.

She won't look at me, but she nods.

I carry Tai inside, and all the way upstairs. I'm overwhelmed with love and sympathy for him, and he must feel it, it's why he responds to me so well. I treat him with respect, requesting that he get into his pajamas and brush his teeth and then climb into bed, and he does it all without a single protest.

I don't feel right getting into the bed where he sleeps next to Jade, so I sit alongside, reading him a story. "Could I have another?" he asks drowsily.

"Of course." I smile and pick up the next book. By the time I'm through, he's asleep. I stroke his face and hair lightly with just my fingertips, not wanting to disturb him.

When I go back downstairs, I see that Jade is ferociously scrubbing the countertops. It looks like she's already loaded the dishwasher.

"Are you all right?" I say.

"He can be so difficult sometimes. You saw it, didn't you?"

"Yes." I saw a poor parenting choice, but I'm not going to say that. I really do want to get along with her, for Tai's sake.

She looks over at me, eyes slightly narrowed. Then she throws the sponge into the sink. "Is he waiting up for me?"

"He was too tired. He fell asleep the second his head hit the pillow." I smile at her. "It's going to be all right. He's a great kid."

She nods, and I can feel her worry. But I feel something else, too. Something dark and foreboding.

Is it directed toward Tai? Or me? Better me. He's just a defenseless little boy.

"I'm tired, too," she says. "Thanks for... everything. See you in the morning."

"Good night, Jade."

Once she's gone upstairs, once I can hear that she's done in the guest bathroom and shut the door to the guest bedroom, I walk over to the bar. I pour myself a glass of Angel's Envy. I love that bourbon, and why should I have to give it up just because Corey was a prick?

I carry the bourbon and a glass outside to the patio. It's full dark, and the floodlights have come on so that the pool has a shimmering blue radiance, like a jewel. I look down at my hand. No more jewels there.

In the first few months of grief over Corey, I made a point of never drinking alone. I didn't want to blunt my emotions; I wanted to feel the force of my love for him through the pain of his loss. It was like a masochistic badge of honor. Also, I was afraid of alcohol as anesthesia. I'd heard stories of other bereaved people for whom substances became a permanent crutch, who turned into addicts. I didn't want to suffer a similar fate.

But I'm not worried about that anymore. I trust myself more now than I ever have. I'm stronger than I ever realized.

I drain my first glass and pour another.

I raise the glass and toast silently. *Hope you're rotting in hell, you son of a bitch. Don't worry, I'll be here taking care of your son.*

And maybe your mistress, too.

THIRTY

JADE

"Oh, sorry," I say, startled to come upon Maren by the pool. "I didn't mean to—"

"Mean to what?" Does Maren sound angry? Or just disoriented? Embarrassed, maybe, at having been caught drinking? Or at having been caught lying, since she's got a bottle of Angel's Envy on the table next to her when she told me that she'd thrown it out.

I've got a glass of Scotch in my hand. I lift it up. "I guess you and I had the same idea. It's been a day, huh?"

"It certainly has." She sounds droll, and a bit slurry.

I want to spin on my heel and go back inside, but I can't run away now. I came here hoping to strengthen my cause and secure that trust for Tai, but it obviously hasn't gone well between Maren and me. Is there a chance that I can turn it around, while she's in a vulnerable state?

I owe it to my son to try.

I stretch myself out on the lounger beside hers. We're quiet for a minute, staring up at the stars. I'm considering my plan of attack when I hear a rustling and glance over.

She's pivoted toward me and placed her feet on the ground,

leaning forward (a bit unsteadily). "Time to compare notes," she says.

"What kind of notes?" I'm asking, though I don't really want to know.

"I was still having sex with Corey. A lot. Right up until the end. Did you know that?"

"I'm not surprised. He told me you had a great sex life."

She shakes her head. "Do you even hear yourself, Jade? Do you get how crazy all this is? He was telling you outright that he loved his wife, enjoyed sex with her, was never going to leave her, and you went ahead and had his baby?"

"Corey and I were more into kink," I say. That was part of it, but far from all. The totality was sacred, and none of Maren's business. My sex life with Corey was various, and deep, and full of tenderness. It wasn't like Maren was the Madonna and I was the whore, though he did have a tendency to put her on a pedestal. I never wanted the pedestal. I wanted equal footing, staring straight into each other's eyes and each other's souls.

"I thought so." I can tell she likes my answer. "But did he tell you that he and I were totally vanilla? Because we had a drawer full of sex toys and a closet full of costumes. Sometimes I was submissive, but sometimes I was very dominant."

I turn my head, eyes back on the Little Dipper or Big Dipper or whatever it is. I feel a stab of pain. I'm supposed to be the one that Corey could do anything with, say anything to.

"So he did tell you that we were vanilla," she says.

"Yes," I say, just above a whisper. *Why, Corey? Why would you lie? You didn't need to do that.*

What else don't I know?

"Do you see now?" she asks me urgently. "Do you see who he was?"

"I'm starting to," I say, and it's mostly strategy, a way to align myself with her, but that's not all of it.

"He shouldn't have treated us like he did. Neither of us deserved to be deceived and manipulated. Nobody does."

Tears are running down my cheeks, and I hope the light is too dim for her to see.

"I'm sorry, Jade," she says. "On behalf of my husband, I apologize."

It's such a power move that I feel a surge of hatred. I want to roll over and spit in her face. Who does she think she is? Who does she think I am?

When it came to Corey, I was a full participant, entirely in charge of my choices and my fate. Maybe they weren't always the best, but they were mine. I'm not like Maren, who skipped along in a blissful ignorance now blown to smithereens, at which point she seems to have decided she's some kind of badass.

I've always been a badass.

But I'm smart, too, and that means that I need to say what Maren wants to hear. For one night only, I'm making the active choice to play the victim.

"I appreciate that, Maren." I don't turn to look at her because it's easier to control my voice than my face. "I think the reason this trip has been so rocky between us is because you're right. I've been fighting against certain realizations. But now I see that Corey did play me. I was a sucker, and I feel like a loser."

I'm still crying. It's almost like I'm telling the truth.

There could be all kinds of reasons that Corey lied about his sex life with Maren. Maybe he just said it one night and I misunderstood and then he didn't want to correct it since I seemed so happy. He must have been protecting my feelings.

I just thought we didn't need to do that. In my conception of our perfectly imperfect love, there was no need for protection. We were perfect equals.

I've always reveled in the irony—that everyone thinks of

infidelity as dishonest or unethical, but our relationship was far more truthful and real than his marriage. We didn't need the state to bless us; we didn't need a piece of paper to legitimize us. Our love was its own justification, its own vindication.

It was, he's whispering to me now. *It was everything. It still is,* and I want to believe so badly.

"Did he tell you we never fought?" Maren says. Corey thought she was so kind but look at her now, kicking me when I'm down.

"Yes," I say, waiting for the blow.

"That was true. If he got angry, he left, and when he came back, he was ready to talk calmly or to apologize. And when I got angry, I stifled it. I pushed it way down inside to keep the peace. I regret that so much."

"Why?"

"Because he got off so easy! He never had to contend with anything. When he was mad at me, did he go straight to you?"

"Sometimes." I wipe at my eyes, dry my face with the back of my hands. I feel a little bit better. I was his confidante, not her.

"Would he talk shit about me?"

"No. He always made you sound totally reasonable. It's like I've been telling you since we first met, he thought the world of you."

"Why did he need two of us then?"

"I don't know." In this moment, I really don't.

"Some people just want more and more. Nothing and no one can ever be enough. Look up 'narcissistic sociopath' and you'll see Corey's picture. He couldn't be satisfied, and he didn't care who he used or who he hurt."

She sounds almost happy saying it, but I'm miserable.

She must be able to tell because she adds, "You'll feel so much better once you accept that Corey was an utter piece of garbage. When you don't have to make excuses for him anymore and, instead, you can think about your future, and about never letting anyone have that kind of power over you ever again. If they ever try, just unleash on them."

I glance over, observing how her eyes are glittering in the moonlight with a sort of vengeful pleasure. Corey really didn't know his wife at all.

"I'm taking your advice," I say. "I'm not going to let anyone have power over me, including you."

"I don't understand." She looks bewildered. She doesn't even know what a bully she is.

"I don't need heart-to-hearts. I'm not looking for your words of wisdom. You and I are not forming a support group. I need money, Maren. Okay? I need you to instruct your estate attorney to write up a settlement. You say you care about Tai? Prove it, once and for all. No more games."

"I haven't been playing games."

"Then prove it. Put it in writing. Have your attorney write an irrevocable trust where all the money goes to Tai."

"But if I do that, you'll be the one making the decisions about how the money is used." There it is, she's finally drunk enough to say out loud what she really thinks of me.

"Yes, I'd be the one making decisions in Tai's best interest. Because I'm his mother."

"I can't do that." She sounds regretful, but at least it's an answer, instead of all the hemming and hawing and delaying and deferring.

My glass is empty. My inhibitions are gone. I can't scrape, bow, cajole, and calculate anymore. It's time for the nuclear option.

"I gave you the chance to prove you really care about Tai, that you're in this for the right reasons and not just for your own gratification, and you couldn't do it. You won't write up the trust."

"Because of how I feel about you, not how I feel about him."

What an elitist fucking bitch she is. Deep down, I've felt that all along. "I'm worried about you, Maren, and about your influence on my son."

She laughs. "You think I'm a bad influence? What about you, Jade? You're rude, you leave messes everywhere, you antagonize children—"

"I'm not the one who's drunk off my ass and slurring my words. I'm not the one who's hoarding all the money for myself when I could be supporting an innocent child." I glare at her. "When we get home, you're going to see your attorney. You're going to have him write up an irrevocable trust or else you'll find that Tai has become unavailable."

"You wouldn't dare." Her eyes widen. "You wouldn't dare try to keep me from Tai."

"I'm his mother. It's my job to look out for him."

"You can't afford to keep him away from me. You can't even afford babysitting."

"There's actually a babysitting co-op in my neighborhood where we moms trade off days. They could use someone for Sundays and Mondays." It's a lie, but I sound pretty convincing, if I do say so myself.

"You wouldn't dare," Maren says again.

"Try me."

I can see her terror. It's apparent just how much Tai has come to mean to her, how lost she'd be without him.

"I didn't believe her," she murmurs.

"Believe who?"

"She told me that women like you just snap one day. I defended you. But she was right all along."

"All I'm doing is protecting my son. You'd do the same, in my position."

She looks over at me, and there's hatred mixed in with the fear. I'm scared, too, though I'll be damned if I show it.

The guns have been drawn, and I can't be sure who's going to fire first.

THIRTY-ONE

MAREN

"Everybody ready?" Emmanuel is trying to sound upbeat as he looks in the rearview mirror at Jade and Tai. I'm sitting next to him in the passenger seat, whereas on the way here, I'd been in the back.

Emmanuel must be able to sense that this trip didn't turn out the way I'd hoped. But he has no idea just how catastrophic it truly was.

"Ready!" Tai says. Then he looks anxiously at Jade.

"Ready!" she says, forcing a smile.

Emmanuel glances at me. "Ready," I say softly, and he starts the car.

Jade and I have been avoiding each other all morning as we prepared to go back to the city. She hasn't apologized for what she said, or rescinded the threat she made. But I was very drunk, and she was drinking, too, so if I'm lucky, she didn't mean any of it.

Okay, so I'm not her cup of tea. She's not mine, either. But we can still salvage this, if she's willing to see reason. Tai needs both of us.

We're speeding down the Montauk Highway and Emmanuel keeps shooting me concerned looks, though I can't say anything now, not in mixed company. Jade's given Tai her phone so he can play games and watch shows. I don't have the energy to try to entertain him, either. None of the adults are daring to speak to each other.

Jade stares stonily out the window. I do the same, my thoughts an anxious jumble. The one thing I know for sure: I can't lose Tai. I will not.

Does that mean paying her whatever ransom she demands? It's like I'm being held hostage, or Tai is. It offends my sense of justice, but really, she's holding all the cards. She's his mother. I'm his dead father's wife, and I'm pretty sure that doesn't come with automatic visitation rights.

An hour and a half later, Emmanuel drops Tai off at preschool, where Tai gives Jade a goodbye hug and then gives me one, too. "Bye, Mommy! Bye, Aunt Maren!" he says, dashing inside.

I try to catch Jade's eye so we can share a smile, but she's not having it. She climbs into the back seat again, and Emmanuel drives to her apartment building.

When he goes to carry her two huge bags inside, she shrugs him off and insists on doing it herself. I don't know what she's trying to prove. It's not like Emmanuel's done anything to her. But then, what does she think I've done? Why am I suddenly her enemy?

I've opened my heart to Tai, let both of them into my homes, given her regular cash infusions, and offered her three months of salary and living expenses. What kind of person keeps demanding more?

A con woman, that's what Alyssa would say. Last night, Jade tried to extort me, plain and simple.

Emmanuel and I get back in the car, and he asks me to tell him what's wrong, but I just shake my head. Telling him would make it real. We listen to classical music instead as I try not to cry.

After we arrive back at my apartment building, I turn to him with moist eyes. "Could you come up, please?" I just can't bear to be alone.

I can see he's uncomfortable, but he agrees.

We're in opposite corners of the elevator, unspeaking, but once the door has swung shut to my apartment, I'm in his arms, sobbing.

"It's blackmail," I choke out. "If I don't give Jade a chunk of Corey's estate—probably a big chunk—she's going to keep Tai from me."

"Oh, Maren," he says, holding me tighter.

"What do I do? Do I pay off a terrorist? And what if I pay her, and then she still keeps me away from him? She's unstable, and she hates me. I don't know why."

"I'm sure she doesn't hate you," he murmurs.

"I can't live without Tai. He's everything."

"Maren." Now Emmanuel's tone is firm, and it's almost like he's compelling me to look into his eyes. "Tai is a wonderful little boy. But he is not everything."

The air suddenly feels charged. Despite the emotional intimacy we've shared since Corey's death, Emmanuel and I have never before had a fraught moment.

But right now, I can envision us kissing; I can feel the pull.

Only he pulls back.

I'm sure I would have, too, if he hadn't done it first. I love Emmanuel, platonically speaking, but I've never once allowed myself to see him in any other light because of Corey and Zauna. Obviously, Corey doesn't matter anymore. But Emmanuel has a family. I would never be a homewrecker like Jade.

Technically, Jade didn't wreck my home; it remained intact

until the end. But still, I'd never be a mistress. I have too much respect for myself and for marriage as an institution.

Emmanuel and I move apart. We're both freaked out by what almost happened.

But it didn't, I remind myself. *Because we stopped. Because we know right from wrong.*

"Take good care of yourself, Maren," Emmanuel says, eyes averted, moving quickly toward the door.

* * *

With Emmanuel long gone and Jade ignoring my conciliatory texts (*I'm sure we both said things we didn't mean...*), I'm at loose ends. Maybe Emmanuel's right, and Tai isn't everything, but he's a lot. He's the reason I want to get out of bed in the morning, the reason I started smiling again.

I can't lose him. If I have to pay out, I will. But maybe there's a way to avoid that.

If only I could find something, anything, to make Jade see the truth about Corey. Then she'd know that she and I are on the same team. She mocked me about the idea of a support group, but women do need each other's support.

I find myself at the door to Corey's office. It's a room I never go in, and I've recently considered turning it into a playroom for Tai. I certainly don't need it as some sort of shrine to my philandering husband.

When Corey first died, I went through his office in a quick and cursory way, just making sure there wasn't anything I needed to address, that there was nothing that could cause me a problem later. The lawyers assured me (over the course of many billable hours) that it was all in order and I had nothing to worry about. I believed them. I believed in Corey.

The room is done up like an old-fashioned study, with loads of mahogany built-ins and a huge rolltop desk. Corey wasn't a big reader, so we just had the decorator fill all the bookshelves with weathered classics to keep up the vibe. Converting it to a playroom would mean a full renovation, but I wouldn't mind. I like the idea of a purge. An exorcism. Out with the old, in with the new.

But first I have to keep Tai in my life. That's the highest priority.

So while I hate being in this space that was so thoroughly Corey's, while this is hardly the moment for a crash course in forensic accounting, while I don't even know precisely what I'm looking for, I'm willing to brave the discomfort.

I go through every last folder and every piece of paper in every drawer. The bottom two are locked, but I've got them open. I always knew where the key was, Corey never hid it from me. I never thought he was hiding anything. I'd assumed him to be an open book.

But the very appearance of trustworthiness is its own disguise. Since I could have gone through his things anytime I wanted, it never occurred to me to do it.

Now, I'm going through it all with a fine-tooth comb, scrutinizing every line of every fiscal document, searching the internet for any terms I don't understand. To my disappointment, it all seems kosher. No unusual financial activity, no mentions of Jade or Tai.

Normally, no news would be good news. But I need something that I can take to Jade and say, "See? He's not the man you thought."

Then I see it, a page accordioned in the back of a drawer.

As I read, my heart drops ten stories. It's from the fertility clinic. Paperwork that I've never seen before, by Corey's design.

I didn't think that he could hurt me anymore. I thought all my illusions about him had already been shattered.

But this is the biggest betrayal of all.

THIRTY-TWO
JADE

While Yvette Buckley is clearly young and new to her solo law practice, she seems competent. Her office is small and nondescript, but it's not seedy. She doesn't seem anything like that dick I saw for my first free consultation, and hopefully, with all that I've learned about Maren, this one will yield a very different result.

"Thanks for seeing me on such short notice," I say.

"You sounded frantic," she says. "Sometimes it helps just to talk." She's kind, too. Nothing like the last guy.

I know she isn't the crème de la crème because the top attorneys aren't doing free consultations, especially not on an emergency basis; you have to pay for every minute of their overscheduled time. But I need someone who can move fast and who's willing to take my case on contingency, with no up-front costs. In my fantasy, there's a quick settlement and then money will be taken out of the equation with Maren. At that point, I'll get to decide whether Tai should be spending time with her or not.

I'm leaning no, but there's no need to be rash. Emotions were definitely running high by the pool, and in the light of day,

I'm not sure she's as awful as she seemed. Maybe she just needs to get some therapy herself.

I hated using Tai as a bargaining chip, but she gave me no choice. What's surprising is that after an initial flurry of texts, I haven't heard from her for the past two days. Why hasn't she caved?

"I thought, by now, this would be over," I say. "That Maren would have wanted to do the right thing."

"What is that, in your opinion?" Yvette asks.

"Tai is Corey's son. He should be entitled to part of Corey's estate. But she's trying to nickel-and-dime me instead of paying out a fair settlement."

"So how can I help?"

"I want to file a claim against the estate. Which isn't the same as suing her, right? Because I'm not trying to make this any more aggressive than it has to be."

"Let's back up a little."

I explain how it all started, what my intention was, and how crazy it's gotten. How much Maren has overstepped and undermined. How she appointed herself Tai's babysitter. That she wants to give me money in dribs and drabs so she'll maintain control.

"She told Tai to call her 'Aunt Maren'!" I say. "Isn't that an admission that Tai is Corey's son? And the money she's already wired to my account—isn't that proof that she knows she bears some financial responsibility for Tai?"

"Not necessarily. Is Corey's name on the birth certificate?"

"No. I didn't want it to be." What an idiot I was. But then, who could have predicted any of this? "I guess I was the one wanting control then." Corey gave me money in dribs and drabs, too. But that had been my choice.

Hadn't it?

Sometimes it's hard to remember exactly how it all went down. It seemed so organic, like Corey and I were in sync.

"Did Corey sign any paperwork to attest to Tai being his son?" Yvette is taking notes on a legal pad. "Is his signature on any contracts or binding documents like for a bank account or preschool? Did he cosign anything for you? Is there anything in writing to indicate that he was taking financial responsibility for Tai?"

I shake my head repeatedly. "He gave me cash when I asked for it or, you know, just to be generous sometimes."

"You mean actual cash? As in, there are no checks with his signature, or electronic deposits from his bank account to yours?"

"Actual cash." Now that I'm saying it, it's kind of weird. Why wouldn't he just use Venmo? I used to laugh that he liked acting like a real sugar daddy, peeling off hundred-dollar bills, but it doesn't seem so funny anymore. It seems like he didn't want there to be a paper trail. Maybe nothing had been as organic as I thought.

"I'm assuming there wasn't a paternity test?" Another head shake. "Is there any way, to your knowledge, of obtaining a DNA sample?"

"He was cremated."

"If we can't legally prove that Tai is Corey's son, then we'd have a real uphill battle when it comes to making a claim on the estate."

The last attorney had said it would be impossible. An uphill battle is actually a more favorable assessment of my case.

I perk up. "There must be some way to present to the court that Maren has a sick obsession with Tai. Just as an example, she won't stop pushing for private school and says she'll pay for that. For that, and for therapy. If Maren's trying to act as Tai's mother, isn't that the same as admitting that Tai is Corey's son?"

"Not in the eyes of the law, no."

"Oh, and she just gave me another twenty thousand dollars. Wired it into my bank account this morning." I hold my phone up triumphantly to show her the notification, like it's the smoking gun.

"And you want more?" Do I detect just the slightest hint of judgment?

"I want a full settlement. I want autonomy. She understood that's what I was asking for, but she gave me this instead."

"Twenty-K is a substantial gift. Plus, you're saying she'd be willing to pay for private school, starting when Tai is in preschool?" Yvette does a little whistle. "That's a sweet deal. Is she willing to put it in writing?"

"I don't want him in private school. I don't want her making parental decisions for me just because it's her money."

"Is the twenty grand earmarked for something?"

"She made me an offer of three months' salary and living expenses, but I said no, I wanted a full settlement. So she wired it to me anyway."

"That's generous."

"She's trying to control everything, can't you see that? I told her that I needed the settlement because I want to reduce my work hours and spend more time with Tai. I said that he's struggling, and he needs more time with me."

"How's he struggling?"

Heat rushes to my face. "He's not. I was just trying to get her to do the right thing."

"The right thing, as you see it."

I feel like this is taking a bad turn. I wish I hadn't just confessed to telling a lie because now Yvette's questioning my credibility, probably wondering what I would be like on the stand.

"If I had a settlement, then I would be the one taking him on amazing day trips all over the city and lavishing gifts on him, not her."

She's studying my face in a way that I find disconcerting. I'm losing her, I realize.

"It's about how she uses her money," I say. "It's manipulative. Like I tell her no, I don't want the three months, and she wires it anyway."

"You could give it back."

"Except that I need it, and she knows that." This is frustrating, how even to Yvette, Maren is somehow smelling like a rose. "There's something about her. I can't explain it. But she's not well. Do you think it's normal for her to want to be this involved with her dead husband's son?"

"If you think she's mentally disturbed, you should deny her access. That's within your rights."

"I already told her that I'm going to deny her access if we can't reach a settlement."

"You mean you threatened her?"

"No. Like you said, I'm Tai's mother. I have the right to deny access if I think someone is a danger."

Yvette looks perturbed. "But are you denying her because she's a danger, or because she won't do the right thing, as you see it?"

"Will this be relevant, like, in court?" It kind of feels like she's interrogating me.

"It could be. It could go to your character."

"*My* character? What about Maren's?"

All I know is, I have to stick to my guns. I can't let Maren around Tai until she makes a deal. Thanks to the $20K, I can afford additional childcare, but temporarily, I'm going to need to take Tai back to my mom's house. Just until I can make other arrangements.

"Do you have reason to believe that Maren would hurt Tai?" Yvette asks.

"Not intentionally. She worships him."

"So you're saying that he's not in any danger when he's in her care, unless you count the danger of being spoiled."

"I guess so."

"Does she harass or abuse you?"

"Not exactly." I don't like where this is going. "She badgers me. She does lots of research. Forwards lots of links and then texts over and over, asking if I've read them."

"That's not harassment or abuse. To be clear, you're the one who approached her initially?"

"Yes." Is this what it would feel like to be on the stand? Maybe she's just trying to get me prepared.

"Because you wanted her money."

"Yes. I mean, no. I wanted Corey's money. And it's not for me, it's for Tai. If I didn't have a son to support, I would never have started this. But now I need to finish it."

"Do you want my advice?" That's why I'm here. But I have a feeling I'm not going to like what she's about to say. "There are worse things than free babysitting and being paid in dribs and drabs. Tai likes her, you said?"

"Because she spoils him."

"And worships him."

I don't answer.

"I have sympathy for you, I really do," she says. "I can see how upset you are. But I'd have a hard time painting you as a sympathetic figure. You went to the widow for money, and she's responded by babysitting your son for free while also providing you with cash infusions, without asking anything in return. She's trying to find a private school for him, offering to pay for educational testing or for therapy, whatever he needs."

"He doesn't need private school! She's a snob and an elitist. She thinks she's better than me."

"Unfortunately, that's not actionable. None of this is."

"How can that be?" I'm hit with a surge of disappointment. Of helplessness.

"You've got a weak case. A nonexistent case, really. You have no proof of paternity, and you'll look like a gold digger, and she'll look like Mother Teresa. You can shop around for other lawyers and maybe find someone who's willing to take this on for a sizable retainer. There are some unethical attorneys out there, but no one could do it in good faith." She meets my eyes. "If you go ahead with this, you're going to lose. Anyone who tells you otherwise is lying."

"In other words, I'm screwed." Yvette can't see Maren for what she is, either. It seems like no one can.

When I first approached Maren, I was so confident. And so underprepared. If I didn't know better, I'd think Corey had somehow set this up. Set me up.

Now Maren's sitting pretty while I have to eat shit.

But only until I can figure out some way to turn the tables on her, outside the bounds of the law.

THIRTY-THREE
MAREN

I'm holding the paper in my shaking hand, nearly blind with rage.

It's telling me that Corey couldn't have children. He was sterile, and he'd known it all along.

At the outset, before we'd even started trying for children, I had us both do medical testing out of what I called "an abundance of caution." I wasn't cautious enough, though, since I never asked to see his results. I trusted him when he told me that the testing had come back fine, nothing out of the ordinary.

Actually, he was diagnosed with azoospermia, meaning his semen contained no sperm. Depending on the cause, this could be treatable or not. His was not.

Yet for years, we continued to try even though he knew we would never succeed. He pretended we were on that roller coaster together, hoping against hope every month, but I was the only one in suspense.

Just when I thought Corey couldn't be more disgusting. Just when I thought he couldn't hurt me any more.

I'm laid out on the floor of the office, shattered, when the realization comes to me: Corey can't be Tai's father.

Jade either cheated on him or they had an open relationship. If she didn't know Corey was sterile, then she might have thought it really was his baby. And maybe he played along?

Jade may or may not have known, but Corey certainly knew he wasn't Tai's father.

Maybe that's why Corey didn't leave any money for Tai. He was willing to give his time and emotions to another man's son but not his money.

Corey was a monster, but I still don't know the full truth about Jade. At best, she's an extortionist; at worst, she's a sociopath, too.

She says she never had paternity testing done, and that's probably true. Why test for what she already knew? Why test and prove that her son wasn't Corey's when Corey was likely wealthier than the other candidate?

I wonder who Tai's father really is, if he knows the truth but doesn't want to be a father or if Jade just never told him. I guess in terms of moral character, he can't be any lower than Corey. Tai might have dodged a genetic bullet by not being Corey's son.

Jade went out of her way to tell me that she never cheated on Corey. She sounded convincing, too.

Her great love story. Ha.

But then, who could have a great love story with Corey? He made it seem like he just changed his mind, that he'd gotten tired of trying to get me pregnant, when really, he'd never tried at all. We could have been investigating other options like donor sperm and adoption when I was still young and fertile because my testing had, in fact, been normal.

He didn't want to tell me the truth from the beginning because he knew I would have left him. Much as I loved him, I would have loved my own family more.

But I don't have one, do I? I have nothing, because of him.

I start ransacking the office, sending everything from his

desk crashing to the floor. Then I'm tossing the books off the shelves wildly, hurling them in every direction, watching them fly through the air like birds and land on the floor with their spines askew and broken.

I feel like a beast that's just been let out of a cage. I'm laughing, enjoying the carnage. The wreckage.

I know it won't hurt Corey, that nothing can now, so what's the next best thing?

Jade.

He loved her enough to love a child who wasn't his. He loved her enough to be a cuckold. Hell, he might have been done wrong by Jade in the same way he did me wrong. Only he stayed with her, when if I had known, I would have left.

He took away my agency and my choices. But never again.

Whether Jade lied to Corey or not, she definitely lied to me. She went out of her way to tell me that she'd never been with another man. She talked up Tai's physical resemblance to Corey, and stupidly, I'd believed it. Thought I was seeing it with my own eyes. That means I can't even trust my own senses.

Corey may have gotten away with his crimes, but Jade won't. I'll see to that.

THIRTY-FOUR
JADE

I'm on edge. I canceled Maren's babysitting and brought Tai back to my mother's (she wasn't necessarily happy to see him, but she was happy that he wasn't with Maren), and Maren didn't even protest. I said Tai was sick, which was a blatant lie, and all Maren texted back was: *Hope he feels better soon.* No exclamation point. She didn't even add any emojis or say she was looking forward to seeing him Sunday.

Did I overplay my hand, assuming her feelings for Tai are more intense than they actually are? Or is she just someone who refuses to cave?

I could almost admire it, if it weren't so nerve-wracking. That $20K might be the last money I ever see from her unless I can figure out some other angle. Applying more pressure seems unwise, but slinking back with my tail between my legs feels like a mistake. It would be like telling her that she can do whatever she wants from now on.

Once I show her she has all the control, it'll be a self-fulfilling prophecy. I really will be at her mercy. Tai might never see a penny of her inheritance.

It makes me so mad. He deserves better.

He deserved better from you, Corey. Lately, I've found myself ranting and raging at Corey more and more. I said I didn't blame him, but I'm starting to rethink that.

I fucked up, okay? If I could have predicted this, I would have done everything differently.

Or so he says, in my imagination. Or so I want to believe.

The things Maren told me at the Hamptons house have been niggling at me. I did think their sex was vanilla, because that's the impression he gave. But if he lied about that...

Maybe he didn't lie. Maybe I just assumed. I can't remember every conversation we ever had. And besides, the sex was great, but it was still a relatively small part of our overall connection. There was so much more, and I'm not going to let Maren sully it. That would be like letting the terrorists win.

But how can I win?

Right now, I have no fucking idea, and Corey's no help at all.

THIRTY-FIVE

MAREN

"So you were right about Jade," I say.

Alyssa leans in, tossing her hair back, assuming her avaricious listening position. We're in her classic brownstone on the Upper West Side. The rooms are small but elegant, and there are so many of them (living room, sitting room, parlor, den, etc.). She and Sean renovated all three floors but kept the original features and fixtures, like ornate moldings, tall sash windows, and plaster medallions from which crystal chandeliers hang. Sean's old money.

Alyssa and I are seated at an heirloom table in what she calls "the smoking parlor." She pours me another shot of bourbon. It's a private label that makes Angel's Envy look like Wild Turkey. But I'd take grain alcohol at this point.

Just one Wednesday without Tai and I'm coming unglued.

I tell Alyssa briefly about my showdown with Jade by the pool. I wish I were talking to Emmanuel, but I could tell how uncomfortable he was with me after the near kiss (not that we were that near; we were still pretty far). So I gave him the week off, with pay, since there are no Tai pickups or drop-offs anyway.

If I were talking to Emmanuel, I'd share what I learned about Corey not being Tai's father. But since it's Alyssa, it seems wiser to keep that to myself.

It's not that I think Alyssa would be smug or self-congratulatory or anything like that. She's capable of being extremely sympathetic, like she was after Corey died. But I know that she would think it was time for me to cut the cord entirely. In Alyssa's mind, if Tai isn't Corey's son, then I've got no business being so devoted to him.

But if anything, I feel even more devoted. Now that I know what Jade's capable of, I have to make sure he's not corrupted by having someone like her for a mother.

Even if you confine the story to just what happened by the Hamptons pool, you have to conclude that Jade is manipulative and dangerous, a view that Alyssa adopted instantly and unreservedly. Maybe sometimes true crime podcasts really can be useful. Right from the start, Alyssa was able to see what I couldn't.

"It really ended with an extortion attempt?" Alyssa asks, eyes wide, bright red lips in an O. "You've told her to fuck off, right? That she's not getting another penny out of you?"

"I wired her a little money," I admit, cheeks flushing.

"How little?"

"Twenty thousand."

"Let me guess. She kept it and also kept Tai from you. She canceled babysitting, right?" I nod again, more miserable and ashamed. "You should have come to me sooner. I would have told you that you never negotiate with total degenerates."

"I wasn't negotiating. I was making good on my offer about three months of living expenses." I'd had to estimate because she never did deign to tell me the actual numbers. She'd been too offended. I sigh. "I know you've tried to protect me since the beginning. You always knew she was a con artist."

"I'm just glad you're seeing clearly. So you're done with her and Tai?"

"I saw an attorney earlier today. She came highly recommended by Bernard, our estate lawyer, and she was willing to fit me in as a favor to him."

"To try to get back the twenty-K?"

"No. To try to get visitation rights." What I didn't tell the attorney? That Corey isn't Tai's father. My claim rests on Corey's alleged paternity, which is why I haven't confronted Jade about her dishonesty.

Jade came looking for me, not the other way around, and she said point-blank that Tai was Corey's son. But what if she decides to come clean to the court about Tai's paternity? I'd have no standing. My case would be destroyed.

I have to hope she keeps on lying. Because I can't lose Tai. Not now. Not ever.

Now Alyssa is the one sighing, her disapproval writ large across her face. But all she asks is, "This lawyer, is she a shark?"

"Oh, yeah. She's definitely a shark." I'd felt pretty uncomfortable in the attorney's presence since she'd practically been licking her chops. "She said that we could make a lowball offer —say, a million dollars—and include visitation rights. That way, we'd avoid going to court and getting into a protracted litigation." Protracted litigation would mean more time away from Tai, and I really don't think I could bear that.

"You can't be serious. You'd give that woman a million dollars?"

"I could live with that. But the shark advised strongly against it. She said that once Jade sees I'm willing to offer a million, that I'm that desperate for Tai's company, Jade will insist on two or three."

Now Alyssa looks approving. "I bet even the shark told you to walk away, seeing how nuts this is."

"No. She told me that I should start with a lawsuit. Any negotiation should begin from a place of threat and intimidation."

"Maren, come on. Do you hear yourself?" Alyssa takes a sip of bourbon and gives me a pitying look. "The shark didn't dissuade you because of all the billable hours. Do you get how much a court battle is going to cost?"

"I don't care. We're talking about Tai."

"Yes, we are. We're talking about Corey's love child with another woman. An unscrupulous woman who's going to try to take you for everything you have. Walk away."

No, not Corey's love child. But I'm not going to correct her on that.

"The shark said we start with visitation rights," I continue stubbornly. "But she thinks I could be awarded joint custody. That probably sounds extreme, seeing as Jade's his mother, but the shark made a good point. She said, 'Jade's his mother in name only, if she's willing to use him as a pawn in her game.'"

Jade's willing to pretend Tai is a dead man's son. What wouldn't she do? That's the real question.

Alyssa's visibly concerned. "I told you weeks ago that you were playing with fire."

"That reminds me, I told you about Tai's burn, right?" She indicates no, so I tell her briefly. "The lawyer said we could really get a lot of mileage out of that with the court, especially if Jade canceled babysitting with me and then took him back to her mother's."

"Don't do this, Maren. You don't want to go to court."

"No, I don't. That's why I'm hoping that Jade's going to come to her senses. I said I want to wait at least another week before we file any papers." Before I officially declare war.

But if I have to declare, then I'll take no prisoners. I won't feel bad for anything the shark does, given what I know about the paternity. Jade didn't have any sympathy for me when she showed up on my doorstep, lying about who her son really is.

"Yes, slow it down," Alyssa says. "Take a week to think about whether this is really worth it."

"I already know Tai's worth it."

And the shark doesn't think we should have any trouble getting a judge to grant visitation. She gave a whole speech about how I'm a wonderful influence and Tai is lucky to have me in his life. "Jade said herself that Tai is Corey's son, so you are, de facto, his aunt. We won't even need to prove paternity. She's making it too easy!" The shark smiled suddenly, for the first time, revealing sharp, pointy incisors. Or had I just imagined that?

Now I'm the liar, pretending that I am Tai's de facto aunt. But the end should justify the means. I will be a wonderful influence, and Tai needs that, with Jade for a mother.

"I never wanted this," I say. "Tai should have a relationship with both of us. But Jade's picking a fight with the wrong woman."

Alyssa doesn't answer, just pours out some more bourbon.

"If I sic the shark on her, I'll feel a little guilty. I bet Jade would have the only attorney she could afford, or she might even have to represent herself. I don't think she's had a super-easy life. She's a young woman who was victimized by an older man. You can tell Corey did a number on her. She's this mess of bravado and insecurity, and no matter what, she's still Tai's mother."

"I think you should walk away," Alyssa says, "but if you don't, then you can't get all bleeding heart about it. You have to stand back and let your shark do her thing. In the end, Jade should be chum."

I don't like that image at all, and I take a big drink to dislodge it.

My plan right now? Wait Jade out a little longer. Show her

that I'm not going to buckle, and she'll be the one to come to her senses. Then I'll have Tai back (for four days, not just two), and Jade and I will find a way to accept that we're in each other's lives for the long haul. I can be a mature adult; can she?

Please, let her come to her senses, because I'm not vicious by nature. But sometimes in life, you need to be the shark.

THIRTY-SIX
JADE

I will be as false and disingenuous as I have to be. I will lie right to that woman's face at every opportunity, because you know what I won't do?

I won't let her call all the shots.

I won't spend the rest of Tai's childhood subject to Maren's whims. I'm no one's puppet.

So it's time to get really dirty. Just full-on lowdown.

All my appeals to Maren's sense of justice and compassion have come to naught, and the law is firmly on her side. Yvette seemed to think it wasn't even just the law as written but that the court would be biased against me. Apparently, I've got a likability problem.

But Maren has to have some skeletons in her closet. She's not who everyone thinks she is; she's not even who *she* thinks she is.

She probably believes she's looking after Tai's best interests, but she's too blinded by her own insatiable need. She meant to have Corey's child, it didn't work out for her, and now she's trying to get her hooks into mine. She's incapable of seeing herself clearly. She thinks she's the heroine in this story.

I know the truth, though: She's deranged, and she has to be stopped. I just need to find something I can use against her.

I've never really been through Maren's social media, even though we are "friends," and I did "follow" her a while back. She's never had a job, so she has no LinkedIn page with coworkers I can approach. Her world was entirely Corey and the finance wives, with their incessant socializing and bogus charity work. I don't think Maren's ever done any actual hands-on volunteering; it was all for show.

There are no recent posts and even when she had a life, it was minimally documented. It seemed like she was doing just enough to promote the idea of perfection. Great lighting, beautiful clothes, handsome and adoring husband, comely friends, backlit food and drink, expensive vacations, lavish events—every wannabe socialite box was checked.

If I want to find dirt, I'll have to look elsewhere. Her social media's scrubbed.

But then I see something surprising. *Someone* surprising. A woman with long ombre hair and red lips. It takes me a second to place her. Then it comes back to me.

Amelia, the hair consult from hell.

I peer at the picture and scan the comments. Her real name's Alyssa, and she considers Maren to be her bestie.

Maybe this wasn't such a waste of time after all.

THIRTY-SEVEN

MAREN

The past few days have been rough. I've had all sorts of thoughts that I'd never say out loud.

I don't like who I'm becoming, but I'm ready to go to extreme lengths for a reunion with Tai.

I texted Jade to say that I'm looking forward to seeing him on Sunday. She marked it with a thumbs-up, though I don't expect her to follow through. Unless I offer a settlement, I imagine she'll keep finding reasons to keep Tai from me.

Earlier today, I went and spied on him at his preschool. I didn't try to interact or anything, I do understand basic boundaries, and adults skulking near preschools are understandably frowned on. I waited across the street pretending to scroll on my phone until all the kids came out into the yard for morning recess. I got to see Tai playing with his friends. As they chased each other around looking entirely carefree, I nearly cried with gratitude and longing.

I miss him horribly. When I got home, I called the shark and told her we should go ahead and draw up the contract for $500K, with protected visitation. Then if Jade tries to negotiate it up to a million, we can make a deal.

The shark told me in no uncertain terms what a bad idea this was. She thinks we can make a strong case given Jade's character (or lack thereof).

But then, the shark doesn't know who Tai's real dad is. I don't either, actually. I do, however, know that it's not Corey, which means my case is far weaker than the shark thinks. So I'd prefer to get this wrapped up as quickly as possible.

The sun is setting. The view from my living room window of Central Park is like a watercolor painting. I'm lucky, dammit. I'm so lucky.

I pour myself another glass of wine. I never wanted to go back to this, to feeling so lonely and desolate.

I've been through every inch of the apartment, searching in every closet, shelf, and cupboard. I don't even know what I'm looking for anymore. Just something that would beat Jade into submission, force her to formalize my time with Tai into a sort of visitation plan without me having to pay her off.

It's not just that she's a con woman, and I'm certainly not cheap where Tai is concerned. (Private school costs a mint.) I'm not even opposed to helping with the cost of living, especially if it would mean moving Tai to a better neighborhood.

But there's no way Jade can be trusted to make sound decisions with large amounts of money. Maybe that's why Corey parceled it out in increments. He might not have trusted her, either.

Could Jade have been involved in Corey's death in some way? I could imagine him wanting to drink to excess when he has to deal with someone like her. She waxes poetic about their incredible love, but if he were here, what would he say? Jade's the kind of woman who could drive a man to death.

What happened to Corey doesn't really matter; what happens to Tai does. I can't go writing Jade a fat check. It's possible that she wouldn't use the settlement on Tai at all. She might go on spending sprees or make poor choices or just otherwise squander it.

I have no reason to trust Jade's judgment or intentions, given the lies she's told me about Tai's parentage and being faithful to Corey. Then there's how badly she's treated me this whole time when I've been trying to help her.

I stare into the gloaming, my mood darkening right along with the sky. Corey left me so much money and no good choices.

I've tried to see it from Jade's perspective, to imagine how she'd explain herself: *Sure, Tai isn't Corey's biological son, but Corey loved Tai and was helping to raise him. So wouldn't it make sense that some of Corey's money goes to Tai? And obviously, Corey's widow wouldn't just hand over that money if she thought there was some other father out there who ought to be on the hook for child support payments.*

Maybe Jade never meant to be so unscrupulous, but one lie begets another. Plus, she's got to be financially strapped. I did a little research, and the average salary for a hairstylist in New York City is $65K a year, with no benefits. In one of the world's most expensive cities! Every time she has to stay home with Tai when he really is sick, she loses the whole day's pay. No wonder she's feeling desperate.

I'm not excusing dishonesty, but I'd prefer if Jade was morally compromised rather than morally bankrupt, seeing as she is Tai's mother.

Maybe there's a way I could repair my relationship with Jade. If I discovered more positive things about her or more specifics about how Corey had manipulated her, that could shift my impression. I mean, I don't want to hate Jade.

But how would I go about doing that? I've already searched this place top to bottom.

Then it comes to me: Corey's laptop. I could pay someone

to hack it. Alyssa would probably have some contact or referral. For the right price, you can get someone to do anything.

No matter what's on there, I'll continue to despise Corey. Sometimes it still eats at me, just how depraved he was, how little he cared for my welfare. It wasn't some sort of benign neglect or abject selfishness. No, what he did to me qualifies as emotional abuse. He gaslit me for years. By keeping salient information from me, he restricted my options. He basically defrauded me, stealing the life that I could have had with some other, more decent man. Sure, he left me all his money, but what he took can't be repaid. I can't get those years back.

When I think about it, I'm consumed by violent emotions. By fantasies of actual violence, even.

This isn't me. I can't let him turn me into a bitter, hateful person.

I want to call Emmanuel, but I gave him time off to spend with his family. At another hour of need, I might disturb him, but on the heels of our almost kiss, it seems doubly inappropriate.

Alyssa isn't ideal, but at least I wouldn't have to fill her in on the backstory. I don't want to tell another friend and have to relive all the pain and humiliation of these past few months.

I call Alyssa, but for once, her phone is off. Since it's an emergency, sort of, I try Sean. "Hey, Maren," he says. "What's up?" From the ambient noise, it sounds like he's at a bar.

"Is Alyssa with you? Or do you know where I can find her?" I'm not above showing up at whatever bar she might be in. I just really can't be alone anymore.

"She didn't tell me where she was going. She said a name, though. Let me think." Long pause, and then I hear a noise like he's snapping his fingers. "I think it's Jewel."

It's like being thrown off a building. And just when I thought I'd hit rock bottom... "Do you mean Jade?" I ask, hoping against hope.

"That's it."

THIRTY-EIGHT
JADE

I hadn't expected Alyssa to get here before me. I didn't think she'd show at all, that instead she'd think it was hilarious to send me on a fool's errand after I'd already been on my feet all day, forcing me to miss putting my kid to bed. Forcing me to have my mother babysit, which still feels like a risky proposition even though she swears she's being more attentive now.

But no, Alyssa's here, at the martini bar she suggested. It's on the thirty-third floor with a glittering view of the skyline and a piano player doing a Sinatra impression in the corner. I don't know if she picked it because it's classic or kitsch, or because no one she knows would be here.

She's at a round table for two, a drink already in front of her. "I figured I'd get started, since you're late," she says.

"By five minutes."

"Which is still late, is it not?" She sets down the phone and makes a big show of turning it off. "I assume you're paying, since you're the one who slid into my DMs, as the kids say?"

As they said many moons ago, but… "Sure, I'm paying." I open the cocktail menu and try not to balk at the prices. On the left side are all the martinis, which range from $30 to $60. On the right side is a variety of bourbon-based drinks, where the cheapest is $100 and the most expensive is $1,200.

Alyssa's drink is brown. She ordered off the right side, and I have a pretty good idea which one.

I can't give her any visible reaction. No signs of weakness. I have to be able to piss with the big boys (and girls). Maren's $20K is burning a hole in my bank account. This night is an investment, and if it goes according to plan, it could pay huge dividends.

"It's good to meet you, Alyssa," I say. "Maybe I'll like you better than I liked Amelia." I smile. This night will go down much easier if she has a sense of humor.

"I doubt it," she says.

The server appears, and I place my order for the $45 martini. Then I ask Alyssa, "Why did you say yes to meeting me? Just wondering."

"I like to live on the edge. And I love free shit." She lifts her glass and takes what's probably a $400 swig. "Salud."

"Does Maren know you're here? Are you planning to report everything I say back to her?"

"I can be discreet, if I'm so inclined."

"Did Maren send you to the salon to try to humiliate me? You should know it didn't work, by the way. I didn't feel worthless; I thought you were."

She smiles. I suspect she likes a formidable adversary, and loves a frenemy. So why is she friends with Maren?

"I have a mind of my own, Jade," she says. "A very inquisitive mind. I wanted to size you up. See what all the hullaballoo was about."

She strokes her almost empty glass with one long red talon, regarding me silently. She makes it clear that she finds me wanting, just as she did in the salon.

My drink arrives, and I sip gratefully. I'm not usually the type who needs liquid courage, but these are unusual times.

"So you know why I'm here," she says. "But why did you invite me?" She adds a cheeky, "Just wondering."

"How well do you really know your friend Maren?"

"Not as well as you knew her husband."

"I'm not someone who goes around sleeping with other women's husbands. Corey's the only man I've ever been with while he was in a relationship."

"Well, that's a fun fact!" she says brightly. "The next time I'm doing Jade Bastone trivia night, it'll come in handy."

"I'm just saying, don't judge a book by its cover. Because I would never do the kinds of things that Maren has. The relationship between a mother and a child is sacred. I would never violate—"

"Oh, come on. Your child *is* a violation. His very existence is an affront to Maren, and yet, she's been nothing but kind to him. Nothing but kind to you."

"You obviously don't know the whole story."

"Well, enlighten me." Even though she's trying to play it cool and look disinterested, I can tell that she's the type who lives for gossip, even about her alleged best friend. Or especially about Maren?

I go through all the mind games that Maren has engaged in since the beginning: the way she's insinuated herself into Tai's life, her manipulative use of money, how she tries to show me up in Tai's eyes, how she works overtime to get me to think exactly what she thinks about Corey, private school education, and everything else. "She's cosplaying a saint, and all the while, she wants me grateful and subservient. She flogs me, and I'm supposed to say, 'Thank you, madam.'"

Alyssa chortles in spite of herself. I'm getting the sense that she likes me, in spite of herself. She's a feisty woman, and she can appreciate that quality in others. So what the hell is she doing with Maren for a best friend? That's the million-dollar question.

"The image of Maren as some kind of dominatrix is hilarious," Alyssa says.

"It would be if she weren't so dangerous."

"Dangerous? Please." She shakes her head. "Just what do you think I'm going to do with this information?"

"You seem very clever. I'm sure you'll think of something."

"Let's get another round," she says, and now I'm smiling. She wants to stay. That means I'm getting somewhere.

"For the next round, you need to order off the left side," I say. "I'm a working gal."

"That you are," she says drily. She pauses, considering. "I'll get the cheapest old-fashioned they have. How's that?"

My smile widens. She does like me.

She signals the server and then, with an exaggerated sigh, "Give me the cheapest old-fashioned you've got. Just for comparison."

"Give me your cheapest martini," I say. "Because I'm broke."

As we await the next round, I'm planning my next move. I can't tell if she's doing the same. What is she really getting out of this? Is she just bored, or could it be that she has her own grievances against Maren?

"How do you really feel about Maren?" I ask.

"She's my best friend. How do you think I feel?"

Well, that was a surprisingly cautious answer from such a seemingly incautious person. But then, she hasn't really given anything away so far. I've shown her mine; she hasn't shown me hers.

"Let me guess," I say. "You feel like you need to protect Maren. Because I'm the Big Bad Wolf and she's Little Red Riding Hood."

She takes a long and deliberative sip.

"That's how Corey felt about Maren. It's how Emmanuel feels about her. Does your husband feel that way, too?"

She stares daggers at me. "What have you heard?"

"What?"

"Have you heard something about Sean and Maren?"

Now we're getting somewhere. Alyssa's insecure. She's worried about losing her husband. But to her fairy-tale princess of a best friend?

"I've heard her mention his name a few times," I lie.

"In what context?"

"I can't recall. I know that she misses the life she used to share with Corey. Living high with a finance bro."

"I've never gotten that impression from her." Alyssa is watching me with narrowed eyes. Shit. Just when we were getting along so well.

"All I'm saying is, Maren has a way with people. They seem to think she's fragile and that she needs them to take care of her. Isn't that what you were doing by coming to see me at the salon? Looking after Maren, the poor wounded bird?"

Alyssa doesn't answer, which seems encouraging. She's neither confirming nor denying. She lifts her drink.

"Doesn't it get on your nerves, having to coddle her all the time?"

"No."

I don't entirely believe her. "Well, I like women who can take care of themselves. You and me, we don't need anyone to fight our battles."

Alyssa's expression is bemused, but again, she doesn't disagree.

Somehow, the conversation shifts. We're talking less about Maren and more about Corey. More about the inner workings of Corey and Maren's marriage, as I understood them. I get the sense that Alyssa has never been let very far into Maren's life and that she'd like to know what was going on beyond the façade.

"One of the strangest things was how Corey talked about

her," I say. "He never said a bad word about her. Can you imagine? A husband having not one complaint about his wife?"

"I really can't."

"They were so repressed together. He couldn't even let himself *think* a bad thought about her. That would have been too disloyal. He was censoring his own mind."

Alyssa lets out a peal of laughter. "Meanwhile, he's having an affair for years!"

"I know, right? I used to say, 'You can tell me what you really think and feel about Maren,' but he didn't come up with anything except that she was the most amazing woman, and he loved her so much."

"Like he was a Stepford husband," Alyssa says. "I noticed that, too. Maren never had a bad word to say, either."

"You were laughing at the idea of Maren as a dominatrix. Didn't you know how kinky Maren and Corey were?" I hadn't known it myself until very recently, and it still rankles. But I've got to use everything I've got to get what I want. This night might cost me a couple of thousand dollars. I need a good return on investment.

"Corey and *Maren*?" Alyssa laughs. "Maren's from Utah. She was raised Mormon. There's no way."

"Oh, there's a way. Maren told me herself. Corey didn't. He let me assume they were totally vanilla."

"Well, there's no way they were chocolate."

I laugh. Then I notice that her glass is almost empty, and I hurriedly signal the server for another. "So she never told you about her sex life?"

"She doesn't like to talk about sex."

"Not with you, I guess." I polish off my martini. "Makes you wonder what else she's left out, doesn't it? What else she might be hiding?"

"Maren's not like that." But Alyssa's red lips have tightened. She's bothered.

"Maybe she's your best friend, but you're not hers. Or she's all about maintaining surface appearances. She just doesn't go very deep."

"She has deep feelings for Tai."

"You mean she's obsessed with him. Would you want someone around your kids acting the way she does? It's freaky."

Alyssa tilts her head. "Maybe not. But then, my kids aren't like Tai. Tai's a mistake."

"Excuse me?" My jaw tightens, as does my hand around the stem of the martini glass. Those are fighting words if I've ever heard them.

"I mean, it's a mistake for Maren to be hanging around with Tai." Bingo! "You're right, it is freaky. That's Corey's son, who he had with his mistress. She shouldn't be babysitting your kid; she should be adopting her own." Bingo again!

"Have you told her that?"

"It's a sensitive subject. She's not really looking for advice." Alyssa takes another sip. "And as you intuited, she's not always the most open person. I have to do a lot of the heavy lifting in our conversations, to be honest."

"Do you normally wait to be asked before you give your opinion? I wouldn't have guessed that about you, Amelia."

"Ha-ha." She's not laughing, though. "Corey and Maren were off having wild sex, and he was having sex with you, too? Where did he find the time or the energy?"

I don't want to talk about Corey; I want to stay on the subject of Maren's weird obsession with Tai. "He was a great dad, and Maren can still be a great mom to someone. She could go to some foreign country and adopt a baby. Or hell, if she wants a four-year-old, think of all the kids who are in the foster system in this country."

"Uh-huh." Alyssa is tuning out. Child welfare isn't the juiciest subject.

"Maren should apply her generosity to people who need it. Tai doesn't. He's already got a mother."

"Or I could give her one of mine," Alyssa says. "Not that she'd want them. Do you know she's never asked them to call her 'Aunt Maren'? She barely sees them."

Alyssa sounds like she's working herself up. It occurs to me that she could be an angry drunk. I probably need to get out of here pretty soon, before this turns. Also, I don't want her to black out and forget this conversation.

"I bet your kids are amazing," I say. I'm assuming that Alyssa would rather head for the hills than talk about her children.

"I don't know about amazing, but yeah, they're, you know, they're kids. She might do things differently than I do, but—"

"That's a good point. Maren is really judgmental, even though she pretends she's not. A lot of times, she doesn't say it outright, but you can just tell. Can't you?"

"You really can, but fuck, I'm not going to blame anyone for being opinionated." Alyssa makes a motion in the air to the server.

Another round? Really? How much free shit does one woman need?

"I've got plenty of opinions, too," I say. "You know where you stand with me because I say what I think. Because I'm honest." Unless I'm trying to use you as a means to my ends, like I am with Alyssa right now. "Maren, though, is opinionated and pretending not to be. It's one of the reasons she and I just don't gel. She's phony."

"I don't know about that."

"Plus, she's majorly up in my business. I can't tell you how many texts and emails I've gotten about private schools."

"Private schools are the worst. All those little assholes in training. My kids might turn out just like their dad, the asshole-in-chief. That's what I call him: Asshole. With a capital A."

I laugh, though really, she's just so awful. And so charmed by her own awfulness. "You call him that to his face?"

"To his face, behind his back. I tell all my girlfriends, 'You want to know what Asshole did this time?' But mostly, it's about what he's not doing. I shouldn't really complain, though. One of the best parts of marriage is getting to take each other for granted."

I'm starting to tune out myself now. Marriage is one of the dullest topics there is.

"...but then something big happens, and it hits you upside the head. You realize that this is your person, the one you can count on when the chips are down, you know? The fact is, Asshole's my soulmate."

That makes sense. Because she's an asshole, too.

I ask enough questions to keep her talking. I want her to think we're bonding. I need to get her to do my bidding, to convince Maren to back off. But I'm fading fast. Four rounds with this woman is a lot. I almost feel for Maren. With a best friend like this, who needs enemies?

On the surface, Alyssa and I probably have a lot more in common than either of us has with Maren. To the casual observer, Alyssa and I are both strong, outspoken women. But the resemblance ends there. I'm only an asshole when I absolutely have to be, and I don't take any pleasure or pride in it.

I wish I didn't have to do what I'm doing, that Maren hadn't taken it to this level. Why couldn't she just set up a trust and then take Tai for occasional outings?

Instead, she needs control. That's her sickness, and I can't let Tai get caught up in it.

"Are you going to tell Maren about this?" I say. "About you and me?"

"There is no you and me." Alyssa gestures between us in the floppy, sloppy way of the highly inebriated. I must be pretty drunk myself, but I'm on such high alert that I barely even feel it. "This was a one-off."

"Fair enough. But you're not going to forget what we talked about, are you?"

"Please. I know how to hold my liquor."

"If you do care about Maren, you should tell her your true opinions. I think you have a lot of wisdom."

"Damn straight," she drawls.

"Like what you said about her adopting a baby? You are so right. Any kid would be lucky to have her." Any kid other than Tai.

Alyssa does a wink. "We'll never see each other again, but I got you, Jade Bastone."

THIRTY-NINE
MAREN

I've been sitting on the front stoop of Alyssa's brownstone for over an hour. I had to come here. I had to see for myself.

Finally, a Mercedes pulls up to the curb, and Alyssa stumbles out of the back seat. I stand up, ready to confront her, not help her inside, though she seems like she could use the latter. "Thanks so much!" she calls to the Uber Black driver.

Then she sees me, and her mouth drops open. I can tell she's thinking frantically.

"What the fuck, Alyssa." It comes out in a growl. I'm almost unrecognizable to myself in my fury. "I know where you were. Don't bother lying."

"Aw, shit." She sits down on the stoop and pats the space next to her.

I glare at her. "It looks like you had a great night."

"Looks can be deceiving. You, of all people, should know that." What the hell does that mean? "Come on, sit down. I'll tell you all about it."

I want to remain where I am and scream down at her, but she has neighbors, and kids. They don't deserve that.

I perch on the same step as her, but far away. Right now, I

feel like she's radioactive. Entirely toxic. Completely untrustworthy.

"How could you?" I demand. "When you know what I've been through with Corey. How he betrayed me."

"You think I betrayed you?" She stares at me with great big moon eyes. "How could you even think that? I went there for you!"

"Went where?"

"To the martini bar."

"You went to *our* martini bar with Jade?" I stare back at her. I don't understand how she's adopted this pure and innocent expression when the location itself is a slap in my face.

"I ordered the $1,200 old-fashioned. And I made her pay." Alyssa smirks; I don't. "She DM'd me, saying she wanted to meet."

"How many times have you met?"

"Just this once. I'm never going to see her again if I have anything to say about it."

"So why didn't you tell me about the DM?"

"Because I didn't want to stress you out more. Come on, you know you would have spent all night worrying."

"I spent all night worrying anyway. After I texted you and your phone was off, I called Sean and found out who you were with."

She rolls her eyes. "Asshole's always the soul of discretion."

"You'd sworn him to silence?"

"No. I didn't figure you'd call him. Why were you so eager to talk to me?"

"I was having a rough night." But I can't really trust her with the particulars, can I? "You shouldn't have lied to me."

"I didn't lie."

"You withheld vital information."

"I was going to call you first thing in the morning and tell you all about it! Tell you all about her. She is a piece of work, no question. Total con woman, just like I've been saying since the beginning."

"So you think she wasn't really Corey's mistress, or the mother of his child?" I'm testing Alyssa, because now I know only one of those is true.

"Oh, no, she's definitely those things. But she's also out to get you. She wanted me to spill all your secrets."

"What secrets?"

"Exactly! I told her that with Maren, what you see is what you get. I told Jade, 'Maren's every bit as good as she seems.' Which is what's driving her crazy. She wants you to be a piece of shit, just like her."

"You really think she's a piece of shit?" I sure do, now that I know she sought out Alyssa.

"Of course she is. Get this: She wanted to dish on your sex life with Corey. How gross is that? She told me lies about how kinky you were. I said, 'Have you even met Maren?'"

I shake my head as if I'm incredulous, though really, Jade's telling the truth. Five years ago, when Corey said we weren't having children, I diligently applied myself to the project of spicing up our sex life. I needed a project because I had nothing else.

But now, I have Tai.

And unfortunately, he has Jade, who is a piece of shit.

"What do I do?" I say. "For as long as I want to be in Tai's life—which is forever—I'm going to have to keep dealing with her."

"And she's going to keep trying to get your money."

"I'm worried for Tai. If she'd do anything for money, if she's out to hurt me, if she'd even try to recruit my best friend, then is she really fit to be a mother?"

"Probably not. She paid for four rounds of drinks tonight. Do you know how many diapers that could buy?"

"Tai's not in diapers anymore." But it does bother me,

thinking that Jade is using the $20K I gave her on expensive nights out. Or is it possible she has some secret source of funds, maybe an account that Corey set up for her before he died? Maybe she's been tricking me this whole time, just faking poverty. I wouldn't put it past her.

Alyssa stares off into the middle distance, and for a second, I think I've lost her, but then she snaps her fingers as if she's got it, she's found the answer, just like Sean did earlier. Like Asshole, like asshole.

I shouldn't be thinking that. She's my best friend. She met with Jade to look out for me. Four rounds of drinks with a con woman, all for my benefit.

I really want to believe that. Because I don't know how I'd metabolize another betrayal.

"Jade paid for tonight, even though she's supposedly a struggling single mother," Alyssa says. "You're the babysitter, but you weren't watching Tai. So who was watching him? Do you think she could have left him home alone?"

"No, she never would have done that. He must have been staying with his grandmother."

"The same grandmother who burned him?" Alyssa might seem self-involved, but she really is a sharp listener. Nothing gets by her, and nothing is ever forgotten.

"Yes," I say. "That grandmother."

"You need to call CPS."

"CPS?"

"Child Protective Services. You can call or, no, I can. Anyone can. They have a whole anonymous reporting system." How does she even know that? Her expression is eager. Excited.

"I couldn't do that."

"You were just questioning her fitness as a mother. Get CPS in there. They can dig around and figure out what's really going on. Maybe there are things you have no idea about. She could have a drug problem, for all we know. You'd be saving Tai."

"But if I do this, she'll be furious. She might try to keep Tai away from me permanently."

"Then you'll sue for visitation. Didn't the shark seem confident?"

"She thinks I'd win, but it could be a long, slow process." I can't imagine going months without seeing Tai. I feel like I'd die, and that's not hyperbole.

"You won't be the one calling CPS. I will. If Jade confronts you, you'll say you had no idea. That I went rogue. She'll believe that because I already did one thing behind your back. I pretended to be Amelia."

"What?"

"I went into her salon and said I wanted her to do a consultation. She was so bad, Maren. You wouldn't believe it. Her recommendations were babylights and sombre." She makes it sound as if that's Jade's biggest crime.

What could Jade's biggest crime be? Would CPS be able to figure that out?

If they declared Jade unfit, then I could become his foster parent.

Am I really considering this? "I don't think so," I finally say. "It's just too cruel. I mean, sending someone in to investigate Jade—"

"This is what CPS is made for. To protect children. I think this woman's a psycho. Just like Corey. Two birds of a feather who flocked together. Bonnie and Clyde."

"What did she tell you?"

Alyssa leans forward conspiratorially. "It's not only what she said. It's her aura. It's just who she is. She's rotten, and it comes off her in waves."

"You really think so?"

"I know so." She leans back again. "But let's just say for the sake of argument that I'm wrong. That we've unleashed CPS on an innocent woman. If that's the case, then the report will get screened out. It'll be called unfounded or unsubstantiated, I forget which."

"You know a lot about this."

She shrugs. "Doesn't everyone know this stuff?"

Not me. But she's making sense. CPS must get a ton of calls, and they can't put resources toward all of them. So if Jade's innocent, nothing bad will happen. If she's guilty, then she'll be held accountable. I could become Tai's emergency foster parent, which would probably be a lot quicker than the regular court system.

"No," I say. "This is just too crazy."

"She won't even know you had anything to do with it. I'll take full responsibility. I'm the one who was out with her. I saw how heavily that woman was drinking, how quick she was to order another round. She might be an alcoholic. And you know that? She didn't text whoever was watching Tai even once. He wasn't remotely on her mind. What kind of mother is that?"

Alyssa's kind of mother. Her phone was off, so she obviously never texted Sean about her own kids.

"Let me do this for you." She meets my eyes urgently. "Let me solve your problem. You can't go up against a woman like this, but I can."

I frown. "I'm not as helpless as you think."

"This woman is wily. She is diabolical. I don't throw around the word *evil* too lightly, but if the shoe fits..." She raises her perfectly tended eyebrows.

"Okay," I finally agree. "If she's innocent, the report will get screened out, like you said."

Alyssa smiles. "You've been through so much, Maren. I'm happy to take care of this for you."

I can't smile back; I mean, this is hardly a moment for exultation. This is Tai's mother we're talking about. I don't like the image of his space being invaded and searched, or whatever it is that CPS does. But Jade's the one who brought me to this point. She's the one who DMed Alyssa. She's the one coming after me and abandoning her son to do it, either leaving him home alone or with his negligent grandmother.

"I could use one more favor," I say. "I need to get into Corey's laptop, see if—"

"Say no more. Sean knows a guy. Leave it to us." Alyssa reaches over and pats my hand. "I'll take care of everything."

FORTY
JADE

"Thank you for coming by," I say. "I appreciate that you're looking out for Tai."

"I'm so glad you see it that way." The social worker smiles. "A lot of parents don't." She's young, and I suspect this is her first job out of college or grad school or whatever.

"You got a complaint. You had to investigate."

"Just between us," she lowers her voice, "you have nothing to worry about. This is going to get screened out."

"Thank you," I say, more sincerely this time. As I shut the door behind her, my expression darkens.

Alyssa.

How had I allowed myself to believe, even for a second, that she and I could see eye to eye? That a gorgon like that could be prevailed upon to do the right thing?

It's the morning after our $2,000 night out. I woke up with my head aching, and then came the knock from Child Protective Services.

It started out rocky between the social worker and me since it was apparent that whoever called in the complaint—most likely Alyssa, though she could have told Maren—had painted me as some kind of wild party girl, spending thousands on a night out when I could barely pay my rent and when my son was... Where was my son?

"He's with my mother," I explained politely. "They're having a sleepover."

I channeled my inner Maren and was nothing but gracious. I said that, yes, I paid for the drinks last night but that it was supposed to be a belated birthday present from my friend Alyssa, who'd forgotten her wallet. "She told me she was going to pay me back later," I said, "but I didn't think she'd pay me back like this." This, meaning a complaint to CPS.

From then on, the social worker was eating out of my hand. It was clearly not the first time she'd had her time wasted on a vengeful, bogus complaint.

She still had to do her due diligence, though, which meant I still had to submit to invasive questioning. She interrogated me about Tai's relationship with his grandmother, and his recent burn.

Maren is either mixed up in this or she'd already told Alyssa about the burn, and then Alyssa decided to include it, for good measure.

I was asked how many drinks I had the previous night and whether I drove; I was asked about my mental health and substance abuse history. Then I had to detail all of Tai's routines throughout the week and give her a tour of the apartment so she could check for any health or safety hazards. She made sure there was enough food in the refrigerator and not too much alcohol in the cupboards. She even went through my medicine cabinet.

Throughout, I was as nice and cooperative as possible. This isn't the worker's fault. She's just doing her job, and I respect people who work for a living.

She also asked about my current childcare arrangements. While I defended Mom, I said that two long days a week was too much for a cancer survivor, and that it's now preschool and Maren. "Will you be calling them?" I said. "Because that would be pretty humiliating."

"No, that won't be necessary. I've got all I need."

Now that she's gone, I'm pacing the room in agitation, still wound up and full of adrenaline. I'm pretty sure I made it through that unscathed, but it's a terrifying prospect, losing Tai. It's my biggest fear, and it could become a reality. I've felt for weeks now that Maren's coming for my son.

I wish I had someone I could talk to. I don't feel like venting to a ghost right now. I'm so tired of doing all this alone. Tired of cleaning up the mess Corey left.

Last night, Alyssa said she had a mind of her own and that Maren hadn't been aware of the salon consultation. It could be that Alyssa's doing this solo, and Maren's totally in the dark.

Or Maren and Alyssa planned it all together. Alyssa could have told Maren about my DM. Had they always intended for Alyssa to file that CPS report? If so, what's the end game? For Tai to be removed from my care and put into Maren's?

I can't ask Maren what she knows or what she's done. For one thing, she could lie; for another, if she had no idea about my actions, then I'd be tipping her off. She'd want to know how I ended up in a martini bar with Alyssa, and from there, she'd realize I'm making moves against her.

Whether it's a tag team or Alyssa's gone rogue, I'm in deep, deep shit.

I have to keep my enemies close and let Maren start babysitting Tai again because it's what CPS expects. If for some reason the case isn't closed and a social worker stops by, I don't want to get caught in a lie.

I grab my phone and start texting: *I NEED TO SEE YOU ASAP.*

FORTY-ONE
MAREN

I loved getting to see Tai today. I loved getting to see Emmanuel, too. I've been missing both my guys.

I was sure Jade would cancel today, even though she'd responded to my confirming text last night with another thumbs-up. I tossed and turned all night, sure that something would go wrong. But then they both came through the door, and I could have wept with joy.

Emmanuel seemed happy, too, if overly formal, which I can understand. But when Tai seemed more subdued than usual, I got worried. I wonder what Jade might have said to him, if she could be trying to turn him against me. I wouldn't put anything past her at this point, not since she went to Alyssa behind my back.

I had an idea, a way to cement my place in Tai's life.

I set Corey's framed pictures up again on the living room bookshelves, knowing that Tai would discover them and ask questions. He didn't seem upset at all to learn that I'd been married to his father. If anything, he liked that we're really related, that I am, in fact, his Aunt Maren.

Now that he's gone, though, I'm regretting what I did. I should have consulted Jade or at least given her advance warning. But maybe he won't say anything. Four-year-olds are easily distracted, and I sent him home with some new toys that he and Jade can play with together.

If the subject does come up with Jade, I'll explain that it was an impulsive decision made in a moment of insecurity. I was just trying to make sure I couldn't get pushed out of Tai's life. He needs my love, and I need his.

Not that Jade understands that. If she did, she never would have gone behind my back and contacted Alyssa.

Of course, Alyssa went behind her back and contacted Child Protective Service. Does that make Jade and me even?

No, I'm worse.

My conscience has been gnawing at me. I can't even imagine how upsetting it would be to have CPS show up at your door, how afraid Jade must have been. I should have told Alyssa no. I want to call Jade, confess everything, and apologize, but it would probably just give Jade another reason to dislike me.

I'm crawling out of my skin. I keep thinking about what Jade might do if she thinks I'm behind a CPS visit. She'll figure out that Alyssa made the call, but she might think I put Alyssa up to it.

I have to hope there wasn't a CPS visit at all. What was that term Alyssa used? Screened out. Maybe Alyssa's report got screened out without Jade ever being contacted.

In hindsight, the whole CPS situation was just so aggressive. So unlike me.

The fact remains, Tai does need some form of protection. Jade has very questionable morals, and she's the air he breathes.

Since the beginning, she's made it clear that she wants Corey's inheritance, and I don't think she's going to stop until she gets it. But I earned that inheritance. I paid with my hopes, dreams, and fast-dwindling fertility. Jade's the upstart. The usurper.

Sharks don't come cheap, and I want my access to Tai to be guaranteed. I'm not about to let Jade keep pulling my strings.

I'm happy to subsidize Tai at my discretion. But Jade will get a big jackpot over my dead body.

FORTY-TWO
JADE

Emmanuel hadn't responded to my urgent text, hadn't been willing to meet ASAP. But he forgot we'd have to meet soon enough, seeing as he's doing Maren's pickups and drop-offs.

"You can't avoid me forever," I tell him.

"It's like I told you in the beginning: I'm staying out of it," he says. He's hovering in the doorway as Tai is running around madly inside, crashing into furniture. I bet Maren gave him ice cream again.

The thing about Emmanuel is that he has impeccable manners. He doesn't want to leave until I give him permission. And I'm not about to let him go.

"Come inside, please," I say.

He looks down unhappily. "Your son needs you."

"My son can watch his iPad or the TV for a while. This is important." I make a show of opening the door wider. Emmanuel steps across the threshold, eyes still averted. I always feel like he should be wearing a fedora and removing it balefully, calling me "ma'am."

But it's an act, isn't it? There's nothing chivalrous about Emmanuel.

I set Tai up on the couch with his iPad, and it's very much like when Maren made her impromptu visit, except that the fort is long gone. I don't need to tell Tai not to listen in on the adult conversation because it's of much less interest to him than literally anything on a screen. Sad but true. Sad but convenient.

I gesture toward the kitchen table. "I don't like this," Emmanuel says, remaining standing. His eyes dart over to Tai.

I sit down and then pointedly stare at the other chair. Emmanuel takes it reluctantly. I wonder what that's like, to be so programmed into politeness that you're practically a robot. It's like he physically can't leave no matter how much he wants to.

"Maren's my employer and my friend," he says. "I'm not going to talk behind her back."

"Do you think I'd be talking to you now if I had any other choice? Do you think I want to be fighting for my son?"

"All she wants is to babysit him." I have the sense that he's trying to convince himself as much as me. "All you want is her money."

"Do you know that her best friend called CPS on me?" I can tell by his face that he didn't, and that he's distressed by the thought. "It's not like Alyssa would have done that out of thin air. Maren must have put her up to it."

"Oh, Alyssa." His distaste is evident, but he also seems relieved that he can blame Alyssa rather than Maren. "Alyssa doesn't need to be put up to anything. Not that Maren would—"

"This is what I've been trying to tell you all along. Maren is obsessed with Tai, and she's lost all perspective. I asked you to talk to her weeks ago so that it wouldn't get to this point."

He's visibly upset, staring down at the table.

"If Maren would do something like that, what will she do next?" He doesn't answer.

"That wasn't a rhetorical question, Emmanuel. What do you think she's going to do next?"

"I don't know." He's speaking barely above a whisper.

"Neither do I. That's why you need to step up. It's not just for my own good, and for Tai's. It's for Maren's, too. She's going down a road she really shouldn't."

"Are you threatening Maren?" His eyes bear down on mine.

"I'm going to protect my son with everything I have. That's all I can tell you."

He shakes his head. "I don't understand this. Why can't you women just get along? You both love Tai—"

"She's not supposed to love Tai!" My voice has gone up an octave and several notches in volume, which seems to confirm for him that I'm some hysterical woman. I glance at Tai—really, a bomb could go off and he wouldn't react—and then lower my voice. "I want Maren out of our lives."

"All she wants is to spend some time with him, while you get free babysitting." Now he sounds pleading.

"Do you really believe that? Because after that CPS call, I'm starting to think she wants Corey's money *and* his son."

I expect Emmanuel to contradict me, but frighteningly enough, he's silent.

"I had no problem with the babysitting"—okay, so I'm lying—"but now I want to end it since I obviously can't trust her. Only how would that look to CPS? What if Maren calls them back with some new trumped-up charge and then claims that I cut her off because I didn't want any witnesses?"

"Witnesses to what?"

"To nothing! I'm a good mother, Emmanuel. A single mother and a widow who doesn't need this stress."

"What do you mean, a widow? Maren's the widow."

"I am, too. In my heart, Corey and I were married. I love and miss him way more than she does. Half that money should have been mine. It should be Tai's."

"Justice is following Corey's wishes. That money belongs to Maren."

I shake my head in amazement. "She really has done a number on you, hasn't she?" No wonder she's upping the ante and involving CPS. She's used to brainwashing people. Only I can see through her.

"I should go." Emmanuel starts to stand up, but I reach out and grab his arm.

"You see what she's doing to me. She's trying to take over my life, to dictate what I can and can't do with my son. Are you really okay with that?"

"Could you remove your hand, please? I'd like to leave now."

I keep my hand where it is. "Can't you think for yourself?" He won't look at me. "You don't want to go up against her because you know she'd turn on you, too."

"No, that's not it."

"You think that if she creates a trust for Tai, she won't take care of your girls." I see that's not it, either. I make my last guess. "Is it because you're in love with her?"

"No." He tries to infuse it with incredulity but fails.

"Does your wife know about your feelings for Maren?" Now he jerks his arm away and gets to his feet. "I think she's in love with you, too." I'm speaking quickly. "That's why you're the only person who'd be able to talk sense to her. Please. Just tell her that Tai isn't the only little boy in the world. She'd be a great mom, so that's what she should do. Find herself a child who'd be thrilled to have her as a mother. The foster system is full of them."

Emmanuel hasn't left yet, so I still have a shot.

"Tai doesn't need another mother; he's got me. Please, Emmanuel." I'm practically begging, and I can see that it's having some effect.

But not enough. He shakes his head slightly, in regret. He wants to help, but he can't.

So I'm going to have to pull out the big guns.

"I'm really sorry about this," I say. "But my back's against the wall, so I guess now yours will be, too."

He's looking at me again, with trepidation.

"Either you convince Maren to write up a full trust for Tai—not just education but the whole enchilada—or I'm going to tell her the truth. I'll tell her that you knew about Tai and me this whole time. She'll never forgive you. You'll lose your job and your relationship with her. You'll be devastated, and so will she."

"Would you really do that?" He seems more sad than angry, as if I've somehow disappointed him.

"If you want to protect Maren, yourself, and your family," I say, "then you need to find your courage. Do the right thing, finally. Persuade her to do the right thing." I stand up. "You have forty-eight hours."

FORTY-THREE

MAREN

"This might not be the best timing, but you know I can't keep secrets," Alyssa says. "Not from you."

Alyssa has summoned me to her house. She said she wouldn't tell me what it was about by text or phone, she needed to see my face. It had to be in person.

I don't want to be here. I'm still upset with Alyssa for meeting with Jade behind my back (even if she claims it was intended for my own good) and then pushing so hard for that CPS call. I still have no way of knowing if CPS paid Jade a visit or not. Alyssa called for an update and was denied any further information. Whatever CPS chooses to do is confidential.

I've been antsy and guilt-ridden. On the ride here, Emmanuel asked what was wrong, but I couldn't tell him. I'm too ashamed. Alyssa made the call, but I'm fully complicit.

What have I done? I might have blown everything with Jade and, by extension, with Tai. Sure, I got to see him on Sunday, but will I get to see him again on Wednesday? It all just feels so tenuous.

It might have been on the verge of blowing up anyway. I have to remember, Jade DMed Alyssa. From what Alyssa's told me about their meetup, Jade wanted to get dirt and turn Alyssa against me. But Alyssa assured me that could never happen. She's on my side, always, and she gave Jade nothing.

I wish I could entirely believe her, but four rounds of drinks? Alyssa must have given Jade something, even if she doesn't recall exactly what it was. And why did Alyssa spend so long with Jade anyway?

With friends like that, who needs enemies?

Is Jade my enemy?

If so, then I can't wait to get Corey's laptop back. I need to dig up some dirt myself. Just for self-protection. And for Tai's protection, too.

If Jade's dangerous and unfit, then it's better for it to come out now while he's young, with Aunt Maren waiting in the wings.

"I can't sit on something this big," Alyssa says. "I'd feel like I'm lying to your face."

My stomach drops. Her timing is indeed brutal, but the truth is always better. "Say it, please."

"Sean just told me that Corey was embezzling from the company. And right before he died, some people were done looking the other way."

"Oh, thank God." I start to laugh with relief. The truth could have been so much worse. "This has nothing to do with me. I've washed my hands of Corey's affairs. Financial, sexual, you name it."

"It shouldn't have anything to do with you, but it could. I mean, it's not likely the company will come after you to recoup the money—the optics of that would be pretty bad, with you being a grieving widow—but it's not impossible, either. I mean, we're talking about tens of millions."

I think back to the conversation I overheard at the Southampton house between Sean and the finance bro all those months ago. Had they been talking about embezzlement then? "Why did Sean tell you this now?"

"I don't really know. Why don't I get him down here? He can talk to you himself. He's home sick, the big baby." She rolls her eyes. "Every time Asshole gets a sniffle, the whole world goes dark." She starts texting on her phone.

A minute later, the elevator opens and Sean shuffles out. He's wearing sweats and has a blanket wrapped around his shoulders, his bulbous nose reddened. His hulking size would make his woe-is-me appearance seem comical if I were capable of further laughter.

"Where's your mask?" Alyssa barks. "Maren's got enough problems as it is. She doesn't need your germs."

He reaches into his pocket and pulls out an N95, placing it over his nose and mouth. "Hi, Maren," he says, slightly muffled. He takes the seat across the table, slouching over piteously.

"Oh, Jesus." Alyssa rolls her eyes again. "So dramatic."

"You're not in my body!" Sean says. "You don't know!"

"Okay, okay," Alyssa says. "We won't keep you long. Maren just needs the details. You know, about Corey's white-collar crimes."

Sean looks around furtively, like he thinks the room might be bugged. "You told her?" he says to Alyssa.

"Obviously! I can't keep secrets from Maren. She's been through enough."

"Do you think it's true?" I ask Sean. "Or could it just be a rumor?"

He looks like he doesn't want to answer, and Alyssa whirls on him. "You told me you thought it was true! You said—"

"All right, all right." Sean looks at me. "But there's nothing official. I mean, it's not like we had an all-hands meeting and it got announced."

"But everyone's talking about it," Alyssa prompts.

Weren't they all talking about it months ago? That was the impression I had at the party.

"Heads are rolling. They think maybe Corey wasn't working alone." There's a long pause as Alyssa and Sean exchange a meaningful look.

"You mean they think I had something to do with it?" I say. "That I'm hiding stolen money? That's crazy!"

"I told Sean that you would never do that," Alyssa says.

"I don't know that they're talking about you specifically," Sean says. "Everyone at the company is under suspicion. We're all walking on eggshells."

"Could I be liable for what Corey did?"

"No," Alyssa says with authority. "Not criminally. I talked to an attorney about this once, just being the curious person I am, and I was told that if your husband commits a crime and you don't know about it, you can't be prosecuted. But you could be civilly liable, if the company or the victims file for a judgment against you."

Sean is staring at Alyssa. "When did you talk to an attorney?"

"Years ago." She waves a hand dismissively. "No biggie." Then she's focused on me again. "If there is a civil suit, you'll have to get an attorney, and they can advise you whether to settle or not. That's part of why you should think twice about retaining that shark over a boy you barely know. You might need the money for, you know, other things."

I'm reeling. I can't believe that Corey has left me in this predicament, and yet, I also can.

"You shouldn't panic," Sean says. "It's highly doubtful that my company would come after you."

"Why's that? They wouldn't want people to know they're suing a widow?"

"No, that wouldn't bother them. But if they sue you, it'll get out that they had an employee who was embezzling. Their wealthy clients need to know their money is safe. This could ruin the company's reputation, and then there'd be an exodus. That's all they care about. Even if Corey stole a hundred million dollars, it wouldn't be worth recouping."

I feel faint. "Do you think it's possible that Corey stole a hundred million dollars?"

"I don't think so. No, not without anyone noticing. It's got to be much less. Half that, maybe."

Fifty million dollars? If that's the case, where is it?

"Oh, and tell her what you told me," Alyssa says. "That'll reassure her." Alyssa reaches out a steadying hand toward me. "Sean said how these things work is that if a company has a suspicion about an employee, they hire a private investigator to look into it. The investigator basically hacks into the system, and if they find anything, they fire the guy. They might even tell him he needs to resign. What I'm saying is, even if Corey had lived, they would have kept it in-house."

"If he'd been guilty and still alive, he would have gone on to work somewhere else," Sean says. "It wouldn't even have followed him. It's a wild, wild world."

I look back and forth between Alyssa and Sean. "Companies just let a criminal go free so he can do the same thing somewhere else, to someone else?"

"Usually, getting caught once will scare him straight," Sean answers.

I think of how Corey left his previous company. One day he was working there, the next he was telling me that he'd had a talk with his boss, and they'd decided to "part ways." He'd seemed cheerful and told me that better opportunities were just around the corner. In hindsight, his demeanor had been strange, his energy more manic than upbeat.

But as promised, he found a new job within a month. He started just after we'd taken an impromptu trip to Bali.

On that trip, he said, "You know how unhappy I was there.

They were holding me back. Now I can really soar." I hadn't known he was unhappy and said as much. He laughed. "I guess I'm a better actor than I thought!"

Why hadn't I asked more questions when he suddenly lost that job? Or when he suddenly wanted to give up on our having a baby? Why had I let him get away with everything?

I look back and forth between Alyssa and Sean. It seems awfully convenient that Alyssa found this out now. She must know she's been in the doghouse with me since her night with Jade and the subsequent CPS call. Now she gets to be my knight in shining armor, telling me what's really going on, and then she can be my rock while I figure out what this really means.

One thing I'm now sure of: Corey wasn't unhappy at that company until he got caught. And clearly, he wasn't like most people; he hadn't been scared straight. He went and did it again.

At least, I suspect he did. Someone else may very well know for sure.

Time for another unannounced visit.

FORTY-FOUR
JADE

Maren bangs open the front door to the salon. All the stylists and clients stare at this woman on the warpath, who's headed right for me.

"Could we talk, please?" she says. "It's an emergency."

I've never seen her with such wild hair, smudged makeup, or unkempt clothing before (well, her shirt has come untucked). She's breathing hard, like she's just run here.

She moves closer and lowers her voice. I smell bourbon. "Did you know what Corey was up to? That he was embezzling?"

In the mirror, I can see my client widening her eyes.

"I'm really sorry," I tell her. She's a dedicated regular, which means she's unlikely to find a new stylist, but the reference to white-collar crime is also doubly embarrassing. "Excuse me. I'll be back in just a minute."

Maren and I step outside. I don't want to have this conversation in front of my place of business, but I don't have the time to go anywhere when I'm mid-haircut.

"I just found out that Corey was embezzling and it's a good

thing he died when he did because he was about to get caught." It comes out of Maren in a rush. "Did you know about this?"

"Let's keep our voices low, all right? I work here."

"Sorry." She looks a bit chastened. "I just—I'm really shocked. I shouldn't be, since I already knew he was a liar and a cheater. But somehow..." She shakes her head as if to clear it. "Is it true, Jade? Did he really steal fifty million dollars?"

I have to say, this is affirming. Even if Maren and Corey had sex a little differently than I'd been led to believe, I'm still the one who knew what he was really up to. I was the one he could trust. He always knew she'd judge him, just like she's doing right now.

All he was doing was leveling the playing field. He had to steal from dickwad clients because his dickwad bosses were passing him up for the promotions he deserved.

But wait—*fifty million dollars?*

The father of my son stole fifty million dollars, and all I got was this lousy t-shirt?

There's no way. If that had been the case, then he'd have set Tai and me up for sure. "I knew he was siphoning," I say. "But where did you hear that amount?"

"Just... around. I guess everyone's talking about it." She stares at me. "Siphoning? Is that really what he called it?"

I hate how she's always acting like some newborn babe. But I should pretend to agree with her about it being immoral because, you know, technically it is. And technically I'm still in a terrible legal position. So right now, I'll catch more flies—or one particular fly—with honey.

"Yes," I say, "he called it siphoning. You know Corey. He was good at explaining things away. He said it was like being in the Tour de France, how the best have to take performance-enhancing drugs. Because if everyone takes them and you don't, then they're going to win and you're going to lose."

She looks disgusted. "Did Corey actually compare himself to Lance Armstrong?"

I can't defend Corey, can I? Not if I'm being strategic. Not when Maren came here looking for a partner in outrage.

"He did," I say. "I guess he had some delusions of grandeur." Maren looks slightly gratified.

Is this how it's going to be from now on? I'm supposed to cosign Maren's every feeling, the two of us slagging Corey together, forever and ever amen, so that she keeps me on her payroll? I'll be an employee, like Emmanuel.

I'm going to say what I need to say because of Tai, but what I really think? That when the whole world is a rigged game, you have to find creative ways to win. Corey and I both believed that.

"If he stole tens of millions, then how many unsuspecting victims are out there, besides you and me?" she asks.

She's determined to turn me against Corey. To destroy my love story because hers was a lie.

What a vindictive bitch she is.

No matter what I say, Corey, I don't mean it. My loyalty is to you. "I wish I knew," I say.

Maren seems to like that answer, the suggestion that she and I are in this together. That we're both dupes.

"I'm sorry," I tell her. "I wish Corey had been more honest with both of us, and that you didn't have to keep discovering things."

She looks at me as if she's touched. Is she really this gullible? I mean, could it really be this easy? "Thank you, Jade. I just haven't known where I stood with you ever since that talk by the pool. That was really rough, and it seems like you've been avoiding me, just texting back thumbs-up emojis."

"*Rough* is one word for it." I give a rueful smile, even though all I regret is that my ultimatum hasn't worked. Which means I'm stuck with her for at least a while longer.

"Is there anything else coming down the pike?" she says. "Because I really don't think I can take much more."

"I don't know of anything else," I lie. "And I'm glad you came here. I've been working my way up to an apology for the way I spoke to you. I've been under a lot of stress—" because of her—"but that's no excuse."

Her relief is palpable. "You are one hundred percent forgiven! I can't imagine how hard it is to be a single working mother."

No, she really can't.

"I appreciate that," I say. "Tai's looking forward to seeing you soon."

"I can't wait to see him!" She looks like she's about to jump and down with excitement. Which is utterly nauseating. "Are you cutting back your hours?"

It feels like a trick question. On the one hand, I can't imagine she wants me around more because then she'd see Tai less; on the other hand, she's checking up on what I'm doing with that $20K. Micromanaging me. Controlling me.

"Soon," I say. It's another lie. I need to hoard that $20K because I don't know when or if the next deposit will happen, if I'll be able to control myself enough to stay on Maren's good side. I'm not sure how I've even made it through this conversation without screaming or bursting into flames.

Maren's positively giddy, and I feel like punching her.

I hate her face, I really do.

I hate how convinced she is of her own rectitude. I hate how disapproving she is of Corey for stealing, even though she's been the beneficiary of his thievery for their entire relationship.

Has she ever considered how she was living so well?

And has she given even a moment's thought to the fact that the entire financial industry is a scam? The exorbitant commissions, the way they manage to avoid paying their fair share of taxes, all the shmoozing and sweet-talking of clients, touting their genius when, really, they're just doing what the algorithms tell them to do. The whole industry ought to be a crime. Just because something's legal doesn't make it moral.

But Maren has never worried about any of that, has she? She's kept her mind clear and her hands clean.

I hate her. Someday, she's going to know just how much.

FORTY-FIVE

MAREN

"These days, I'm not the biggest fan of surprises," I say, shooting a glance at Emmanuel. He's in the driver's seat, and I'm riding shotgun. He knows where we're going, I don't.

"This will be a good surprise," he says. "Ultimately."

Hmm, that's intriguing. But I have to trust someone, don't I? It's too exhausting otherwise. So I fall silent and let my lids droop. I'm resting my eyes, as my mother used to say.

I haven't told my parents about Jade or Tai. I don't want to worry them when there's nothing they can do from across the country. Also, they raised me with pretty traditional values. They'd been so disappointed when I told them years back that there'd be no kids in my future, but I can't even imagine their faces if I said to them now, "Meet Corey's love child, Tai!" Or if I explained Tai's not *exactly* Corey's son. Or if I added that Corey had been embezzling.

I've been thinking more about the fact that Jade already knew about the embezzling. Knowledge, as they say, is power. And it's always struck me as odd that a man with as much ego as Corey would have been totally fine with raising another man's child.

Maybe it wasn't that Corey stayed because he loved Jade and Tai so much. What if Jade had been blackmailing him? She'd seemed awfully comfortable with that tactic out by the Hamptons pool. That might be because it wasn't her first time.

Let's say Corey stole tens of millions of dollars, like Sean said. Or even if it was a lot less, like $10 million total, Jade could still take a healthy percentage and be set. Corey might have hidden his share in an offshore account and done the same for Jade. She just hasn't started spending it yet because she wants to look poor. That way, I'll feel sorry for her and will donate my inheritance to Tai.

Once I've done that, she can let loose. She can create an extravagant, lavish life for her and Tai, and she'll be able to afford the best lawyers, who can deny me access to Tai. She'll have everything and I'll be left with nothing.

Maybe that's been her endgame all along. She's been talking about how she was never jealous of my relationship with Corey, how she's always wished me well, blah blah, but it sure doesn't look that way. The last time I saw her, she'd acted like she had some kind of change of heart, as if she was ready to see Corey for who he really was. I'd be a fool to take such a sudden conversion at face value.

I didn't sleep well last night. How can I feel safe when I don't know who's going to knock on my door next? It could be creditors or clients that Corey defrauded or his bosses. Maybe it'll be some goons demanding repayment.

That's not even counting the threat posed by Jade.

Obviously, Corey wouldn't care that he left me in the eye of a hurricane. Hell, he and Jade might have planned this together.

Learning that he embezzled in both his jobs confirms that he didn't just turn bad along the way. It wasn't like he saw everyone else doping around him and decided to take a performance-enhancing drug to keep up. No, Corey must have been born bad, out for himself from the very first.

Thankfully, he never got the chance to raise Tai in his image. For Tai, Corey's death was a blessing in disguise.

But was it really an accident?

Corey didn't normally drink massive amounts of Angel's Envy by himself in his office. I was told that if he hadn't choked on his own vomit, he likely would still have died from alcohol poisoning. Yet the police hadn't seen fit to investigate further.

If people were closing in on Corey and they weren't willing to look the other way this time, if he'd been fingered as the criminal that he in fact was, could he have killed himself?

That would be a true nightmare for me because it would invalidate the insurance policy.

Far better would be murder.

Maybe the powers that be at his company threatened him—*stop what you're doing or else, give back the money or else*—and he kept right on going because his ego was just that outsized. He was convinced he could get away with anything in his professional life, just like he did in his personal life.

What if Corey finally flew too close to the sun and got burned?

Someone could have tied him up and forced him to drink a gallon of alcohol. Or they might have tricked him somehow, or dosed him with some sort of poison that the police couldn't detect. I don't know, this isn't my area of expertise. But powerful people know how to get away with murder.

Unless it was someone who felt powerless. What if Jade's the one who wasn't going to let him walk away scot-free?

He could have been thinking of ending things with her once and for all and she snapped. Or it could have been premeditated—an ultimatum or a threat. Had it been: *Marry me, or else? Pay me off, or else?*

She knew about the embezzling, so that could have been her ammunition. But when he wouldn't cave, she resorted to something else.

Or she could have reached the same conclusion I just did, that Tai's better off with no dad than with Corey. Jade tried to get Corey out of their lives, but he wouldn't go, so she got desperate.

How desperate is she feeling now? How far will she go?

My eyes fly open. "I want to tell you something," I say to Emmanuel. "Corey was in trouble, and now I might be, too."

I relay the conversation I had with Sean and Alyssa, watching closely to make sure Emmanuel seems surprised.

He does, which is a relief.

As I continue to ramble, I reveal that Corey was sterile. Again, more surprise from Emmanuel, and some anger, too.

"This is part of why we're taking this trip today," he says. "Because I've become increasingly disillusioned with Corey. He's not the man I thought he was."

"No, he's not. But he might be the man Jade thought he was. They might have been like Bonnie and Clyde." That's what Alyssa had said, though she didn't attempt to back it up in any way. I'm still not sure she's told me everything about the hours she spent with Jade. Whether she's keeping secrets for my protection or for some other reason, it doesn't feel good.

"My gut tells me that Jade is a decent person," he says. "She's made mistakes, but she can be redeemed."

"I really hope you're right. But I don't think I can just wait around and hope."

"What do you mean?"

"I've made my decision." Right now, in fact, while talking to Emmanuel. I can't just sit back and wish for people to be better than they are. Corey was helping to raise Tai, but he wasn't blood. I'm not blood, either, but that shouldn't be disqualifying, especially if I can keep the court from finding out.

There was no paternity testing. If Jade gets up on the stand and claims that Corey wasn't Tai's father, it could easily look like she's lying as a way to weaken my case.

I'm the credible one, not her.

"I'd make a really good mother, don't you think?" I say.

"Absolutely."

I smile. "I think so, too, and Tai deserves that. So I'm going to sue for full custody. Jade can have visitation."

I can tell that Emmanuel is disturbed by the idea, but then, he's traditional, like my parents.

When Jade and I first met, I could tell she was looking down on me for being too stodgy and conventional. Well, that's not my problem anymore.

I'd say she's the one with the problem now.

FORTY-SIX
JADE

Emmanuel had called me just in time. He'd taken the full forty-eight hours, but that's okay, so long as the job gets done.

But as I look up toward the entrance of the café, my stomach corkscrews. He didn't come alone.

He's holding the door open for Maren, who's walking in ahead of him. She sees me and then looks back at him. He says something in her ear, and then she gives a nervous smile in my general direction.

I've got a bad feeling. I don't think Emmanuel did as he was told.

They confer for an extra minute, and then he stands in line at the counter while she walks over to me.

"Good morning!" she says, way too brightly.

"Good morning," I say. I'm fuming. How dare Emmanuel ambush me? He could have at least texted to say she'd be here.

"Where's Tai?"

As if she hasn't committed his schedule to memory. "He's at preschool."

"Are you happy with how much he's learning there?" So

apparently, we're going to engage in small talk until her driver/manservant brings her drink.

"Tai loves it," I say. Then I start to tell amusing little anecdotes. It's all just filler, seeing as I have no desire to engage in big talk with someone as shifty as Maren.

What the hell is Emmanuel up to?

Finally, he comes to the table with two mugs. "Thank you," Maren says, with one of her patented gracious smiles.

Anxiety settles over the table. Emmanuel seems to be feeling it as acutely as Maren and I are. We're both looking at him expectantly.

"What's going on?" I ask when I can't take it another second.

"I'm very troubled by what's been happening between the two of you," he says. "I'm here to broker a truce."

Maren lets out a very fake laugh. "It's not like we're at war!"

"I fear it's coming to that." His expression is grave. "Corey placed you both in an unfortunate situation. Perhaps you're making each other pay because Corey can't."

"You don't know what you're talking about," I say, annoyed. "I want her to pay, literally, because I have a son to support."

"Corey betrayed you both," Emmanuel says. "He betrayed me, too. He made me an accomplice."

Wait, is he intending to confess to Maren with me here in order to take away my leverage?

"Corey could be very persuasive." There are tears in Emmanuel's eyes. "He was my dear friend, and I loved him. But I shouldn't have covered for him." He looks at Maren. "I'm very sorry, Maren. I should never have kept this secret."

"What secret?" she asks.

Emmanuel makes her wait for it because now he's looking over at me. "Corey betrayed you as well, Jade."

So he's not going to confess. He's here for something else.

"Corey wasn't who any of us thought he was," Emmanuel continues. "He was the man of many faces. Sleeping with multiple women, for the entire time I knew him."

I glance at Maren, who looks unmoved. She doesn't care anymore about Corey's affairs. But I still do. I still love him.

"He was with quite a few women for one night only. But there was one other full-blown affair that lasted months. It was with Alyssa."

Now Maren has a reaction. "Alyssa, as in, *my* Alyssa?"

"Yes." He nods. "As in, Sean's Alyssa."

"So Corey betrayed me and he betrayed Sean," Maren says slowly. "And Alyssa betrayed me, too."

"Yes," Emmanuel confirms.

But more importantly, Corey betrayed me! If this is true. *Is this true, Corey?*

Answer me, you prick!

Give me a sign! If yes, knock something on the floor.

Nothing falls. But I know that doesn't mean anything. Nothing I had with Corey meant anything.

He was lying to me the whole time, when he didn't even have to. I already knew about Maren, I could have handled the idea of a bunch of anonymous hookups. Or maybe even that horrid Alyssa.

Corey lied because he was a liar who had no respect for anyone, least of all his mistress. That's what Maren's been trying to tell me, but I've refused to listen. I'm flooded with hot shame.

"I don't want the two of you to be at each other's throats anymore," Emmanuel says. "You've been through enough because of Corey. You both deserve peace."

"I've never wanted to be at your throat," Maren says to me.

"Then what about CPS?" I can see by her instant reaction that she was in on it. She knew. She either incited or enabled.

"What do you mean?" she asks, but it's a terrible acting job.

I shake my head. I'm not even going to dignify that. Besides, I've got other problems right now. I'm dealing with true heartbreak. The worst pain since I found out months ago that Corey had died. Now it's like he's dying all over again. The man I thought I knew, the man I loved, never existed.

I'm as stupid as Maren.

"It's time to let go of all the personal animosity," Emmanuel says. "You need to reach an amicable agreement about Tai."

If he's talking about a financial agreement, then I'm all ears.

"I'd love that," Maren says. "I truly would. But I'm afraid lawyers are going to need to be involved, and they're not known for keeping things amicable."

She's *afraid* they need to be involved?

Bullshit. She wants them involved, because then she knows she'll win. She has the money to hire the best, and they'll paint me as a gold-digging whore. I'll get offered some lowball settlement, probably what she spends on shoes in a year.

THIS WASN'T THE PLAN! I told Emmanuel the plan! But he thought he was smarter and turned the tables and now look at her, shyster that she is.

"Do you see what she's doing?" I ask Emmanuel. "How she's playing innocent? She was behind the CPS visit! She manipulates everyone!"

"You're the one who went to Alyssa behind my back," Maren says. "Why do you care who Corey was with anyway? You were both sleeping with other people."

"I was not."

She does a dismissive head shake. "Please. Stop insulting my intelligence."

"I was completely faithful to Corey." But I can see she doesn't believe me. I look to Emmanuel, as if he might defend my honor.

"Maren's just upset," Emmanuel tells me. "She only wants what's best for everyone."

At that, I explode. "She does not! She wants what's best for her!" Then I hiss at Emmanuel, "This was not the plan."

He was supposed to persuade Maren! To tell her in no uncertain terms to stop trying to steal another woman's child and go adopt her own! But this is what he does instead? How much Kool-Aid can one man drink?

"I'm hoping this conversation can be a fresh start," he says. "A new beginning. Then there won't be any need for a custody case—"

"Wait, what?" I look from Emmanuel to Maren. "You're going to sue for custody of Tai?"

"I am his aunt, and some of your behavior has been a little, I don't know, erratic."

That's not a denial. She hasn't said, *No, of course I'm not, because suing for custody of another woman's son—of the son that her dead husband had out of wedlock—is completely insane.*

"Did your lawyer tell you to get a CPS report filed?" I say.

"No, that was—" Then she clams up, realizing what she's just admitted.

"You think I'm unfit? Well, you know who's unfit? You're a total lunatic!" Then I turn on Emmanuel. "You might be even worse because you know this is wrong and you're not doing anything about it."

"I came here to do something about it. That's why I'm telling you both the truth about Corey."

"Why don't you tell the whole truth, Emmanuel?" I say. "Tell her that you knew about Tai and me while Corey was still alive. That you knew about us the entire time. Where was your conscience then? Where was your loyalty to Maren then?"

I've dropped my bomb, but I don't even wait to see the mushroom cloud. Hopefully they're both incinerated.

I stumble out onto the pavement, stricken. Not about Alyssa

or the other women, though I'm sure that'll come later. The more immediate pain, the sheer terror, centers on Tai. Because the worst-case scenario has been confirmed. Not only am I not getting Tai's inheritance, but she's suing for custody.

It's official: Maren's coming for my son. We are definitely at war.

FORTY-SEVEN
MAREN

I can't even look at Emmanuel.

I haven't felt pain like this since I found out about Jade and Corey. Now I know about Jade and Emmanuel.

I thought Emmanuel truly cared for me. That he even loved me a little, but in my life, that might just be the prerequisite for betrayal.

Emmanuel and Corey. Jade and Emmanuel. Corey and Alyssa.

Not one person in my life can be trusted.

"Please, say something." Emmanuel's voice sounds like it's from some faraway realm. "Tell me what you really think of me now. I deserve every insult."

Only he doesn't deserve my words.

"I'm so sorry, Maren," he says. "Jade insisted we meet two days ago. She wanted me to 'talk sense into you,' as she put it, or she was going to tell you that I'd known about her and Corey all along. I could see that she was coming unhinged, and I actually felt for her. So I decided that this was the better course. But I know that best of all would have been going to you years ago and telling you the truth. Back then, I still thought Corey was a good man doing bad things. Now I know—"

"You acted like you didn't know about the embezzling. Was that a lie, too? Were you covering for him?" He shakes his head. "I bet he told you he was a good man stealing from bad men. He's Robin Hood. He's Lance Armstrong."

"I swear on my girls, I didn't know." Emmanuel looks ravaged.

"I can't believe you. I can't believe a thing you say."

"Believe this: What's going on between you and Jade is toxic. It could destroy you both, and Tai, too. Write her a sizable check so she'll go away and you can move on. Adopt a child. Be a mother. Live your dream. That's all I want for you. Love and happiness."

I glare at him. "Oh, really? She gets to have Tai all to herself, plus my money? I bet she already has plenty of her own, hidden away. There's probably an offshore account with her name on it full of siphoned cash. She's been living in squalor to fake me out."

"Why would anyone do that? Why would she put herself and Tai through all of this if she already had money?"

"Why would she sleep with someone else's husband for six years instead of finding her own? Because she's always working an angle. Because she always wants more. Because millions aren't enough for her to feel worth anything. Or because she's just plain hateful. How's that for a reason?"

People are staring at me, and I don't give a shit.

"She hates that Corey loved me and never offered to leave me, not even after she tried to trap him with a baby."

"I know you're hurting, Maren, but—"

"I can't begin to understand the mind of someone as conniving and horrible as Jade. Or someone as disgusting as you."

His face falls. "You're not yourself—"

"How could you know all that about Corey and still love him, Emmanuel? How could you have been so faithful to a monster?"

"I don't know, Maren." Emmanuel's voice comes out low. Small. "I'm very ashamed. I got caught up in his stories because he looked so sincere. So earnest. Even tormented, as if he wanted to be a better man than he was able to be. I felt for him."

"Same as you felt for Jade? Well, didn't you feel for me, being saddled with a man like that? By keeping his secrets, you took away my ability to make choices." I'm too angry to even cry. "I could have divorced him! I could have a family of my own by now!"

"I'm very sorry, Maren."

"He ruined my life," I say.

"No, your life is still going on. You're young and beautiful and—"

"I'm ruined! How could I trust anyone after what he did to me? After what you did to me, too?" I stare at Emmanuel while he struggles to meet my eyes. "Someone killed Corey, and honestly? I wish it had been me."

Emmanuel looks up, alarmed. "No, Maren. The police ruled it an accident."

"You think the police never make mistakes? That they can't be bought off?" His naïveté is stunning.

"You're not thinking straight. You're all turned around."

"For all I know, Jade did it," I say. "For all I know, you did."

Corey, Jade, Alyssa, Emmanuel. What a crew. What a life I've built for myself.

Anything I have to do now will be entirely justified. It's self-defense.

"Obviously I never want to see you again," I say. I don't even feel anger; I'm numb. "You're fired, effective immediately."

He nods miserably, getting to his feet. "I understand, Maren. Please know that I could not be sorrier."

I don't know how I'll ever be able to trust my judgment again. I can't spot a bad man when he's right in front of me. Or a bad woman.

Jade's been playing me from the start, pretending she was meeting Emmanuel for the first time. She was hoarding this information so that she could blackmail Emmanuel, and when that didn't work, she sprang it on me as cruelly as she possibly could.

A person that vile shouldn't even get to be a mother. At this point, I'm not sure I even want her to have visitation rights.

I *will* be a great mother, and nothing—and no one—is going to stand in my way.

FORTY-EIGHT
JADE

I walk blocks in a stupor. Then I sit down at a bus stop, shivering though it's not cold.

Maren really is going to try to take Tai, through the courts. That's how people like her do it because they know that the law will always be on their side. It's made for well-coiffed, prosperous women like her.

Her lawyer will look into my past and spin everything I've ever done. Have I made mistakes? Of course. Am I perfect? Of course not. But I'm a good mother.

I love my son, and I show him that all the time. I've never put my hands on him in anger. I never would. But I do yell sometimes, like many parents do, and on rare occasions I've sent him to his room without dinner, and on even rarer occasions I've refused to tuck him in because I'm mad. I've also failed to tuck him in when I couldn't hold it together any longer, when I needed to cry alone in my room from stress and heartbreak. I don't want him to see me like that because a child shouldn't have to comfort his parents. This past year, I've had moments of nearly debilitating sadness, but I've always picked myself back up to meet my responsibilities, to take care of the boy who I love more than life itself.

Yet I have no doubt that Maren and her lawyer will manage to present me to the court as unfit. Who knows what was written up in that CPS report? What witnesses could she find if money (and honesty) is no object? What stories will her lawyer tell?

Even my potential lawyer, Yvette, thought I was unsympathetic. I'm pretty sure she'd say the opposite about Maren.

Maren's probably been plotting this since the beginning, and all this time, she's been taking notes of my supposed wrongdoings. I gave her a front-row seat to my relationship with Tai during the Southampton trip, and I'm sure it didn't look stellar. But that wasn't because of him or because of me; it was Maren. She distorts everything. And she'll continue to do so in order to achieve her sick ends.

She wants my son all to herself.

How do I get us out of this? How do I keep him safe? How do I keep him, full stop?

She's a control freak with a god complex. She'd do incalculable damage if she were to get custody.

That'll never happen, though. Rich people can't just steal poor people's kids, can they? I'm Tai's flesh and blood; the court will ultimately have to side with me.

But Maren has the money to drag it out and to drag me through the mud. The $20K she gave me might cover the retainer, though I bet that'll go fast. Then what? My mother's retirement savings? And what if I use all that up and still lose my son? What'll happen to Mom then? Or to me? Or to Tai?

I can't go up against Maren in court. That would be a disaster.

I have to think what to do, how much time I have. If TV is to be believed, the courts are backlogged and slow. Fortunately,

I haven't even been served with papers yet. There might be a way to delay, some sort of stalling tactic. Should I call Yvette and admit I haven't taken any of her advice? That instead, I tried to turn Alyssa against Maren and it backfired, ending in a CPS visit, and then I tried to blackmail Emmanuel, and then…?

No, I can't contact Yvette. If this ever gets to court, I'm fucked.

I've been fucked ever since I chose Corey to be the father of my child. Or rather, he chose me.

Corey, how could you?

Tears flow down my face, dripping from my bowed head onto my clasped hands. I can't deny the depth of the betrayal anymore. No more pretending Corey was a good man in a morally ambiguous world.

Corey didn't care what happened to me or to Tai. He treated Maren like a pretty, pretty princess all those years, leaving her everything without opening so much as a savings account for my son. Not our son—*my* son. And now it's turned out that he cheated on me with Alyssa, and countless others.

Alyssa, of all people?

I was clearly open to polyamory. So why not tell me the truth so we could have worked it out as consenting adults? Why conceal it when the heart of our relationship was brutal honesty?

Because he got off on deception, on lying to both Maren and to me. Double the pleasure, double the fun.

I was supposed to be his safe haven! The woman who could accept all of him!

This calls into question everything I thought I knew about him and about our love. Was it even love, for him?

I'm as much of a cuck as Maren. It turns out we've always been in the same boat when I treasured feeling different. Maybe Corey figured that out. It was my Achilles' heel, and he exploited it. I fell for every one of his lines.

Through the haze of shame and humiliation, I think about what Maren said in that café. No, not just what she said but how she said it: her absolute certainty that I'd been sleeping around.

Why would she think that?

I take deep breaths, forcing myself to think slowly and methodically. I have to retrace my steps, to consider anything that's out of place or out of the ordinary. Anything Corey did that was unusual, even if it hadn't struck me that way at the time or if I hadn't dwelled on it because I was so used to suspending belief and giving him the benefit of the doubt. He'd conditioned me to accept any explanation or excuse he gave as some sort of gospel.

Maren wasn't the only member of the cult of Corey, was she? Turns out I'd been the fucking president.

I choke on bus exhaust as I review my love story. When I get to the circumstances around Tai's conception, my blood runs cold.

Could it be? Is it even possible?

I look at the transit map inside the bus shelter and realize that I'm not far from where it all began, in a matter of speaking. From where Tai began.

I bolt for the subway. In less than thirty minutes, I'm pulling open the door to the fancy fertility clinic Corey had insisted upon and asking the receptionist to see my medical records. Hands shaking, almost hyperventilating, I sit in the waiting room and pore over the chart, which confirms the terrible truth.

At the time, I'd assumed that Corey was worrying way too much since he and Maren had had so much trouble. I told him that I was much younger than Maren, that my eggs were fresh and would make excellent omelets. He didn't smile. I teased him about that phrase he was using, "an abundance of caution," and how Maren-esque it sounded. He didn't laugh. Instead, it had turned into an argument.

I'd wanted to get pregnant the old-fashioned way, saying it would be more romantic, and besides, we were in no rush. He felt differently, saying he couldn't wait to be a dad. I eventually agreed to be inseminated at the clinic where he was buddies with the head doc. Corey invested the guy's money and they played golf together.

"If it's that important to you, then all right," I said. I decided to be flattered that he was so desperate to be the father to my baby. It seemed like a vindication and a confirmation. See, I really was superior to Maren! See, he really did love me way more!

I blindly trusted Corey and, by extension, the doctor. But now I see from these notes that I shouldn't have.

My chart doesn't start from the day I first met the doctor. It started when Corey went in and revealed that he'd be unable to impregnate me due to a medical condition. They discussed how to select and procure donor sperm. Corey told the doctor that he would relay this conversation to me and that he and I would choose the donor together.

Needless to say, that never happened. I was inseminated in the clinic. With another man's sperm. Without my consent.

My suspicion? That Corey and his buddy were winking behind my back, if not outright laughing. What a woman doesn't know won't hurt her, right?

I never met with the doctor alone; Corey was there for my two visits. The doctor addressed nearly everything to him, I realize now, though, at the time, it had seemed normal. They were buds, after all, and Corey had assured me that the doctor was at the top of his field. "Only the best for my baby," Corey said.

But he knew it wasn't his baby.

This is betrayal on a colossal scale. We're talking about my womb. My child. Only I don't even know who Tai's real father is.

I put my file under my arm and walk out. *How could you, Corey?*

I wanted a baby with you more than anything, I can almost hear him saying. *That's why I went to such extreme lengths. I didn't do it for Maren, did I? She would have been more than happy to use donor sperm. But I wanted you, Jade. That's how much I love you.*

You didn't respect me, though. If you did, you never would have done this to me.

What he loved and respected was his freedom. And his control. Our arrangement made it so that he could participate as little or as much as suited him.

I wasn't as stupid as Maren. I was stupider.

Did she know about Corey's sterility all along? If that's the case, then she knew from the second I showed up that Tai wasn't really Corey's child. Yet she cultivated that relationship anyway. Because this whole time, she's been scheming to make Tai hers.

Maybe Corey and Maren were a perfect match all along. A couple of conniving liars.

Corey had painted a picture of Maren as the feminine ideal: kind and generous and, above all, loving. Maybe he'd always been lying to me, thinking it was some kind of lark. If he knew all along what Maren was, then that explains why he never wanted to have a child with her. But she'd been great at keeping up appearances and serving his ambitions.

Corey had been my enemy all along. That's what Emmanuel was just trying to tell me.

But then, Emmanuel's a coward who was also trying to get himself out of hot water. He said himself that he was Corey's accomplice, his partner in crime. For all I know, Emmanuel was being rewarded for his loyalty with some of that embezzled money because I never saw any of it.

Corey's dead, so I can't make him pay. The doctor has covered his ass with those notes, so I can't make him pay, either.

But I can still get to Maren. It's not too late.

She's trying to take my son. So there is no greater enemy.

FORTY-NINE
MAREN

I fire off a series of rage texts to Alyssa:

Everything you said about Jade is doubly true about you. You're the liar. You're the con woman. You're the danger.

How do you sleep at night?

I know what you did.

I KNOW WHAT YOU DID.

I want to tell her she's not going to get away with it, but then, she already has. I don't believe in justice anymore.
Still, there's no harm in an empty threat, is there?
You won't get away with this, I add, for good measure. *I'll make sure you pay.*
My phone starts ringing. It's her, of course. She's been gaslighting me for months, and it stops now. I hit ignore and then block her.

I want them all to pay. Alyssa, Jade, and Emmanuel. Sure, Emmanuel lost his job, and he'll have to explain that to Zauna. Or will he just lie? It turns out he's excellent at that.

Well, I'm about to tell her what kind of man she married.

I haven't seen Zauna in a few months, and it's not like I expect a warm reception when I show up at her school. But the utter ferocity and hatred in her expression still throws me off balance. The contrast between that and her brightly colored outfit and the beads in her cornrows is striking.

"Outside," she commands, and I do as I'm told, following her from the principal's office down the corridor. She pushes open the front doors and now we're on the concrete basketball court. It's deserted and feels disturbingly like we're facing off in a prison yard.

"I called and asked what time your lunch break was," I say. "I didn't want to pull you out of class—"

"Save it, Maren." She crosses her arms over her chest and glares at me. She's so angry, though I'm only here as a courtesy.

"A wife deserves to know who her husband really is. If someone had done that for me years ago, I—"

Her laugh is brisk and hostile. "I already know everything."

"You knew about all Corey's affairs? And about Jade and Tai?" I'm taken aback. I'd always thought of Zauna as a feminist. Her daughters certainly are.

"Of course. Emmanuel tells me everything. Do you truly think infidelity is the worst thing that can happen to a woman?" Her expression is derisive. "There are more important things than where Corey put his dick, Maren. I have children, and now their father has no job. Emmanuel won't even ask you for severance because he's too ashamed."

"He should be ashamed."

"No!" she flares. "You should be ashamed! Take responsibility for your own life. You didn't know your husband. You didn't understand the bargain you'd struck. That's not Emmanuel's or anyone else's fault."

"I couldn't know what I didn't know!" I raise my voice.

"Shush. There are children learning here. You came to my place of work, and you will respect it."

I lower my voice, but I'm choking with anger. "I can't believe you're blaming the victim."

"You're not the victim! You're a multimillionaire who has nothing but options and time on her hands, with no compassion for others."

"Others meaning Emmanuel?" Now I'm the one being derisive.

"Emmanuel, for starters. Did it ever occur to you what a difficult position Corey placed him in, that Emmanuel was in a vise both because Corey was his employer and his friend? I bet that if Emmanuel had gone out on a limb and told you about Corey's affairs, he would have been punished for it. You would have gone to Corey, Corey would have lied or explained it all away, and you would have realized just how much you had to lose if you acted with integrity. So you would have stayed, and Emmanuel would have been fired for being disloyal to his employer."

"No. I would have left."

"You say that now, but you didn't leave Corey five years ago, did you? Not even when it cost you the chance to have the child you so desperately wanted. You chose money and privilege instead."

I'm speechless.

"You might not have liked every choice you made, but you did make them, Maren. You have no one to blame but yourself."

"People were lying to me!"

"Oh, grow up, Maren. There are worse offenses than that. But if you want to talk about lies, about pretending, let's talk about how you and Corey treated my husband. Emmanuel is a true friend, through and through. He was always defending you and Corey, always supporting you. But I knew that when push came to shove, neither of you would have a shred of loyalty to him. And you proved me right by firing him just like that." She snaps her fingers.

"He betrayed me." My voice is quavering.

"Are you incapable of listening? Incapable of seeing others' perspectives and struggles? Corey had my husband in a vise! I hated when we had to host you for dinner, the way you went on and on about how amazing my girls are. And those huge gifts to their college funds—that was all for show, too."

"That's not true! I do think your girls are amazing, and I do want to help them with college. I want them to succeed."

"But now I assume all the gifts will stop, right? Now that Emmanuel has displeased you, my girls can go to hell."

"It's not like that!" But what is it like? I don't even know anymore. I'm just so turned around, and so alone.

"You kept dangling the idea of educational trusts in front of Emmanuel until Tai showed up and suddenly you were too busy to visit the attorney. Now those trusts are out of the question, aren't they?"

"I haven't thought that far."

Another laugh. "Of course you haven't. As soon as Lady Maren gets hurt, she doesn't have to consider anyone or anything. No, wait, it's Aunt Maren, isn't it?"

"I can't believe you're mocking me after all Corey put me through. And Emmanuel just let it happen. He never even—"

"You have no clue what Emmanuel did or didn't do. Your husband was a horrifically selfish man. A criminally selfish man. And you're not much better. You've been preying on Emmanuel's sympathies for months, treating him like a surrogate husband. I know you tried to seduce him—"

"No, that never happened."

She barrels forward, right over me. "He came home that day extremely upset, saying that the two of you had almost kissed, and he's been looking for a new job ever since. But they're not easy to come by, and now I assume you intend to give him a terrible reference. Do you even care what this will mean for my family? For my amazing girls?"

"I do care, and I never tried to seduce Emmanuel. You have it all wrong."

"Emmanuel has been more loyal to you than you could ever know. He's been defending you ever since Jade came into your life despite how reprehensible your behavior has been."

"Reprehensible?" I stare at her in shock.

"How dare you try to come between a mother and a son? How dare you take Tai out on grand excursions, showing up his mother? You've been trying to buy that boy's love since the first, and at whose expense? The mother's, of course!"

And how dare *she* take Jade's side? She doesn't even know Jade.

Unless she does. Emmanuel did.

"Have you met Jade?" I ask ominously.

"No. But I've heard all about her. For years." Zauna enjoys that last remark, reminding me that everyone knew what I didn't. They all kept it from me, and she's not remotely sorry. "I understand that Jade is an excellent mother."

I shake my head. I can't believe this.

"Don't shake your head at me, Maren. I'm not your employee. Unlike my husband, I'm at liberty to tell you exactly what I think. You should have created trusts for my kids months ago when you promised, and you should have created a trust for Tai when you first found out about him. Then you should have gotten the hell out of the way."

"I love him!"

"If you love him, then help his mother provide for him. Stop trying to control everyone with your money."

"I'm not like that."

"Of course you are! People show themselves through their actions. You say you care for my daughters? Then give Emmanuel a generous severance and a favorable reference. You say you love Tai? Then draw up his trust."

"It's a lot more complicated than that." I can't trust Jade as far as I can throw her. How responsible would it be to hand Jade a million dollars with no oversight? What'll happen to Tai once his mother blows through it all?

How lovely it must be for Zauna to sit on her high horse and simplify. To make me the villain in this story.

"Tai is entitled to his father's money," she says. "Period."

"Except that Corey isn't Tai's father!" I nearly shout. "Corey couldn't be anyone's father! He was fucking sterile!"

I can tell by her face that she hadn't known that. So Emmanuel didn't tell her everything after all. He keeps some things confidential. Despite everything, he does still have some loyalty to me.

I feel a twinge. Not of regret exactly but of longing. It's like I'm losing everyone I've ever cared about.

But I can't lose Tai. I will not.

Zauna and I are staring each other down, and as it occurs to me what I've done, the terror sets in. I'm intending to tell the court that Corey is Tai's father. I can't let Zauna throw a wrench in that plan.

If this gets out, then it would undermine my legal claim to Tai. I wouldn't be Aunt Maren anymore, but a virtual stranger trying to steal Jade's son.

It's not like that, obviously, but people see what they want to see. I know that better than anyone.

I step closer to Zauna, lowering my voice. "If you tell anyone about Corey's medical situation, I'll make sure Emmanuel never works again."

"This might surprise you, but New York is a very large city. You don't know everyone—"

"Try me." Adrenaline is coursing through me, and I might not know who I am anymore, but I know what I have to do. "If this information gets out, I will destroy you. Mess with my family, and I'll mess with yours."

FIFTY

JADE

The texts come from Emmanuel's phone, and the leadoff is, *This is Zauna, Emmanuel's wife. You should know, Maren is out of her mind.*

Zauna says that in a custody battle, she'd be happy to serve as a character witness, or rather, a witness attesting to Maren's lack of character.

It's a great offer, but I can't let this get to court. Somehow, Maren would find a way to manipulate the situation and the system, to make herself look like the victim. From what I can tell, that might be her only true skill in life, but it is a potent one.

Zauna agrees. She confirms in her text what I've come to know: that Maren is, in her way, as sociopathic as Corey turned out to be.

I can't rely on the law to fix this problem. I've been wracking my brain, and there really seems to be only one solution.

Maren needs to have a little accident, just like Corey did.

FIFTY-ONE
MAREN

There is to be no contact between you and Tai, effective immediately. You have no legal rights. I am his mother.

We'll just have to change that then, won't we?

Jade's text came in yesterday; I showed it to my shark attorney today. She made time in her schedule for me yet again. That bodes well. She likes me already, and so will the judge.

In light of the recent escalation between Jade and me, my shark said the case is more complicated now, which I took to mean more expensive, and I assured her that money is no object. I'll spend whatever I have to in order to destroy Jade and protect Tai.

I still can't believe what Zauna said to me, that she was so thoroughly on Jade's side. What must Emmanuel have told her about me, and about Jade? And what was that insanity about me trying to seduce him? It had been a mutually fraught moment. A mistake that we quickly rectified.

Zauna's just jealous and threatened by Emmanuel's feelings for me. She should be tending to her own backyard, keeping her own side of the street clean, or however the saying goes.

I will not be gaslit anymore. I know my truth.

Now I just need to prove it, in court.

I get a special delivery from the private investigator/hacker extraordinaire who came highly recommended by Alyssa and Sean. I can't help being a little frosty toward him. Wary. Can he really be trusted, given the referral source?

As he gives me a tour of Corey's laptop, I relax. He seems like a total professional. He was able to crack a number of Corey's passwords, which means that I now have the ability to explore at my leisure.

He'd been able to get into Corey's internet history—even what Corey thought he'd erased—and has a site list for me. He shows me the accounts for banking, investment, and crypto.

I recognize them all, can access them all. That means I still don't know where the missing money is.

My suspicion? That Jade has it.

Could she use it to fund her custody battle? Is it possible that this won't be as easy as I've been imagining because she can afford a shark of her own?

I thank my hacker and say I may very well be in touch soon. I'll consult with my attorney, see if she thinks it's time for me to commission a full dossier on Jade.

Once he leaves, I'm left alone with my panicked thoughts. And Corey's laptop.

I'm sure there will be more dirt on Corey. The man was truly filthy. After learning about Alyssa and the others, I went and had a battery of STD testing done. On that front, at least, I'm all right. Emotionally, though—that's another story. I feel like I've been hit by a truck and then run over a few more times by everyone else I know. But I'm getting back up because of Tai. He needs me.

It's Wednesday, and I miss him so badly. Soon, though, every day will be ours.

But first...

Going through Corey's laptop is a daunting proposition. I have to steel myself since there's so much that I just don't want to know anymore. No more revelations, please. About Corey, that is. But I have to find out all I can about Jade.

In my dream scenario, I discover something that will deliver the knockout blow, and we'll be able to wrap this up quickly, without even going to court. That's best for Tai and for me.

I go through everything, program by program, app by app. Nothing seems out of the ordinary, except for a single Word document named "Manifesto." Could this really have been written by Corey? I never knew him to journal, but then, I never knew him to do a lot of things. I never knew him, period.

If you're reading this, you shouldn't be. Eyes on your own paper.

I know at least a few people have been watching me for a while. You know who you are. If you've managed to find this, congratulations. You win.

All the rumors are true. I'm weak and selfish and cowardly. I've done so many things—good and bad—just to hide those facts. But I can't do it anymore.

I don't know how to be a man, and I'm not equipped to raise one. Tai's going to be better off without me.

It's stunning to learn that before Corey died, he'd actually reached the same conclusion that I have. But is he saying what I think he is? Is this a suicide note?

I didn't know narcissistic sociopaths killed themselves. I thought they just brought down everyone around them and had a great time doing it.

My whole life, I've felt antsy, like I had something to prove, and I never could, no matter how much money I earned or how much I siphoned. But now I'm almost at peace. What a ride it's been, and I'm ready to get off.

For the last few months, Sean and Alyssa have made it clear that they're going to get me, one way or another. They've developed a shared bloodlust that passes for passion. This is the most in love they've ever been. And they're determined. They want me dead.

When I look over my shoulder, one or the other of them is often there. They hate me like I've never been hated before, except by myself.

I can't blame anyone else. This is my fault. I should never have been sleeping with Alyssa. I don't even like her, never did, and every time, I had to be shitfaced just to go through with it. One time I got so drunk that I told her about the embezzlement. It came out during pillow talk, which was weird because she and I never had pillow talk. We had quick frenzied sex in a closet or somewhere while Sean and Maren were in the other room.

It was disgusting. It made me feel disgusting. But after the first time, Alyssa assumed we'd just keep going and crazy as this sounds, I didn't want to disappoint her.

I felt bad, doing that to Maren, but I also felt stuck. And it only got worse, what with my loose lips. Alyssa and Jade were the only people who knew I embezzled from my previous company, that it was how I afforded a driver, the apartment, the Hamptons house, and Maren's spending. How I can afford to keep up appearances. The money's in offshore accounts, and I've used it gradually over the years. It couldn't look like a sudden windfall since that might attract suspicion, especially Maren's.

Not that Maren's ever been suspicious. I could have told her anything and she would have believed me. That's a big source of guilt. But sometimes? It's a source of frustration, too.

Some part of me has always wanted to get caught. I'm dying for accountability.

Is that why I told Alyssa, because she couldn't remotely be trusted? Because I knew everything was likely to come crashing down? I don't know, I'm not a psychiatrist.

Even when I got caught at my last company, it turned out to be no big deal. I got let go suddenly, but it didn't cost me a thing. I just walked away and found a new job.

But I did learn my lesson. I decided to be honest going forward, and I was. At work, that is. Everywhere else, that's a different story.

So Corey hadn't been embezzling when he died? Was that just a rumor that Sean and Alyssa spread?

Maren and Jade deserve infinitely better. But I don't have the decency to let either of them go. I keep us all trapped.

It's coming to an end, though. I have this feeling like my days are numbered.

I still don't know why Alyssa tapped me for an affair. Maybe it was to get back at Sean for something, or because she's always been jealous of Maren. Now she knows she doesn't have any reason to be since I'm garbage. I'm Maren's Asshole. Jade's, too.

I couldn't end it with Alyssa because of how vindictive she is. I didn't think she'd tell Maren since that would mean outing herself, too, but if I crossed her, she'd find some way to punish me, I was sure of that.

Then one day, out of the blue, she says it's over, and I'm relieved. Only the next day, Sean comes looking for me. He says that Alyssa confessed, her conscience was getting to her. He says, "She was just trying to get my attention however she could." He took it as a wake-up call and realized just how much he loves her. "But you didn't love her," he says, "you were just using her."

I tried to tell him it wasn't like that, though I couldn't really explain what it was like. That I hadn't been attracted to her, but she seemed so determined? That I was scared of her? That I didn't want to hurt her feelings? That I gave in because it was easier than resisting, and I always wind up taking the easier path? That I'd been glad when it ended?

Sean didn't believe any of it. He thought I was either in love with Alyssa or out to get him or both, and he held me responsible for everything. He was GOING TO hold me responsible, that's what he said.

The affair's revitalized their shitty marriage, and Sean's convinced that's the whole reason Alyssa did it, like she's some genius mastermind. They finally have something in common. They both think I'm the devil, and they want me to be punished. They've said it outright.

Sean's framing me for embezzlement. My guess is that the company's going to hack my computer, unless they already have. I wouldn't put anything past Sean and Alyssa. They could have planted "evidence," seeing as they always know a guy. It feels like I'm on borrowed time.

Sean can't stop, not when he's being egged on by Alyssa. Not when he feels like his whole marriage and family hinges on vengeance. He's defending her honor; he's saving his family. He's finally feeling like a real man.

Makes me wonder how many lives have been ruined in the pursuit of real manhood.

I've never heard Sean talk like this before. He sounds like he's had a religious conversion, like a fucking zealot.

I'm tired of looking over my shoulder. I'm tired of trying to outrun my crimes. Sure, I didn't embezzle this time, but I did it before. I cheated on Maren with Jade, cheated on both of them with Alyssa, cheated on everyone with the nameless hordes.

You live by the sword, you die by the sword. I played with fire and now I'm gonna get burned. I'm every cliché.

I don't want to be around when Maren finds out everything. I don't want to see the look on her face. I don't want to know how badly I broke her heart.

Someday, I would've had to see Jade's heart broken, too, and Tai's.

You'd think it would be fun, loving and being loved by two incredible women, and in moments, it was. But it's also a prison. You've got these two silos, and you've got to cover your tracks.

Better to have no lives than two.

The problem is, no one knows the real Corey. With Maren, I performed lightness; with Jade, I performed darkness. At work, I was whatever was needed in a given situation.

I love only Maren and Jade, but I have to be attractive to other women, too. Pursuit and conquest, that's what I've always done. Rinse and repeat.

When I found out Jade was having a boy, I was pretty down. I couldn't show her that, though. So... more pretending.

In my life, in my work, you can't act like a girl. People will think you're weak. Women might pretend they like a sensitive man but it's not true. In finance, you can't be truly close because everyone's your competition. You need to be always winning, amassing greater trophies and promotions and money. Always ascending to greater heights. Get the power, and then the real struggle begins, because you've got to keep it.

Jade and Maren might say they love me for me, but they want me on the rise, too. Sometimes it's like there's an invisible wall between us. Behind that wall are all the things I can never show them, all the things that would make them recoil.

I always thought love would be the antidote to loneliness, but it's not.

I always wanted to be a father, and that's what I told Maren right from the beginning. It's a big part of why I was drawn to her. I knew she'd be a great mom. But as the years went by, I was a lot less sure how I'd be as a father.

I started to think that I wouldn't really be up for full-time fatherhood. I wasn't even man enough to impregnate a woman, which is one of the great shames of my life. Too great for me to ever tell Maren or Jade. They'd never see me the same way. I'd be forever weak in their eyes, and that would have been the beginning of the end. Even if I didn't lose them, I'd lose their respect, which might be worse.

If I'd had a baby with Maren, I would have had to show up

all the time, every day, as a father. The stakes would have been too high.

But Jade was already used to part-time from me, and she likes it that way. She wants me coming and going rather than staying. It's who she is.

She'd been low maintenance and low pressure through our entire relationship. She's got a rough exterior, but she's a loving person. I knew she'd be the kind of mother who could deal with anything life threw at her. Hopefully, I'm right about that.

I tried to be the best father I could for Tai. I read through all the donor bios and picked someone as different from me as could be, someone gentle and sensitive. An artist.

Back then, I was feeling hopeful. Becoming a parent was a second chance, a lifeline.

What kind of father would I be? I didn't know, but I'd get to figure it out, without commitment. I could be a father on my terms. If it turned out it wasn't for me, I could bail out, and Jade was still young and beautiful. She'd find someone who could take over as Tai's stepfather. Or if she didn't want that, then she'd make up the difference herself.

I'm a small-doses dad. That's all I've got in my tank. And lately, I'm running on empty.

I fooled myself for a long time, told myself I was bigger and better than other people, that I couldn't be contained. I had two homes, two full lives, when other men couldn't even manage one.

Two homes, and I belonged nowhere. Part this and part that equals 100 percent fraud.

I hate myself, I hate my life. I'm angry at Jade and Maren because they can't see through me. Because they're too good for me, and they don't even know it.

I love my son, but I'm no role model. I can't even control my own mind. I'm unbearably, repulsively weak.

Sean and Alyssa already know that, and they've been trying to expose me at work, but I get the feeling that it's not happening fast enough for them. They want retribution, now.

The end's near, I can feel it. And maybe I don't deserve to feel happiness, but right now, I do.

I can't believe this.

I can't believe that I'm actually feeling sorry for Corey. That I'm actually wondering if I should have done more, if I could have been a better wife. There was so much I missed, so much that I chose not to see.

All the questions I never asked, no matter how troubled he seemed. All that I was determined to overlook.

He wanted me to figure it out. He wanted accountability.

Maybe he's right, I didn't really want to know him. Could I have been, on some level, complicit? Have I been actively choosing denial for years?

Before I read through the document again, I uncap the Angel's Envy and pour myself a huge glug.

Corey was obviously distraught when he wrote this, but he sounded lucid. I don't think he was drunk himself. He was no writer, I do know that much. It would have taken him a while to produce a document this long. This wasn't just a snapshot; this is what he felt over time. He was gaining in clarity as Sean and Alyssa were closing in.

Could they really have murdered Corey?

Or could this have been his attempt to frame them? Maybe he committed suicide but left this behind to point in their direction. That way, I'd still be entitled to his life insurance benefits.

It doesn't make sense, though. If all he wanted was to frame them, why make himself look so awful? Why detail all his own dastardly acts? Like about inseminating Jade without her knowledge or consent? Also, he didn't exactly make this manifesto easy to find.

Jade was telling me the truth. She was faithful to Corey. She thinks Corey is Tai's father.

I can't believe that I'm feeling this, but I want the whole truth. I want justice for Corey. I want justice for us all.

As I start reading again from the beginning, there's a knock on my door.

FIFTY-TWO
JADE

I'm dressed all in black, which isn't unusual for me, though I am wearing sneakers, which is practically unheard of. I was all in black the very first time I met Maren, so I guess we've come full circle.

I was in mourning for Corey back then. Will I mourn Maren next?

I won't miss her, but I will grieve, as much for myself as for her. Because I'm about to become a murderer.

I have to remember that she forced my hand. She brought this on herself. I would never even contemplate something like this if Tai's future didn't hang in the balance. She's a danger to my son.

That's what I keep telling myself, over and over, as I do my little ninja routine. I'm staying out of sight while peering into the lobby, waiting for just the right moment when Javier steps away from his post. I'm beside the awning, and when pedestrians walk by, I pretend to be on my phone.

After an excruciating hour of this, Javier disappears into a back room. Heart racing, I dash into the lobby and onto the elevator.

I allow myself a tiny smile. Rich people think they're so protected, but it's by people who make little more than minimum wage in an astronomically expensive city. What kind of allegiance can anyone really have to those who exploit them?

This is no time for social commentary. I'm inside and unseen, hurtling upward toward an unsuspecting woman.

At least, I hope she's unsuspecting. I sent her that one text yesterday, and she hasn't responded. I thought she'd protest being fired, but I'm guessing her lawyer advised her not to.

Maren fashioned herself a tour guide, nanny, and fairy godmother all rolled up into one, and turned her apartment into a high-end toy store. She buys Tai ice cream every time she sees him. No wonder he was crabby today when I told him there'd be no Aunt Maren.

I canceled my clients to stay home with him, and he definitely struggled with the change in routine. He was in withdrawal from his drug dealer. No matter what I suggested, he fought me. He didn't want to be pent up in our apartment, he wanted to get out and do things and spend money, but I can't do that. I have to be frugal. Because of Maren.

And because of Corey. Corey didn't love us; he screwed us over. Let's face it, I wouldn't be here tonight if it weren't for him. Maren's blood would be on his hands, if he still had them.

On the subway, I kept hearing his voice in my head. He was trying to talk me out of this. *You're not a killer*, he said over and over.

Well, people change.

I refuse to talk to Corey anymore. If he is somewhere watching and listening, I hope he's suffering.

But he won't suffer, will he? Only we will, Tai and me. People like Corey have no heart and no soul. They can't be hurt. In their way, they're invincible. That's why they have all the power, always.

I thought I was so smart and in control. I thought I had it all figured out.

I don't want to kill anyone, but what choice do I really have? I can't just wait for Maren to serve me papers. If this gets to court, there's a very good chance she'll win. I'm an unsympathetic figure, remember? Even my own lawyer said so.

Maren's poised to take my son. I don't want to do this, but I'm running out of time.

I'm not a killer. Yet I have to kill Maren.

And I have to do it in a way that won't take me away from Tai. That means it either has to look like an accident or self-defense. Could I drive her to suicide instead?

I doubt it. She's resilient and tenacious, like me.

I don't know how people train for this, how they choose the scenario and the weapon. How they find rare and undetectable poisons, or manage to get in just the right kind of physical fight that can lead to a conclusion of self-defense. Based on watching police procedurals, I need to decide what story I'm telling and then make sure the resulting scene fits the crime. Means, motive, and opportunity, that's what they're looking for.

I need Maren dead quickly because once she files the paperwork, I'll have a motive. Before that, she's a woman who's been generously babysitting my son, a woman who's planning to write up a trust for him. Our relationship hit a rough patch, but I know how much she cares for Tai and that she'll come through for him. Why would I want her dead before she's completed the paperwork? How could I know that she had such violence in her?

I had to kill her, Officer, because she attacked me suddenly and viciously. I knew she was highly engaged with my son, but I didn't realize until that moment that she was obsessed. That she was willing to do anything to have him all to herself.

Zauna will back me up on how nuts Maren has become. That means Emmanuel will, too.

I'm shaking as I walk down the hall to Maren's apartment. What if I'm shaking too badly to coordinate my movements? What if instead of killing her, she kills me, in actual self-defense?

I'd be dead, and Tai would likely wind up with Maren anyway.

There's so much that could go wrong. Maren's way tougher than Corey ever gave her credit for. But I'm tough, too. I will not let Tai down.

I knock sharply, and Maren opens the door. I don't know what I expected, but this is more terrifying.

She looks happy to see me.

FIFTY-THREE
MAREN

I can't believe how grateful I am to see Jade. But then, who else would care what's in this manifesto as much as the two of us?

I don't want to be alone in this, deciding what to do about Sean and Alyssa. I feel like Corey: Tired of being alone. Tired of keeping up appearances.

The manifesto exonerated Jade. That means that there's hope for us to work this out like reasonable people. I mean, historically, I've been a reasonable person.

Corey's manifesto was a cautionary tale, and I'm going to heed it. When you try to seem perfect, you sow the seeds of your own destruction. Authenticity, honesty, and decency will set you free.

I can do this. I can get back to my real self.

"Come on in." I usher Jade inside. "There's something you need to see." The laptop is already yawning open on the dining room table, which seats ten. I've decided to reclaim the room now that there are no more dinner parties. And since I'm not a hostess anymore, I don't offer Jade anything to drink or eat.

Her eyes immediately stray to the open bottle of Angel's

Envy and my half-empty glass, so I grab another highball for her. Who likes drinking alone?

"Sit," I say. "You need to read this."

She's watching me warily, and I can't entirely blame her. Things have gotten completely out of hand between us, and it's time to set the record straight.

I'm having the most unusual experience right now. I feel compassion toward Corey; no, it's empathy. I actually feel close to him. I feel like I do know him. Like in some small way, I am him.

What he said about pretending your whole life resonated with me. I didn't even know that's what I was doing throughout our marriage. Superficiality was second nature to me. I'd been raised with certain ideas about masculinity and femininity, about men and women and our respective roles, and I didn't question them. I was supposed to support my husband no matter what, and then I was supposed to be a mother. But when Corey said no to having children, I went into a tailspin. He was the breadwinner and the boss. So instead of talking to him about my feelings, I just did as I was told.

So much falsity. I was pretending to be the perfect wife, and Corey was pretending to be my perfect husband. The tragedy is that in the end (or since the beginning), we barely knew each other.

Corey was selfish, and he did some terrible things, but he wasn't an unrepentant sociopathic narcissist. He was misguided and frightened.

The manifesto is laced through with terror—not about being murdered, which he treats as an almost welcome inevitability—but just about being himself, whoever that was. Corey was afraid of his true self, and that was his undoing.

I might not know who I am at the moment, but I do know right from wrong. Since meeting Jade, I've been acting in more and more outlandish ways. Now I'm ready to declare a truce, and I'm not afraid to admit to what I've done wrong.

But first things first.

"Could you read this, please?" I say, gesturing again toward the laptop. "Everything makes so much sense now."

Jade's still standing awkwardly, not moving a muscle. "What is it?"

"It's a document Corey wrote."

"Corey didn't write. He barely read."

I force a laugh, like we're old friends instead of... whatever on earth we are. "True. But that's how you know he really had something to get off his chest."

She shakes her head. "I've had enough of Corey's bullshit to last a lifetime."

"I would have said that, too, before I read this. Please, Jade?" I'm not above pleading, and I'm not about to take no for an answer. She must be able to see that because she finally sighs and sits down. "Thank you."

She's skimming quickly. "So he's guilt-ridden and paranoid. I've seen that side of him when he's had too much to drink. Yep, more delusions of grandeur. Does he really think he's so important that Alyssa and Sean would risk going to prison and orphaning their kids just to get even with him? He can't be the first man that Alyssa fucked behind Sean's back."

She pushes the laptop away in disgust.

"I can see how it might be true," I say. "I mean, Sean did neglect Alyssa for a long time, and she is an incredibly forceful and nasty person." She convinced me that she should call CPS, for example, though I'm not going to bring that up.

Jade takes a tiny sip of bourbon. I wonder what brought her here tonight, and who's watching Tai (though I wouldn't dare ask her the latter question, not after the whole CPS debacle).

"I believe him," I say.

"That's because he's a salesman. Don't you get it? It's all in there." She stabs a finger in the direction of the computer. "He sold you one bill of goods and sold me another. He fed us what we were starving for so he could stay in control. You're the one who's been telling me how evil he is!"

"He was finally facing the truth. He wanted accountability, that's why he wasn't even going to the police about Sean and Alyssa. He let them punish him. This manifesto was for him. He wasn't crafting a narrative for you or me or anybody."

"Then how did you so conveniently find it, Maren?"

I'm not going to tell her that, since it might be a crime to hack the computer of a dead man. "It wasn't that convenient."

"You found it because he wanted you to. Then you could feel sorry for him and share it with me so I could feel sorry for him. But there's no excuse for what he did. He had me *inseminated*. I don't even know whose sperm it was." She looks at me, her green eyes bright with pain. "Can you even fathom that?"

"No." Time for my first apology of the night. "I'm sorry that I accused you of cheating on him. I just didn't know what else to think after discovering he was sterile."

"I accept your apology." She finishes off the rest of her drink. "But don't ask me to care about that motherfucker ever again."

"You don't have to. But just because he was a motherfucker" —the words feels awkward in my mouth—"does that mean Alyssa and Sean should get away with murder?"

Alyssa slept with my husband behind my back and lied to my face for months. I texted her to say she wouldn't get away with it, and it was an idle threat, but maybe it doesn't have to be. How sweet it would be to bring her to justice, especially since murder wouldn't invalidate the life insurance policy.

"I could bring this to the police," I say. "See if they can reopen the investigation. There might have been things they overlooked."

"You are really something, Maren." That is not admiration

in Jade's tone. "You've been telling me for the past month that I should hate Corey, and now you want to avenge his death?"

"I want you and me to be on the same page again."

"Again? We've never even been in the same book."

"Well, let's get there." I'm trying to meet her eyes, but they're shooting all over the room, almost frantically. "We can decide together what to do about Corey. And about Tai."

At Tai's name, her face assumes a fierce expression.

"I understand," I say. "You don't trust me, and it's not helping my case that I'm pleading Corey's."

She doesn't answer. She's still looking around. What is she hoping to find, I wonder?

"I'm not saying you should forgive him. I'm not saying I forgive him." What am I saying then? I don't even know, except that, in defending Corey, I'm somehow defending myself. He didn't know how to be a genuine person, and I've had a hard time with that, too, but now I'm different. I'm showing her my true colors.

So why won't she look at me?

"When it comes to Tai," I say, "you and I have gotten off track, but we can get back to where we need to be. We can strike some kind of deal—"

"Enough," Jade says, slamming her hand down on the table so loudly and suddenly that I jump. "I've had enough of your tricks and manipulations and about-faces, Maren. You're just like Corey. You have too many fucking faces. This ends tonight."

FIFTY-FOUR
JADE

Maren looks stricken, but I need her angry. Angry enough to attack me physically, and then I can kill her in self-defense.

I'm angry, too, but not so much at her. That manifesto makes me want to kill Corey with my bare hands. Hopefully I can transfer that to Maren and get this done.

It's all there, in his confession. He did play me. He told me what I wanted to hear, claimed that he was showing me everything, that I was the one who got to see the whole Corey. But there was no whole, unless you count the one true thing he said. Corey was 100 percent fraud.

He wasted years of my life, just like he wasted years of Maren's. I didn't have his child, and neither did Maren. Maybe we're both lucky to have dodged that bullet.

But I can't go empathizing with Maren now. I have to kill her. And that's Corey's fault, too.

Keep emotion out of it; this is business. I'm a hitwoman, and I'm working for my son.

Why should I be making any kind of deal with her when he's my flesh and blood? Who does she think she is?

I have to incite her to attack me. I want her to land the first blow, and then once it starts, I need to finish her. Otherwise, she'll live to tell her own story. I'd wind up in prison for attempted murder, and she could wind up with Tai.

I glance at the laptop, trying to gauge its heft. If I swung it with all my might at Maren's head, what kind of damage could that do?

It would definitely stun her, and probably wound her. But to kill her, I'd have to hit her again and again, probably with some heavier object. It would have to look like she'd been getting back up, ready to come at me again, maybe with the broken neck of a bourbon bottle in her hand?

I'm starting to feel sick, imagining the kind of brutality that's required.

Maybe I can still talk sense to her. "You know that Corey was sterile," I say. "Since Tai's not Corey's son, you're not his aunt. You're not his anything."

"I'm someone who loves him."

"You barely know him, Maren. What kind of a lunatic tries to steal another woman's son?"

"Maybe I haven't always made the best choices, but I'm perfectly sane."

"You're filing for custody of my son even though you know I'm a good mother. Even though now you know you shouldn't have any claim on him at all, given that Corey's not his father. How do you sleep at night, Maren?"

"I'd make a great mother." There it is, Maren's assumed superiority. I can tell from the set of her jaw that she's still planning to file for custody despite Corey's manifesto. Maybe she's going to conveniently lose it before we go to court, destroy all records of his sterility. Or she'll just find some way to spin things. Women like her are always believed. Women like me are another story.

"You're untested," I say, disgusted. "You've never been a mom. You've never done the hard stuff, just the fun stuff. You take Tai for trips and buy him things. Me, I'm in the trenches every day."

Her face tightens. "If he were my son, I wouldn't talk about trenches. I wouldn't make it sound like motherhood is fighting a war. I'd be grateful, every day."

"You don't know that."

She drains her glass. "I don't want to argue with you anymore. I just want to do what's right for Tai."

"Which is what?"

"Joint custody. We can share time."

My eyes bulge. I was right about her; she is utterly insane. "I'm not even going to entertain that. He's my son. Mine."

"We don't own people, Jade. It takes a village to raise a child."

No one will blame me if I swing this bottle at her head after that.

"You want to take Tai away because I don't parent the way you would," I say. "Because I can't parent the way you would since I'm not a rich widow." She is disgusting, and she deserves to die.

But can I kill her?

"I don't agree with all your choices," she says, "but I wouldn't say you're negligent or unfit. We can work something out."

"Oh, gee, thanks."

"It's better if we don't involve lawyers. There are custody forms online. We could fill them out ourselves. We could do it right now, if you want."

"Here's the deal." If she accepts it, she gets to live. "We're at an impasse. Because if the courts learn that Tai isn't Corey's son, then there's no inheritance claim. But you also have no custody claim."

"What are you proposing?"

"You leave Tai and me alone while you adopt a child in need, and I get half of Corey's estate."

"Why would I ever agree to something like that?" She looks amazed and also (amazingly) hurt. How could she have believed that I'd want her to stick around?

"You should agree because you love Tai, and you know legal battles will only drain everyone's energy and money. If you want what's best for Tai, you'll cut me a check and cut yourself out of his life." I don't have much leverage, and I can't even claim Tai is Corey's heir. I just have to hope that she really does love Tai.

"He lost his father, and now you want him to lose his aunt?"

"You're not his aunt! He's only known you for two months. It's time to step away before he gets any more attached. Let us get on with our lives, and you get on with yours."

She shakes her head sadly. "I can't do that."

"I thought you said you wanted to settle this now, that we could fill out the forms tonight."

"For joint custody. I can't do what you're asking. I can't just bow out."

"Because you're as selfish as Corey was." Now fury is coursing through me, which is going to be useful. I have to channel that to get this done.

The time for talking is over. Once she's dead, Corey's whole estate is up for grabs. Or maybe she's already amended her will to make Tai the beneficiary. I mean, who else would it be? Emmanuel? She's constructed a life where the closest person to her is her driver. Or he was, before she fired him. That tells you everything you need to know about her.

I stand up, my hand closing around the bourbon bottle.

That's when there's a knock at the door.

FIFTY-FIVE
MAREN

Another unannounced guest. What is it with Javier tonight?

Jade's basically fled down the hall, saying, "I'm using your bathroom!" I guess she's giving me privacy, or she doesn't want to be seen in my presence. Whatever.

She really is impossible. I made her *another* generous offer, and she threw it back in my face. How do I work with someone like that?

I look through the peephole and my heart begins to race. It's Sean.

"Alyssa and I split up," he says, looking sorrowful. "She doesn't know I'm here. Could I come in?"

He's wearing a dark cap and a dark outfit, like he's in mourning.

"Please?" he says again, staring up into the fisheye. Staring right at me.

He might have murdered Corey. If I let him in right now, I could find out for sure. Alyssa's always said that Asshole isn't the brightest bulb, that he's easily fooled. Maybe he's finally done being manipulated.

By Alyssa. But I haven't even begun.

If Alyssa murdered Corey alone, I could convince Sean to turn her in. A husband doesn't have to testify against his wife, but he can choose to.

Even if he does intend to do me harm, he's in for a surprise. He doesn't know that I've already got company. I've got backup.

I open the door, and he strides in like he owns the place, heading right for the living room. But then, he and Alyssa have been here plenty of times. I can't believe how hospitable I've been to those people. How many times were Corey and Alyssa together while Sean and I sat in the other room, blissfully unaware? Alyssa probably got off on that; from the manifesto, it sounds like Corey barely did.

Sean sits down heavily on the sectional. "You know about Alyssa and Corey, right?" he asks. I nod. He pats the seat next to him. "We've got a lot to talk about."

I sit near him, but not too close for comfort. "How long have you known?"

"I just found out."

He's already lying. The manifesto said he's known for months. That he terrorized Corey for months. "Alyssa just told you?"

"I saw your texts. You know, the ones asking how she sleeps at night. So I pushed and pushed until she confessed."

"Confessed to what?"

"To an affair with Corey."

He's not saying anything about murder. Jade didn't seem sure there had been a murder; she thought Corey might have just been drunk and paranoid. I guess he could have drunk himself to death.

I just want to know the truth. Can I get it from Sean, when he opened this conversation with a lie?

I study him and realize something, how he might have gotten to my apartment. He's dressed like some sort of handyman. The dark clothes are a quasi-uniform. He could have used the back entrance and the service elevator to avoid detection. Above his pocket is stitched a name: Adam.

I shift farther away from him on the sectional. I don't want to make any sudden movements because if he panics, this could get really bad. He might not have come to kill me, but with this outfit, it seems like he's leaving himself the option.

Where's Jade? Should I call out to her, just to let Sean know that we're not alone?

If I do, then it'll shut him down. There's no way I'll get any sort of confession at that point.

"I don't think there's anything useful that I can tell you," I say, trying to look sorry. "You've come to the wrong person."

"I don't want information," he says. "I was hoping for comfort." He slides closer. "I've always found you really attractive, Maren. But unlike Corey and Alyssa, I would never have acted on it."

"No, thank you." Even now, in a moment of mounting fear, my instinct is to be polite. But should I be running from him in my own home? Or screaming for help?

He's surprisingly agile for a man of his size and build, leaping on top of me, one hand over my mouth, the other around my throat. For a second, I'm frozen. I can't tell if I'm going to be raped or—

No, he's not here for that. He's here to kill me, his hands tightening around my throat.

Alyssa must have shown him my texts, and they took my idle threat seriously. They decided that they needed to eliminate me before I could go to the police about Corey's murder.

I writhe and try to call out, but I'm pinned. I can't make sounds. I'm still breathing, though. He hasn't managed to completely block my airway. I suspect he's not using his full strength, that some part of him doesn't want to be doing this.

My right arm is free. I feel around on the floor, my fingers closing around something hard. It's Tai's ukulele. He's been learning songs and wanted to play them for me.

Tears fill my eyes. This could be it for me. I'll never see Tai again, never see anyone again.

Sean is grunting, and I realize he's also crying. He wants to stop, but I can't talk him out of it. I can't talk, I can't shout.

Where is Jade? She must be able to hear this. Is she too scared to do anything? She might have called the police already, but by the time they arrive, it'll be too late.

A ukulele isn't much of a weapon, but it's all I've got.

I land the hardest blow I can to the side of Sean's head, and in that second's pause, I kick off with both feet. His bulk smashes through the glass coffee table.

He's not moving, but he's not dead. So I pick up a large piece of glass and plunge it into his throat.

That's when I hear Jade say, "Oh my God."

"I had to," I choke out. I can barely talk, after what he did. "He was strangling me. If I hadn't killed him—"

"You did. You killed him." She seems to be in shock. I guess it is a grisly scene, but shouldn't I be the one in shock?

"Listen to me," I say urgently. "I had to, or he would have killed me. You know that. You saw it."

"Did I?"

FIFTY-SIX
JADE

I'd crept back down the hall and heard the whole interaction between Sean and Maren. When the talking stopped and the struggle ensued, I peered in.

It had been hard to do nothing. Hard to root for a murderer to claim another victim, even if those victims had been Corey and now Maren.

Sean was doing what I'd come here to do. What I hadn't been able to bring myself to do. Let's face it, I'm no killer.

But it had been excruciating, bearing witness to such violence, and not stepping in to do anything about it. I have some scruples left.

To tell the truth, I'd actually run back to the kitchen and picked up a large chef's knife. I wasn't sure that I was going to intervene, but I like to have options. I got back to the living room just in time to see Maren finish Sean off with that glass shard.

She is, indeed, one tough bitch. But so am I. I can play hardball.

She glances down and notices the knife. "What are you

going to do with that?" she asks. I see a dawning realization. "Is that why you came here tonight? To kill me?"

"No." But I don't sound very convincing. "I picked this up to help you with Sean. But I guess you didn't need my help." I look meaningfully at the body. "You do now, though."

"What are you saying?"

"You need me as a witness. You're going to tell the police a story about self-defense, right?"

"It's not a story!" She's breathing heavily, indignant.

"From where I was standing, you looked like the aggressor. He was down, and he wasn't moving. Who has glass sticking out of their throat, you or him?"

"You wouldn't!"

"You've got your vantage point; I've got mine. If you want them to match up, then maybe we really can make a deal." I walk a little closer to her. "That's what you wanted earlier, right? For us to draw up paperwork tonight."

She's quiet a long moment, calculating.

"I know that you went to Zauna, and you were pretty aggressive then. She actually texted to warn me about you. She said you were crazy. And dangerous. Capable of anything. She offered to testify against you in a custody battle. I imagine she'd be very willing to talk to the police."

"I just survived an attack on my life! Are you really doing this right now?"

"I don't think there's a better time." I could feel sorry for her, but I won't. "You threatened me with CPS. You threatened to sue for custody. I'm not going to wait around to see what you threaten next. We finish this tonight."

FIFTY-SEVEN

MAREN

It's brutal, the way Jade's pressed her advantage, but I can almost understand it. She thinks she's protecting her family. To her, I'm the ultimate danger.

I can't stop crying as I plead my case. I tell her how much I love Tai and that I want to enrich his life. I'll enrich hers, too. I'm prepared to sign over millions tonight to ensure my freedom and Tai's future.

"But please, don't put in that last clause," I say. "Please don't say I can never contact Tai again. I just want to watch him grow up. Let me have visitation. That's all I want."

"You don't know how to just watch, Maren. You want to participate. You want to control. I can't give you that opportunity anymore." Does Jade sound a little bit regretful? A tiny bit remorseful? Maybe I'm just imagining that. I want to think that she sees some good in me, that she knows my feelings for Tai are real.

"I'm a loving person," I say. "I have a lot of love to share."

"And I hope you will. But not with my son." She turns the laptop toward me. To add insult to injury, she's writing up the contract using the same website that I'd found for us to do the joint custody document. "You have to e-sign fast because I bet the police will be here any minute."

I don't even care about the money; I'm hesitating over that final clause.

"Don't worry," Jade says. "I'm going to hold up my end when they get here. Hurry up and sign. Then we'll both say it was self-defense."

"And if I don't sign?"

"I guess you'll find out." As if on cue, the police are banging on the door.

FIFTY-EIGHT
JADE

Six Months Later

I love my new salon, and my new work hours (only weekdays while Tai is in school, with a maximum of four clients a day). It's good to be an independent woman, earning my own money, even though it's also great to have a cushion. I've started an investment fund, retirement fund, and a college fund for Tai.

He's in kindergarten at an incredibly selective public school, a magnet school—Maren was right, he tested off the charts—and it's right here in Brooklyn, walking distance from our brand-new condo, paid for all in cash.

I've also signed him up for after-school enrichment programs. I was never opposed to enrichment; I just didn't like having it foisted on me by Maren.

Money is freedom. I love my freedom. Life couldn't be better, really.

I approach the building where Tai has been taking a kindergarten cooking class. It's only the second day, but he really enjoyed the first. I like the idea of him developing basic skills—

including safety skills—nice and young. No more burns in his future if I can help it.

Just as I open the door to the classroom, he dashes out. I guess he's been lying in wait. He's ebullient, covered in flour, and I start laughing immediately.

I notice a little girl is scampering right along with him. She's adorable, blonde and blue-eyed, with a braid on either side of her head.

"She's new," he tells me, indicating the girl. "Can she come over to play? I told her we can walk to my house!"

"It's all right by me. But we have to ask her mother first."

"I'm right here," says a familiar voice from behind me. If anyone overheard, they'd think she was entirely pleasant. Gracious, even.

I turn slowly with a sinking feeling just as Tai lets out a gleeful yelp of recognition.

"Maren," I say. "Fancy meeting you here."

A LETTER FROM ELLIE

Dear reader,

I want to say a huge thank you for choosing to read *The Secret Mistress*. If you did enjoy it, and want to keep up to date with all my latest releases, just sign up at the following link. Your email address will never be shared and you can unsubscribe at any time.

www.bookouture.com/ellie-monago

I hope you loved *The Secret Mistress* and if you did I would be very grateful if you could write a review. I'd love to hear what you think, and it makes such a difference helping new readers to discover one of my books for the first time.

I love hearing from my readers – you can get in touch through Goodreads.

Thanks,

Ellie Monago

goodreads.com/elliemonago

ACKNOWLEDGMENTS

First of all, thanks so much to you for reading this book all the way through to this page! Thank you for being curious about who's helped me get to this point. I hope you've enjoyed this novel and that you'll find it worthwhile to check out my others. I very much value the time you've spent on my work.

I'm profoundly grateful for all the readers in the world, for everyone who continues to appreciate the art and craft of the written word.

Much appreciation goes to Bookouture. I've been in the publishing industry a long time—both traditional and non—and I can really feel the difference with this team. The culture is stellar, and in my recent dealing with Jenny Geras, the managing director, I could see that it's emanating from the top. Richard King, Kim Nash, Jess Readett, Alba Proko, Hannah Snetsinger, and Peta Nightingale are all fantastic as well.

Then there's my editor, Harriet Wade. She's kind, wise, insightful, erudite, accessible, enjoyable to talk to… in other words, the complete package. So glad we're back together and hope we can keep this beautiful collaboration going and going. I am tremendously grateful for you every day.

I'm also blessed with amazing family and friends. Life isn't always easy, but I'm a lucky woman. I love you, and I thank you all.

PUBLISHING TEAM

Turning a manuscript into a book requires the efforts of many people. The publishing team at Bookouture would like to acknowledge everyone who contributed to this publication.

Audio
Alba Proko
Sinead O'Connor
Melissa Tran

Commercial
Lauren Morrissette
Hannah Richmond
Imogen Allport

Cover design
The Brewster Project

Data and analysis
Mark Alder
Mohamed Bussuri

Editorial
Harriet Wade
Sinead O'Connor

Copyeditor
Ian Hodder

Proofreader
Lynne Walker

Marketing
Alex Crow
Melanie Price
Occy Carr
Cíara Rosney
Martyna Młynarska

Operations and distribution
Marina Valles
Stephanie Straub
Joe Morris

Production
Hannah Snetsinger
Mandy Kullar
Ria Clare
Nadia Michael

Publicity
Kim Nash
Noelle Holten
Jess Readett
Sarah Hardy

Rights and contracts
Peta Nightingale
Richard King
Saidah Graham

Made in United States
Cleveland, OH
17 June 2025